"So she is dead?" Clara asked. Her brother, Wade, had gone quiet about Faith in recent weeks, but for a while Faith had been all he'd talked about. Her parents didn't respond one way or the other—an ordinary single pulse, who cared? Well, *Clara* cared. Clara cared a great deal.

"I don't see her much," Dylan said. "But she's not dead. At least I don't think she is."

Clara was pleased to hear Dylan wasn't with Faith and surprisingly enthusiastic about the fact that Faith was alive. She fantasized about killing her quite often. Now, it would seem, her wish might come true. It was only a matter of when.

PATRICK CARMAN

TREMOR

KATHERINE TEGEN BOOKS
An Imprint of HarperCollins Publishers

Katherine Tegen Books is an imprint of HarperCollins Publishers.

Tremor
Copyright © 2014 by Patrick Carman

Library of Congress Cataloging-in-Publication Data
Carman, Patrick.
  Tremor / Patrick Carman. — First edition.
      pages cm
  Sequel to: Pulse.
  Summary: "In the year 2051, one group of telekinesis masters attempts
to use their powers to stop another group of telekinesis masters from
destroying the world"— Provided by publisher.
  ISBN 978-0-06-208581-8 (pbk.)
  [1. Science fiction. 2. Psychic ability—Fiction.] I. Title.
PZ7.C21694Ts 2014   2013015453
[Fic]—dc23   CIP
                                                                        AC

Typography by Joel Tippie
15 16 17 18 19   PC/RRDH   10 9 8 7 6 5 4 3 2 1
❖
First paperback edition, 2015

No problem can be solved by the same consciousness
that caused it in the first place.
—Albert Einstein

Contents

PART ONE: October Road   1

1 ▶ Leaving on a Jet Plane   3

2 ▶ Bowling Ball Spin Cycle   12

3 ▶ The Looney Bin   26

4 ▶ Supermax   50

5 ▶ October Road   67

PART TWO: Prison Bound   99

6 ▶ Hey, Dad, How's It Hangin'?   101

7 ▶ Cell Block D   125

8 ▶ She's a Little Unpredictable, This Girl   141

9 ▶ Trust Me, Grandma   170

10 ▶ Wanna Play Asteroids?   186

11 ▶ Sasquatch   212

PART THREE: State of Chance   235

12 ▶ Departing Is Such Sweet Sorrow   237

13 ▶ Buckshot and Fishtail   267

14 ▶ Personally, I Like the Javelin   281

15 ▶ Doctor Doom!   307

16 ▶ Universal Donor   320

17 ▶ Now You Must Run   334

18 ▶ The Last Light of Day   344

part one

OCTOBER ROAD

Chapter 1

Leaving on a Jet Plane

Long before Faith Daniels and Dylan Gilmore found each other on the ragged edges of the broken world outside, a woman was lying on her bed alone, thinking about leaving the one she loved. The thought was like one she'd had a long time before, and it surprised her, because, really, in all the intervening years, the idea had never crossed her mind again.

What would become of me if I left this place and these people behind?

But once the idea was in there, bouncing off the tender walls of her mind like a bee trapped in a cloth sack, she knew her time with these people was coming to an end. She concluded without a hint of emotion that it was the pregnancy. That was the thing that had led her to this bouncing bee of an idea. It was a course of action that would do more than just sting if she followed its pull on her imagination. It would, in due time, spill some serious blood.

Oddly enough, it was the exact same thought some ten years earlier that had led her to Hotspur Chance in the first place. It was during a time in her life when she was two essential things at once: ruthlessly intelligent and disastrously unwise. She did not see eye to eye with her parents about what the future held, not only for them, but for all people. And when she debated with coworkers, she wielded her ideas with cunning and vigor. Eventually, no one wanted to argue with her, and after a time she became something of a loner. Clutching a ticket in her hand, trying to imagine what it would be like to fly through the air, her brilliance and her lack of experience were about to get her into some real trouble.

There were still a small number of airplanes flying between airports in those days, and she had found herself singing a very old, melancholy song as she fled from the place of her birth, away from her parents. The song was about a girl, or so she imagined, who was leaving on a jet plane and was hoping that the one she loved would still be there if she ever returned.

It was a love song, she knew, and not having a person to leave behind had made her feel sorry for herself. For all her intellectual power, she had failed to attract the right person at the right time. Love was like a velvet-lined box locked with an unsolvable combination. It had completely eluded her, this all-important aspect of adult life, producing a sort of simmering sadness she couldn't shake.

She wiped her tears in the nearly empty airport and tried to focus on the fact that in a world gone mad, at least she had been chosen, and not by just anyone, but chosen by the man who had envisioned the States and, by all accounts, was well on his way to saving the planet. He was not waiting at the gate when she arrived, as she'd hoped he would be. Someone else was there. He was about her age, with dark hair and a big, awkward smile.

"I'm so glad you decided to join us, really I am. You're going to be so pleased."

They exchanged pleasantries and names, and he escorted her to a white van, the kind that usually picked up those who wanted to enter the Western State. More and more people were streaming into the States, simply leaving everything behind, not turning back. And there was no room inside the States for a U-Haul full of personal belongings. It was part of the deal with the

States: come as you are, bring your Tablet, leave everything else. Her own parents had talked of leaving, and it struck her as she stood outside on the cracked pavement that she might never see them again. She could return home and find that they, too, had abandoned the outside world without her.

The white van deposited them in the desert, where the young man with the gleaming smile opened her door, touching her elbow softly as he pointed toward a low-slung building sitting all alone. The desert heat took her breath away, like stepping into a sauna, and she hoped the building had air-conditioning. She would never forget how white the van looked against the endless, sandy wasteland as it pulled away and left her behind.

"There are no rules in there. You can't imagine what he's like, what he's accomplished."

"I don't know. My imagination is pretty big," she said.

"Not this big."

And it turned out that he was right. Hotspur Chance, the man who had solved the global climate problem and invented the States, had turned his attention to human biology and the mind. When someone as brilliant as Chance started meddling with DNA, the results were bound to be astounding.

Chance had heard the prevailing idea that humans use only 10 percent of their brains. He knew this claim was patently false, because any part of the brain that isn't used quickly dies. People use only 10 percent of their brain's *potential*. Not so with Hotspur Chance. He used 90 percent of his brain's potential and was said to help others do the same. And it wasn't through mind-enhancing drugs or rewiring or shock therapy. He simply knew how to unlock astounding levels of human potential in certain individuals.

"I was hoping you would take me up on my invitation. I'm very pleased you've decided to join us. Come, sit down."

Those were Hotspur Chance's first words when she arrived. In hindsight, they were eerily similar to the greeting she'd gotten from the man who'd picked her up at the airport. Chance's mention of the invitation reminded her of how she had come to be standing there in the first place. She had taken an unusual test on her Tablet, one that everyone was being asked to take, and apparently her results were promising. The test involved looking at objects on what appeared to be a static picture of a table. There was a green apple, a red ball, a Coin, a knife, a picture. The test had asked her to move those objects with her mind, and while she had assumed it was a trick, she had been successful. She had even sent the knife flying up in the air, turning, and stabbing into the wood of the table.

"How about we see if you can do it for real, shall we?"

Hotspur Chance seemed to read her mind, to understand what she was thinking. Or maybe it was just obvious, given that he was sitting behind the very table from the test and the same objects awaited her. What else would she be thinking about?

"Think about the object you want to move," Hotspur said. "Look at it. Now control it."

Besides his prematurely gray hair cut very close to his head, Hotspur Chance didn't look a day over thirty-five. Everyone knew he was at least sixty, but the skin on his face was tight and crisp, his eyes bright and youthful. He assumed that Meredith was distracted, so he narrowed his instruction.

"Think about the apple," he went on. "Look at it."

It wasn't what she would have called a proper introduction, and looking around the room at the faces staring at her, she began to wonder why she'd come at all. There was another woman in the room. She was tall, with severe, striking eyes that seemed to be saying something.

Why are you looking at me? He told you to look at the apple. Look at it.

She glanced at the young man who had picked her up at the airport, appreciated his warm smile, and turned her attention to the work at hand. It was then that she noticed the one difference about the objects before her: the apple in the test she'd already taken had been green. This one was red.

"Move the apple," Hotspur Chance said. "Bring it under your mind's control."

That was how it had begun, all those years ago, as the apple wobbled and rolled and fell off the table.

"It's too bad," the woman with the severe eyes said. "Not what we hoped for."

"It's enough," said the dark-haired young man with the winning smile.

As time went on the isolation bothered her, but the experiments didn't. In fact, she rather liked the attention as her powers grew more profound. In time she mastered the movement of larger objects with her mind: barrels of water, a motorcycle, even a car. They never spoke of the red apple, and it never really crossed her mind that the only other red objects she ever saw during her time there were attached to Hotspur himself. He wore a red lab coat over a pressed white shirt and red tie, but somehow the color never came up.

The training was enough to distract her from the slow and nearly unnoticeable descent into what could only be described later as worship. She came to see Hotspur Chance as everyone else did, as something more than a man. Nearly a decade later, as the world outside continued to empty into the States, she had the first inkling that she may have stumbled into a cult of the most dangerous kind.

"The States aren't exactly what I imagined them to be," Hotspur confessed. "We may need to make some, how shall we say, *alterations*."

Hotspur filled their minds with ideas she knew were wrong. But it wasn't long before she had fallen in love with the dark-haired young man, and he was the one to assure her that everything Hotspur was telling them would all make sense in the end. Hotspur Chance had saved the world and given them these remarkable powers. He fed them, clothed them, kept them safe. He knew what was best.

And so she hung on. She grew more powerful in the ways in which she could. She tried to withstand Hotspur's overpowering will. She hoped certain events would never come to pass, terrible things that these people were plotting. Until one day she woke up pregnant and the buzzing bee of an old idea got stuck in her head once more.

What would become of me if I left this place and these people behind?

She had a man to leave now; and kissing him as he slept, she imaged him kissing her back, smiling for her, saying that he'd wait for her. She stepped outside and sang the old song in her head, but she knew there were no more planes to catch. Those days were gone. And this turned out to be all right, because she didn't need an airplane to put some miles behind her. By then she could fly away all by herself.

The man she left behind was Andre Quinn.

The steely-eyed woman who would take her place was Gretchen.

The children who would be born in her absence were the twins, Wade and Clara Quinn.

This woman who flew away was Meredith. Seventeen years later, she would become the rogue leader of a nearly hopeless resistance.

And the baby she was carrying grew into a young man who had not one but two pulses. His name was Dylan Gilmore, and though he asked many times, Meredith never told him who his father was.

A time was coming when Dylan would need to know.

Chapter 2

Bowling Ball Spin Cycle

Faith Daniels was standing in the middle of a large, empty meat locker when the first red bowling ball lifted off the floor and began turning from side to side. The holes where her fingers and thumb would have gone if she were actually bowling looked like a round nose and two vacant eyes boring down on her from thirty feet away. Faith steadied her nerves, shifting her weight from side to side as she focused her mind, and ran her hand through the air in front of her.

"Let's see if a little noise throws you off," she whispered, not loud enough for the five drifters standing behind the floating balls of urethane to hear what she was saying. She hadn't touched all the empty hooks hanging down into the room, but she'd made them dance like chimes in a hot summer wind.

Four more red bowling balls rose up in the air, surrounding her from every side in the soft light and the clanging metal hooks.

Each of the balls weighed ten pounds or more, and they suddenly moved as if they'd been shot from five cannons, fired into the center of the room.

Faith had only recently mastered red objects, a color that presented serious problems for second pulses when they were new to the craft of moving objects with their minds. First pulses, like the drifters in the room with her, didn't have any trouble at all with the color red. It was one of the ways that Meredith, the leader of the drifters rebellion, had known Faith had two pulses even before Faith knew it herself. Meredith had never forgotten how easy it had been to move the red apple so many years ago when she'd first met Hotspur Chance. It had told him Meredith would never have a second pulse. Not so with Faith Daniels. Faith could deflect anything and everything that came her way. She was invincible.

Everything inside Faith screamed *Move!* But she knew moving wouldn't solve anything. These drifters were among the most experienced fighters in the rebellion. They knew how to zero in on a target whether it was moving or not. The best way to deal with red, Faith knew, was to stay still. She closed her eyes, balled up her fists, and held her breath. When the five bowling balls surrounded her in the middle of the meat locker all at once, she felt them nudging her, but only barely. She turned them away like marbles bouncing on pavement, returning fire at twice the speed. The drifters, all of whom were in mortal danger with no second pulse to protect them, dived for the floor as the balls ricocheted off metal walls and slammed into fluorescent lights overhead.

"Take it easy!" one of the drifters yelled.

Faith gathered all the bowling balls and lined them up like train cars, setting them in motion. They moved so fast it was like watching a ring of fire encircling the wide perimeter of the space. The drifters tried to take control of something—anything—but found that Faith was far too powerful to overcome in a confined space. She picked up all of the five drifters, one by one, and hung them on meat hooks by their long trench coats.

"Don't overdo it, Faith. I mean it."

Meredith's voice over the loudspeaker had the tone and quality of a drill sergeant. It was unmistakable.

Faith appeared not to be listening as the bowling balls changed course.

"Faith," Meredith said. "I know red makes you

angry. You have to control your rage. Understand?"

The bowling balls hovered several feet over the heads of the drifters. They were wearing football helmets, which they'd procured from the sporting goods store in a nearby deserted mall. The meat hooks clanged louder and louder as Faith made the balls spin in place and began lowering them toward the people who had thrown them.

"Don't say I didn't warn you," Meredith said.

The doors to the meat locker burst open, a streak of bright light bathing the room. Faith unlatched two of the long hooks, carrying one in each hand as she walked out into the light. As soon as she reached the opening, the real onslaught began. Dylan and a troop of drifters had recently raided a Sears down the street, where thirty or more washers and dryers had been lined up. For a person with the pulse, they were a very nicely sized object for throwing. The appliances were the equivalent of a softball for a normal person and even felt about that big in Dylan's mind as he threw one after another, raining down metal on Faith as she dodged out of the doorway. She used the bowling balls like antiaircraft fire, slamming them into washers and dryers as they came near her. Shards of metal flew past her on all sides, and anything that made it through was slashed and chopped by the meat hooks she carried.

Faith was out of control and loving every second of it, taking everything Dylan threw at her and shoving it right back down his throat.

A drifter was standing off to the side of the training area, and when he decided to pick up a truck tire and throw it in Faith's general direction, Faith turned on him. The tire flipped through the air, and Faith sent a bowling ball through the hole, slamming it into a concrete pillar the drifter was hiding behind. Had it connected with its target, the drifter might not have lived.

"Enough!" Meredith yelled. She was standing on a grated platform overhead, staring down over a paint-chipped rail.

All the washers and dryers and bowling balls fell to the floor at once, and with a brush of her arm, Meredith cleared away the mess. It was as if a giant broom had swept across the floor and pushed everything away.

"Too bad you don't have a second pulse," Faith said, staring up at her as she dropped the metal hooks with a loud clang. "You'd be one badass mother—"

"Let's reset and try the storm simulation," Meredith interrupted. "And this time, how about we dispense with the theatrics?"

"But it's easier to concentrate if I put them on hooks," Faith complained. "Otherwise they're harder to contain."

A huge, bald-headed drifter of Samoan descent walked by, holding a red bowling ball. His name was Semana, and he was wearing a football helmet that did nothing to hide his wide, black eyebrows. His head, which was unusually large, barely fit inside the protective gear.

"I don't mind hanging," he said through the guard on the helmet. "Just don't hit me with my own bowling ball. That would be crossing the line."

The training session was reset as Meredith watched. Up high it was relatively safe from any flying object she couldn't see in time to deflect. They'd been at this for nearly four months, almost entirely focused on getting Faith as far along as possible in the short time they had. She was remarkable, but Meredith was still having trouble containing Faith's reckless outbursts. Half a dozen drifters had been injured in sessions where Faith went too far, too fast. They were like sparring partners in a boxing match with an invincible opponent. They never complained, but hanging them up on meat hooks? It was just one in a string of such events that worried Meredith.

The rest of the drifters emerged from the meat locker, all of them holding red bowling balls, which they'd retrieved from the pile of rubble. As they brushed past Faith, some of them threw a shoulder in her direction, and none of them were smiling.

"We're on your side, you know," one of them said. She was the only woman among the five drifters pouring out of the room. Faith caught her eye, her nostrils flaring ever so slightly as their eyes met.

"And I'm on *your* side," Faith said, walking away without so much as a glance. "I'd say that makes you pretty lucky."

It was as close as Faith was going to get to an apology, and it served only to drive a wedge further between her and the rest of the resistance movement. She had the real power, the rare second pulse. Nothing could harm her. All those drifters? They could throw cars up in the air with the power of their own thoughts all day long. But if they didn't get out from under that thing fast enough, they'd end up the same as a normal, everyday person: dead.

The drifter shook her head and kept walking.

"Better play nice," she said over her shoulder. "You might need us one day."

Doubtful, Faith thought. She was at least smart enough not to say it out loud as she walked into the meat locker and slammed the metal doors shut with her mind.

Meredith watched the drifters span out around the edge of the warehouse, and she knew how badly they wanted a second pulse. She understood because she wanted one, too. From the time she'd stood before Hotspur Chance and that godforsaken table full of objects, she'd longed to take a hit as well as she could dish one out. At least she had been taught how to coax a second pulse into existence, a skill of highly selective use out in the real world. Finding single pulses was hard enough. In all her searching Meredith had encountered only two people with second-pulse potential: her own son, Dylan, and Faith Daniels.

Dylan flew up to the landing and rested his elbows on the rail.

"Assessment," Meredith said. It was not a question but a command.

Dylan shifted back and forth, scratched the back of his neck as the black T-shirt he wore folded up along his bicep.

"It didn't go as well as I'd hoped," he admitted. "Her powers are off the charts as usual. And she's not only overcoming five drifters, she's *controlling* them. She's holding them in place with her mind even while they're trying to escape. She's shutting them down. It's incredible. I don't know how she does it, and she still won't tell me."

"I know how she does it."

Dylan looked at his mom while she stared at the

metal doors of the meat locker.

"Are you going to tell me, or do I have to guess?"

"She's not upset, Dylan. She's furious. There's a difference."

"Emotions haven't got anything to do with power."

Meredith almost smiled, but not quite. *Is my son
really this naïve?*

"You're just not angry enough," she said. "And you
probably never will be."

"What's that supposed to mean?"

Meredith sighed deeply.

"How long have second pulses been understood?
Twenty years? Less? We think we know the powers we
possess, but what do we really know? Maybe Faith's
second pulse is more highly evolved, or maybe the force
of her emotions is like a witches' brew, altering the way
her system operates. The truth is, we don't know; and
since we're not in a laboratory with lots of free time on
our hands, I'm going with rage. She's an angry girl out
for blood. It's having an effect."

Dylan was feeling, as was often the case, that his
mom didn't appreciate his talents and intellect.

"She wouldn't even be here if I hadn't spent all those
months training her."

"You're a good teacher," Meredith agreed. "No . . .
you're a *great* teacher. But the fundamental question

remains: do you have enough to fight for?"

Dylan ran a hand through waves of black hair in frustration and then ticked off the score.

"Clara Quinn killed Faith's best friend in cold blood. Her Neanderthal brother murdered ten drifters without batting an eye, and two of them were Faith's parents. If they could find you they'd kill you, too. Trust me; I've got plenty to fight for."

Meredith raised her eyebrows and turned to her son. *Are you sure about that?*

Times like these Dylan wished Hawk were there to defend him. Outside of Faith, he was Dylan's closest friend and confidant. Hawk was younger, scrappier, goofier, and also the smartest guy he'd ever met. A guy like that could be useful when being undermined by your own mother, but it was way too dangerous in the training area for a guy as small as Hawk without even a single pulse to protect him. And besides, he was on a scouting mission with Clooger anyway. Last he'd heard they were somewhere near Denver, a thousand miles away.

"What do we know for certain about the second pulse?" Meredith asked.

"Very rare," Dylan said. He understood from experience that it didn't matter if the complete answer was obvious. His mother wanted to hear it anyway. "We can move things, including ourselves, by thinking about them. That's the first pulse, which is more common. We've got a dozen single-pulse drifters. A second pulse gives us the power to deflect things coming at us— a wall we're flying into or a semitrailer being thrown at us—so, in theory, we can't be harmed."

"And how many of you are there?"

"Two on our side—me and Faith—and three on their side: Gretchen, Wade, and Clara Quinn."

"Rare. Very, very rare."

"Is there a purpose to this conversation?" Dylan asked. "Because if not, maybe we could do this whole quiz thing later. Everyone is in position."

"You know, Faith's not as strong as she thinks she is. There are surprisingly simple things that could get her into real trouble she couldn't get out of on her own."

Dylan wanted to disagree, but the teacher inside him couldn't bring himself to defend Faith. She'd always been stubborn, all the way back to her first training sessions on the roof of the old Nordstrom building. But the depth of her resolve grew unfathomable after Clara took a hammer to Faith's best friend's head. For all Faith's astounding power, it often felt as if she was focusing only on the instruction required to complete a cold, hard task she was destined to perform: killing her enemies.

"I've been training her awhile now," Dylan said. He

was acutely aware of Faith's shortcomings as a student; and as much as he hated to admit it, she needed the kind of push only Meredith could provide. There was also, at the front of his mind, the confusing fact that he was in love with the girl he was training.

"Throw the kitchen sink at her; she'll figure it out."

"You sure about that?" Meredith asked.

Dylan didn't have time to change his mind before Meredith began lifting washers and dryers up in the air with the force of her own thoughts. She was, everyone knew, capable of some pretty scary shit when she was trying to prove a point. Thirty smashed-up washers and dryers slammed into the meat locker doors, piling up like a Montana snowdrift. All that remained for the training to start was for the person hiding inside to come out. The washing machine on the top of the pile tumbled to the concrete floor, followed by a breathless moment of silence.

The echo of a cough was heard.

Then all hell broke loose.

When Faith blew open the two metal doors, it was like a bomb going off: washers and dryers were ripped to shreds; shards of metal and knobs and wires flew everywhere, exploding into the air. But Faith's show of bravado was her first mistake, because Meredith had secretly placed a dozen more bowling balls in the meat

locker. They were black, which had made them harder
to notice in the dim light of the room full of meat hooks.
Before Faith could turn around, all ten balls were slamming into her back one after the other, pushing her out
onto the warehouse floor like a tin can being kicked
down the street.

"Hey, take it easy—" Dylan started to say.

But Meredith was having none of it.

"Stay out of this."

As soon as she had Faith off guard, she started piling
the appliances on top of her, quickly burying her under
a mountain of junk. There was silence in the warehouse
as the drifters looked on, unable to stop themselves
from smiling. The pile began to move, slowly this time,
as Faith glided up through the tower of metal. She hovered in the air, holding a ball and staring at Meredith as
if she was planning to knock her down like a bowling
pin. She was about to say *Is that all you got?* And she
would have, but Meredith had one more trick up her
sleeve, and the time had arrived to use it.

A giant swath of netting dropped from behind an
exposed beam in the ceiling, then spun like a cork-
screw, tangling into a knot around Faith's body. That
was followed by a thick rope, which spun around and
around Faith so fast she couldn't stop it. She hung in the
air, struggling to get free, like a caterpillar helplessly

trapped in a cocoon. She flew back and forth, banging into walls and concrete pillars, a rage-fueled menace without a chance of setting herself free. When she finally gave up and fell to the floor, Faith was so exhausted she couldn't even scream in frustration.

Meredith looked at Faith and thought of the first words Hotspur Chance had said to her all those years ago:

Think about the object you want to move. Look at it. Now control it.

Meredith rolled and tumbled Faith across the floor like a sack of potatoes, hauled her into the meat locker, and hung her on a hook. Then she slammed the metal door shut.

"She's going to be pissed off," Dylan said. "I'm not sure the hook was such a good idea."

Meredith turned toward a door behind her, opened it, and disappeared inside.

"Clean up this mess," Dylan heard her say. "We'll try again tomorrow."

Chapter 3

The Looney Bin

A half hour later Dylan had freed Faith from the tangled netting and together they'd cleaned up everything. Faith didn't say a word until they were finished, and when she finally did speak, it was short and to the point.

"She tricked me."

Dylan agreed, but he also knew they were living on borrowed time. The day was coming when the luxury of training days would come to an end.

"She's only trying to make you better. We all are."

"Easy for you to say," Faith mumbled. "And stop acting like my teacher. I thought we were past all that."

Dylan knew better than to push too hard when she

was angry. She had a certain look that said *Are you seriously doing this right now?*

"Come on; let's head over to Six Flags. It'll be dark soon. We can take a break like we talked about."

"I've got somewhere to be," Faith said. She leaned in close and gave him a kiss on the lips, which felt about as warm as a handshake on the receiving end.

"Where are you going?" Dylan wanted to know.

"Just something I need to do. I'll catch up with you later. Promise."

"Look, I'm sorry, okay?" Dylan said. But by then Faith was already walking away in the same skinny jeans she'd worn at Old Park Hill all those months ago.

Three states away, in what remained of Florence, Colorado, Hawk and Clooger were hiding out in a cemetery. The city was what they called *zeroed*, or 100 percent deserted. There were plenty of vermin and wild animals roaming around, especially at night, but the only humans were buried under the ground where they were hiding out. They had to be careful in places like this, because there tended to be packs of wild dogs and wolves roaming around. They could be vicious, but more importantly, the wild dogs barked like crazy if they so much as smelled a human. Sound traveled surprisingly well in a zeroed city, because the normal layers of noise Florence used to have—cars going by, the hum of streetlights, voices—all that was gone. A pack of wild dogs could be heard for miles, and that's exactly what they didn't need.

"Any heat out there?" Clooger asked.

"Yeah, plenty," Hawk replied, glancing at a Tablet screen covered in a geological map. There were tiny hot spots of glowing orange in some areas. "But we've got four or five miles of perimeter. We're okay for now."

Clooger was talking about large animals. One of the scariest things about zeroed cities and deserted quadrants was the predators: cougars and wolves and bears prime among them. Something had happened to these species in the emptiness of North America. Predators didn't avoid humans like they used to; they aggressively sought them out in remote locations. People hypothesized that officials of the States had something to do with this phenomenon, but no one could prove it. Had they used DNA-altering drugs to make certain species more aggressive in order to help keep those areas zeroed? It sure seemed like it.

"I remember when a guy could walk around in the woods all day and never see so much as a chipmunk or a deer," Clooger groused. "The big animals were out there, but the last thing they wanted to do was cross paths with a human."

Old Park Hill and places like it were spared, because the last thing the States needed was a lot of bad press about a whole town of people on the outside being attacked by wild animals. It was more evidence that they, the States, were in control of whatever was happening on the outside.

Hawk was along for the journey with Clooger in order to make sure they stayed hidden from people and the occasional presence of something that could rip their limbs off, such as a mountain lion. Clooger also liked a little company on an expedition when he could get it, and Hawk was a good traveling companion. They had a nice routine going, and Hawk often had information Clooger needed.

"Distance to target?" Clooger asked. He was staring through a pair of infrared goggles, which covered most of the exposed skin on his face. Between the dreadlocks, the beard, and his enormous size, it was fair to assume Clooger's first cousin was, possibly, Bigfoot.

"It's 2.4 miles by road," Hawk replied. "But you could trim that to 1.5 miles if you cut across the open field. Let's say you walk at a brisk pace, keep it real quiet. With your stride, you'd travel the road in about thirty minutes, an hour round-trip; figure ten minutes to observe the location and take a few pictures. That's seventy minutes."

"And the shortcut? How long would that take?"

"Assuming you don't get eaten by a pack of wolves, you're all in at forty-five minutes."

"Risk assessment?" Clooger asked.

"You're doing that *Star Trek* commander thing again."

"Am I?" Clooger hadn't noticed.

"It's okay; I like it. *Distance to target, risk assessment*—you're cracking me up. I think you could have been a comedian, actually."

No one ever called Clooger funny, and he hated the idea of making people laugh for Coin, especially if it was at his own expense.

He glared down at Hawk and asked for the risk assessment again, which only seemed funnier to Hawk.

Hawk sniffed the air like a bloodhound.

"I smell a skunk, and if there's one, there's a hundred. Getting that smell out of your hair if you end up crossing a skunk in that field—no way—it would all have to go. Dreads, beard, the whole crazy mess."

"Stink risk if I take the shortcut, high. Got it."

"Or a shaving risk, depending on how you look at it."

"Anything else?" Clooger asked.

Hawk took a bite of a protein bar, his third one of the day, and tapped commands on his Tablet. He'd set the screen to dim, so it barely put out any light at all, but he still used it sparingly. Light was scarce at night outside the States, and they were, he hoped, in enemy territory.

"Access on the field side is darker; that's a plus. But there's no doubt about it; the shortcut will have animals in it. You could run into a mountain lion or a cougar. Either one of those things could be watching us right now, just waiting for you to wander into a death trap. Still, the field side is faster; always better to be out in the open as little as possible. Overall, I'd say fifty-one percent for the shortcut, forty-nine percent for the road."

"Elections have been decided on thinner margins," Clooger observed, returning his gaze to the collection of buildings huddled together off in the distance. He scratched his beard thoughtfully and looked down at Hawk.

"Be ready to leave in forty-five minutes."

Hawk was happy to hear Clooger's decision, because the idea of standing alone in a cemetery at night at the edge of a ghost town wasn't exactly on his list of things to accomplish before his fourteenth birthday, which just happened to be right around the corner. The faster this was over, the better.

After ten minutes of waiting alone, he snapped his

Tablet to pocket size and put it away, then sat down on a gravestone and took off his shoulder pack. Inside were more protein bars, a bottle of water, and a printed copy of the picture book *The Sneetches and Other Stories*. He'd had to go back to the old grade school library in Faith's neighborhood and take the only other copy, because Faith had ripped up the one he'd had before. *Thank God for libraries that kept multiple copies of popular titles,* he'd thought when he'd gotten his hands on it. For all Hawk knew, it was the last copy of *The Sneetches and Other Stories* on Earth. It had become his most prized possession through everything that had happened in the intervening months. By now some of the pages were torn, and the corners of the cover were marred by damage.

The half-moon cast a pale light strong enough to read by, and Hawk made the mistake of turning to a story in the *Sneetches* book called "What Was I Scared Of?" In the story, the narrator repeatedly meets up with an empty pair of pale green pants. Given Hawk's situation, it was, quite possibly, the scariest thing he had ever read. By the time Clooger reappeared a half hour later, Hawk was ready to jump into his arms and cry like a seven-year-old. And he might have done it were it not for the fact that Clooger smelled like something out of a horror movie.

"If it hadn't been for the skunk attack, the expedition would have been a complete success," Clooger said.

"You gotta be kidding me."

Clooger began walking through the cemetery, which put Hawk downwind of a soft breeze.

"You smell like zombies," Hawk said.

Clooger didn't say anything until Hawk jogged closer beside him, pulling his T-shirt up to cover his nose.

"I found what we came looking for," Clooger reported without a hint of emotion. "Time to go home."

While Clooger and Hawk were preparing to leave Colorado, Faith and Glory were sitting in a mostly empty Claire's jewelry store in the abandoned mall just south of their headquarters. Only one light was on, right over the top of them both, and everything outside their little halo of light was quiet and lonely. Empty mall stalls stood like tombstones in the shadowy light as the buzzing of a tattoo needle started.

"Tell me why you want this, and I *might* do it for you," Glory said. She was testing out the instruments, making sure everything still worked as she rummaged through her bin of inks and dyes.

"Is there some unwritten code of tattoo ethics I don't know about?"

"You mean, do you have to tell me?"

"Yeah, that's what I mean."

Glory stopped looking through her bin of supplies and focused her attention on Faith. *Such a pretty girl,* she thought. *Blond haired and blue-eyed and tall as a Kansas cornstalk, like someone out of a magazine.*

"What's goin' on inside that head a yours, Faith Daniels?"

Glory's eyes were large and bright against her dark skin, and when she looked at Faith this way, it was always hard to keep secrets. But on this night Faith was particularly uninterested in any kind of criticism about her motives or her feelings. She didn't answer.

"So the hammer didn't hurt enough?" Glory asked. "Now you wanna put a tattoo on your tattoo?"

She'd asked Glory to add a white letter *C* over the ball and chain she already had etched into her skin. The chain ran circles around her forearm, tangled with green ivy, and the ball at the end lay on the softest part of the skin on her wrist. That's where she wanted the white letter *C* tattooed, right on top of the ball.

"The *C* is for *Clara,*" Faith whispered, her voice cracking under the weight of the words. Her heart was like a cauldron of sadness and rage whenever she thought about Clara Quinn. She'd killed Faith's best friend with a hammer throw, killed her without thinking twice about it. "It's for Clara Quinn."

Glory didn't reply; she just sighed and shook her head softly. She quietly went about the task of preparing a small portion of the titanium dioxide she would need to etch the white letter, and then she went to work on Faith's wrist.

"You ready?"

"Yeah, I'm ready."

As a second pulse, Faith had to clear her mind in a certain way in order to let the needle in, and this she did.

It wasn't a lot of work, just a simple letter *C*. And it wasn't very big, only a half inch high and thin. But Faith had never felt such a shock of pain in her life. Faith was sure Glory was digging the needle deeper than she needed to, but she couldn't bring herself to tell her to stop. The searing pain lingered across Faith's wrist, and, looking up, Glory saw how much pain she was inflicting.

"Revenge hurts, don't it? And not just the one on the receiving end."

And still Faith said nothing. She would endure this pain, even take pleasure in it, until the deed was done.

"We through," Glory said a few minutes later. "You know the drill: keep it clean; give it some air."

Faith's hand was shaking as she brushed away a

tear. Her wrist felt as if it were on fire, as if the mark were burning a *C*-shaped hole all the way through to the other side.

"I'm sorry," Faith said. She didn't know why she said it, but there it was. She got up and walked alone through the empty corridor of the mall, farther into the darkness, and, looking back, saw that Glory hadn't moved at all. She looked like an angel who wasn't quite strong enough to break through the shadows and save Faith from herself.

Six Flags Magic Mountain had been, at one time, one of the more popular Southern California theme parks for teens. Disneyland was fine if you were a kid, but Magic Mountain had the really badass thrill rides, the ones that made your pulse race just by looking at them. With names like Viper, Dive Devil, and Drop of Doom, these were rides with the kind of muscle that routinely turned varsity football players into babies screaming for their moms.

As Faith flew over the wide, looping roller-coaster tracks, she wondered what it would feel like to ride the rails, looking down at the park as she screamed and laughed. It was possible. She could get the coaster moving with the power of her mind, but the risks had been deemed too high by the almighty Meredith. What if someone saw them, reported them, came looking for them? There was too much at stake to risk revealing their hidden location to take chances on something as stupid as a glorified fair ride. And so Faith had been careful not to let herself think too much about sitting next to Dylan, hanging upside down at the top of the world, holding on to each other for dear life.

Faith landed in the park and felt an immediate surge of adrenaline that put her senses on alert. It was always dark at night in the park, and it was pushing midnight. She hadn't seen any patrols from the white State vans in weeks, and they'd settled on the location so close to the rising tide of the ocean for a reason: no one had stayed. Valencia, and Magic Mountain along with it, were zeroed. It wasn't people Faith was worried about; it was animals. Wolves, coyotes, packs of rabies-infested dogs, and some alarmingly huge cougars that had taken over the whole city long before Faith and the other drifters had arrived.

"Here kitty, kitty, kitty," Faith whispered, walking down the main thoroughfare of the park. There was something altogether wrong about a theme park with no lights or throngs of people, but it was also peaceful in a way that she could never quite explain. Maybe it was the idea that it was a place that should have been full of life but wasn't that had a heightening effect.

She felt a presence and knew, before she saw it, that she was being tracked by at least one cougar. They were stealth creatures, quiet as mice when they wanted to be. And they were big, seven or eight feet long and loaded with claws and teeth for killing.

The attack came from behind, and the jaws were wrapped around the back of her neck before her face hit the pavement. Faith felt her shirt ripping, the slight pressure of teeth against the skin. It was a big cat, the jaws clenched tight as they reached all the way around to the front of her throat. Faith raised her back, and the cougar moved as if it had been blown out of a rocket launcher. It flew end over end into the air, and, looking up, Faith deposited the beast inside a stranded roller-coaster car on the highest part of Goliath, a ride with a peak turn at twenty-six stories high.

"Maybe next time you'll think twice before hitting a girl from behind," Faith said. She stood up, felt the shirt on her back.

"Damn. I really liked this one."

It was a blue-and-gray-plaid shirt from Old Navy, the only one like it she'd found at the mall.

Maybe Glory can sew it back together again, she thought.

She'd arrived at the edge of *Bugs Bunny* World, where the kiddie rides were located. She and Dylan had grown to love this part of the park because the rides were small and harmless. They could make the rides move without much risk of being seen, because the rides were so quiet and low to the ground and because *Bugs Bunny* World was hidden away, deep inside the park, below the big rides that dominated the night sky.

"Dylan?" Faith searched with her voice. "You in there?"

She felt nervous, never having gotten totally used to the idea that she couldn't be harmed, not by a big cat or a piano falling on her head. She kept walking, past a boarded-up concession stand and the WONDER WOMAN Lasso of Truth, a glorified fair ride guarded by a twenty-foot-tall wooden Wonder Woman. She had a very serious look on her face.

"I know exactly how you feel," Faith said. "Weight of the world on your shoulders, right?"

She saw movement ahead, but it didn't worry her. Faith knew the soft, whispery sound of a ride being operated without the power of electricity.

"Sorry I'm late," Faith said as she saw Dylan glide by inside a teacup, turning circles as he spun the wheel with his hands.

"It's okay; I've been having a pretty good time all by myself. Good ride."

Dylan leaned his head back, staring up into the night

sky as the cougar screeched from its roost far overhead, the sound echoing through the park.

"You didn't," Dylan said.

Faith, a little embarrassed that she'd imprisoned a giant cat, turned around so Dylan could see her shirt in the dim light.

"The crazy thing attacked me. It's not helpless. It's a monster."

"Whatever you say," Dylan said, half smiling, as the ride carried him away and back again. He brought the ride to stop with his thoughts and held out his hand. His gaze fell on Faith. It was a look that pushed the rest of the world into shadow, leaving only the two of them in a place that was just their own. Belonged only to them. When Dylan looked at Faith with a smile that told her she was his everything, her prickly mood melted away.

"Come on," he said. "Let's ride this crazy thing."

Faith climbed into the same cup in which Dylan was sitting, the Pepe LePew's Tea Party, and sat down, laying her head heavily on his shoulder.

"You okay?" he asked, slowly starting the ride and letting it turn the teacup in a gentle circle. They'd decided it was one of their favorites, because it was easy to make it move and it made them feel like kids again. Faith lifted her head and pushed the dark strands of thick hair away from his forehead. He kissed her, and she closed her eyes, feeling the softness of his lips and the spinning of the teacup as one unbroken sensation. She couldn't say which was making her light-headed, the kiss or the turning of the ride.

"Do you ever wonder what this place was like before the States?" Faith asked, pulling away as their eyes met.

Dylan put a hand on Faith's knee and let his mind send the cup spinning in circles.

"They have better theme parks than this in the States. Disneyland West is supposed to be a million times better. I don't think humankind is hurting for rides."

"But this is different, isn't it?" she asked.

"How?"

She couldn't figure out how to put it into words, so she just sat there, feeling a slight faintness as the teacup moved around and around. A theme park outside the walls of the States was different from one inside. It just was. Like the library they used to go to. The books were different from the stories on the Tablets.

"You wouldn't understand," she finally said.

"I'd like to fight you on that, but I think you're probably right," Dylan said. "Magic Mountain is the same inside or out. They *have* a Magic Mountain inside the States. The difference is, this one is empty and the rides aren't as good."

Dylan let the ride come to a stop.

"In there we'd be fighting off an army of five-year-olds trying to get inside one of these teacups," Faith said.

"Yeah," Dylan agreed. "And they'd be making a lot of noise."

"Some of them would be crying for their moms."

Dylan looked up into the night sky and thought about what the park might have been like. "But most of them would be laughing. People would be crowded around, eating cotton candy and taking pictures. And the big rides would be going by, making everyone look up. Our friends would talk us out of these dumb kiddie rides, and we'd work our way through the crowds until we found ourselves standing in line for Goliath. I'd be nervous, but I wouldn't let it show; and when we got on, we'd all be laughing. We'd go up that first long climb, all of us looking over our shoulders at the people and the lights down below. And then we'd reach the top, flatten out for a few seconds, and you'd squeeze my hand really hard. Then we'd start screaming."

This was one of the reasons Faith loved Dylan. He found his way to what she was trying to say without her having to say it.

"It's lonely out here sometimes," Faith whispered. She hated crying, but she was so angry and sad about so many things the tears were starting to form.

"I'm not going anywhere," Dylan said, taking her hand as Faith made the teacup spin around in a soft circle. She closed her eyes and imagined them at the top of the roller coaster, the wind just about to start blowing her hair back, her best friend, Liz, in the front seat. She imagined Liz leaning back, the curls of her dark hair flopping over her shoulder. And reaching out to her, she held on to Liz's outstretched hand, like Liz had always liked.

The cup started spinning faster, and the ride was moving along its usual route again. The ride kept going around and around, faster and faster. In her imagination, they were all flying down the roller coaster, laughing and screaming. Faith leaned back, let her hair fly in the wind, and then her little fantasy turned dark and terrible. In her imagination she looked down at the ground, but it was too late. The hammer was already flying through the air; Clara Quinn was already smiling up at her. The two parts of the hammer—the ball and the chain—slammed into Liz's head. She didn't even see it coming, so the last thing Faith heard in her mind was Liz laughing. Liz's head moved violently sideways, an anvil carrying the rest of her body out of the ride, because of course they weren't wearing seat belts—who wore seat belts in a nightmare? The last thing Faith felt was the soft skin of Liz's hand as it pulled free.

"Faith, I'm going to slow this thing down now," Dylan said.

Faith couldn't feel the tears leaving the corners of her eyes as the wind pushed them back into narrow tracks. She couldn't see that she had let go of Dylan's hand, that she was groping in the air, trying to hold on.

When the ride came to a stop, Faith rolled over into Dylan's lap and took a deep, exhausted breath. She was like a girl with a split personality: either sad beyond all hope or trying to hold back a furious rage. Both threatened to destroy her, and keeping them in balance was wearing her down.

"Take me to the Looney Bin," she said. "I need to lie down."

Dylan kissed her cheek softly and then took Faith in his arms; and, rather than lift her up in the air, he walked like a normal sixteen-year-old. He wanted to feel his body heating up from the effort, to match the heat of frustration and tears coming off this girl. He passed by the darkened rides—*Elmer's* Weather Balloon, *Taz's* Trucking Co., *Tweety's* Escape, *Yosemite Sam's* Flight School—and imagined the echoing, distant sound of small children laughing.

"We need to fire up *Foghorn Leghorn's* Railway one of these days," Dylan said. "I think you'd like that one."

He used his mind to open the door to the area called

the Looney Bin, which was actually called the Looney Tunes Lodge, and carried Faith inside, closing the door behind him.

"Don't forget to let the cat out," Faith said, half asleep already.

Dylan turned back with Faith still in his arms and looked up through the grated metal fence that surrounded the Looney Tunes Lodge. The cougar was a predator he should probably let fall to its death. It could take out a single-pulse drifter, and they were down to so few. Every person counted. But he couldn't bring himself to do it once he had the big cat moving through the air. Besides, there were thousands of wolves and big cats out there. Killing one wasn't going to make much of a difference either way. He flew the beast in close, a few feet away, letting it hover in the air like a helpless rag doll. Then he looked it in the eye and it looked back, confused and afraid. He dropped the cougar the final ten feet, where it landed on all fours.

I could have killed you, Dylan thought as the two stared at each other. *Don't forget that.*

The animal turned and darted away with dazzling speed, disappearing around a sharp corner.

"I was just thinking you and me, we're like cartoon characters," Faith said. "That's why we like this place so much."

"Are you saying I look like Elmer Fudd? Because that's not cool."

Faith yawned, smiling softly, and Dylan carried her into the darkness. The Looney Tunes Lodge was, essentially, a glorified McDonald's play place. Larger, and with a few more plastic balls, but otherwise filled with the same kinds of slides and ladders and secret rooms.

"You do look a little like Fudd," Faith said as Dylan set her down on a wide trampoline.

"Be thankful you're not a wascally wabbit," Dylan said. "I'd have to shoot you."

Faith rolled forward and Dylan lay down beside her, curling around her and smelling the rose-petal scent of her hair.

"I mean we can't get hurt," Faith said. She was drifting away, Dylan could tell. "Like earlier, I was thinking a piano could fall on my head and I'd just pop right up, like nothing happened. Like Daffy Duck."

Dylan wanted to remind her that Daffy Duck was, more often than not, gravely injured before he shook off the damage and charged ahead. But he didn't see what good it would do. And besides, Faith had rolled over in his direction, unexpectedly more awake, and there were far more enjoyable activities to attend to.

They kissed, long and passionately, and Dylan's

hand found the softness of skin through Faith's ripped shirt.

"I'll have to thank that tomcat when I see him again," Dylan said, moving his hand along her spine until it rested on her bare skin just below her neck.

"You boys are all in this together," Faith said. They kissed again as he pulled her close. "I should have made you leave him up there."

"He's got a lady friend somewhere around here," Dylan joked. "Think of the trouble he'd be in if he stayed out all night."

Faith pulled off Dylan's shirt and ran her hands up the length of his back and then down his muscular chest.

Dylan smiled, and his lips stretched playfully along Faith's own. She loved it when he smiled and they were kissing, as if his happiness were seeping into her, making her whole.

"How long before we make our escape?" Faith asked. She'd asked this question many times before, like a story she wanted to hear over and over again.

Dylan didn't hesitate. He pulled back and looked into her eyes, touched her cheek.

"One day, Faith Daniels, this *will* be over. We won't be a part of something we didn't ask to participate in. We won't be counted on to fix anything we didn't break.

We'll be free. Free of the rebellion and the States—all of it."

"And then what?" Faith asked, feeling her pulse quicken as she kissed him again and again. "Where will we go?"

Dylan rolled her over on her back and leaned in close.

"We'll go to the mountains, high enough where no one can find us. And we'll build a cabin together. We'll stay in bed until noon, get up, and make omelets full of wild mushrooms. We'll take long walks in the woods."

"We'll need chickens," Faith said as she stared deep into his golden-brown eyes.

"And a house cat. Should we bring the cougar?"

"Whatever you say."

They rolled playfully across the trampoline, and Faith ended up on top. She looked down at Dylan, her hair falling in waves.

"I love you," Dylan said, pulling her closer.

Faith's breath caught in her chest. It was the first time he'd said this to her, and she hadn't expected it. She hesitated in her reply, instead going in for an embrace that left her lips touching his ear. Her emotions were a bottled-up mix of revenge, love, anger, and fear that confused her and made her defensive.

"I love you, too," Faith said. It came out as one word

without any space in between. She hoped it hadn't felt rushed or insincere.

"Let's stay out here all night," Dylan whispered back.

And so they did, dreaming of a cabin in the woods on a mountain peak, far away from all their troubles and responsibilities.

Chapter 4

Supermax

They woke simultaneously to the sound of a voice. Some-one was calling their names from outside the Looney Bin.

"Dylan? Faith? You two in there?"

Light was streaming in as they both sat up and real-ized they'd slept through the night.

"What time is it?" Faith asked. Dylan pulled his Tablet out of his pocket.

"Whoa, eight twelve. We slept in a little bit."

Faith was already slipping on her boots before the call came again.

"Come on, you guys; I know you're in here. Why you gonna hide from old Semana?"

"At least it's not your mom," Faith said, pulling her long blond hair into a ponytail. "That might have been a little awkward."

"Hang on, we'll be out in a second," Dylan shouted, but Semana had entered the Looney Bin and found his way to the trampoline.

"You two should let someone know if you're not coming in for the night. Least I knew where to look."

"Thanks, Semana."

"How pissed off is she?" Faith asked as she bounded across the trampoline and stepped out onto the floor. He was a big guy, round and soft around the middle, and he put his arm on Faith's shoulder.

"Let's just say your timing could have been better."

The entire rebellion had long since taken to extreme measures with their Tablets. Hawk, a genius-level Intel, had hacked into all their Tablets and turned off the communication and GPS features, just in case Andre and the rest of the Quinns had tapped into the system. He'd been working on a secure communication system for months, but so far he hadn't found a safe way for them to send information back and forth without potentially being detected.

"We better fly, no time to waste," Semana said. "Stay low, like we talked about. And don't move anything else."

The standing rule was no flying in daylight hours.

There was no telling who might pass through the area and see them, and the second that happened their cover would be blown. It wouldn't take long to figure out they were living in an office park a few miles off the coast.

"What's going on, Semana?" Faith asked as she dodged around a telephone pole and they all three flew a few feet off street level.

"The recon team pulled in an hour ago. They're waiting for you to show up before they report."

Dylan and Faith knew exactly what this meant, and it made both of them smile as they flew through an intersection with streetlights that hadn't worked in decades.

Hawk and Clooger were back.

"Nice of you to join us."

Meredith didn't look up from whatever she was working on. She was writing something down the old-fashioned way, with a pen on paper. Hawk jumped up from one of the three couches they'd moved into the planning room from a furniture place they'd found in a strip mall. He fist bumped Dylan as Faith threw an arm over his shoulder.

"If we'd known you were coming, we would have baked a cake," Faith said, pulling him close like a little brother. His mop of curly hair had grown even longer while they'd been in hiding, and he'd put on a full inch and approximately three pounds. Otherwise, he was the same old Hawk.

"Or maybe you would have had the courtesy to let everyone know where we could find you," Meredith said. She looked up from her work. "Every second counts; don't let it happen again."

"We won't," Dylan said. He was relieved his mom wasn't doing a full inquisition regarding their whereabouts or activities during the previous night.

"Where's Clooger?" Faith asked. "Wait, let me guess—kitchen?"

Clooger loved to eat, and they'd been stuck with protein bars and bottled water for a bunch of days in a row. The thought of a frozen Eggo waffle, nuked and smothered in syrup, made Faith's stomach growl with hunger.

"Do me a favor and don't make a big deal about the new look," Hawk said, scratching his tangled, curly hair. "He's a little sensitive about it."

But it was too late for that, because Clooger walked in carrying a plate of lasagna and Faith screamed. It was not the most subtle of reactions.

"Holy shit, Cloog—what happened to you?!"

"Lasagna? For breakfast?" Hawk asked as the smell of Italian food wafted into the room. "I'm in."

Hawk brushed past Clooger and more or less ran out the door.

"Make it fast!" Meredith shouted, shaking her head as she thought about the ragtag group of misfits she'd gathered to save the world.

Dylan looked Clooger up and down. "Who did this to you? I won't rest until they pay."

Clooger pointed his fork toward the door. "He went thataway."

Clooger's head was shaved right down to his noggin. The dreadlocks, which had been two feet long in some places, were gone. The beard, which had covered his face for as long as anyone could remember, had been reduced to a few hours of stubble.

"You two must have gotten really bored out there," Faith said, going in for a hug that never materialized. When she got within a foot of Clooger, she smelled the lingering remains of a serious skunk attack. "Oh, wow, that's bad."

"I've gotten used to it," Clooger said, sucking in a giant sniff of air. "Smells like roses."

Faith took a long look at Clooger, turning her head from side to side, taking in the strong chin and the round moon of his head. Then she went on in and gave him the hug after all.

"You look ten years younger."

"Twenty," Meredith said, smiling at Clooger in a way that mildly suggested something more than commander and soldier.

"Can I get some lasagna?" Dylan asked. He was hungry enough that Italian was starting to smell pretty good even at eight thirty in the morning.

Meredith rolled her eyes and tapped a button on an old-style phone that sat on her desk.

"Hawk?" she said.

There was a pause, then a small, mouse-like voice answered.

"Yeah?"

"Bring the whole pan and hurry up."

"And some forks," Dylan added.

Five minutes later Faith, Hawk, Dylan, and Clooger were sitting around a coffee table that held a pan of Costco lasagna, stabbing it with forks as Meredith stood before a whiteboard. She watched them take three or four bites each, tapping her foot on the slick concrete floor.

Meredith was clearly concerned. A few hours before, when Faith and Dylan turned up missing, she had genuinely wondered if they had decided to run away together. That stupid, sappy old song had been playing in her head ever since, and she'd honestly thought they'd taken a serious left and turned their lives in a different direction. She could hardly have blamed them if they had. She'd been known to do such things herself. Then Clooger had arrived, shorn like a poodle and smelling like a skunk. And now this, the ragtag team she had assembled, more interested in eating a block of lasagna that had been frozen for decades than in tracking down the most dangerous enemy the world had ever known.

She'd had it.

"Can I bring you anything else?" Meredith asked. "Some pizza, perhaps?"

"We have pizza? What kind?" Hawk wondered, stuffing his face with lasagna.

Meredith raised her hand, and the tinfoil pan of lasagna wobbled back and forth on the table. She flicked her finger in the air, and the square tin flew across the room as if someone had picked it up and used it in a pie-throwing contest. The pan hit the far wall with a squish-filled pop, then slid down and landed on the floor, leaving behind a greasy orange skid mark.

"That's the saddest thing I've seen all day," Hawk said.

Dylan had forked faster than the rest and felt nearly full. "The day is young; give it time."

"Thanks a lot, Hawk," Faith said through her last bite of breakfast. "I was really enjoying that."

The forks went next, all four of them jerked out of their hands and stabbed into the ceiling overhead.

"Clooger, please begin your field report," Meredith said. Veins were pumping blood behind the paper-thin skin of her forehead, and her willowy eyebrows were furrowed, her eyes staring down at the bald-headed man seated on the couch.

Clooger cleared his throat and, feeling a phantom beard, ran his fingers through the empty space beneath his chin. Finding nothing there, he resorted to running his large, meaty palm along the warm surface of his head.

"We've tracked Andre to a maximum-security prison facility in Colorado. Odds are his entire team is there, including Gretchen and the twins."

"Is there any chance they detected you?" Meredith asked. "*Any* indication you were followed?"

"I can answer that," Hawk said, raising his hand about halfway in the air before remembering he wasn't in school anymore. "We were not detected, impossible. And we were not followed; I made sure of it."

"What are we waiting for?" Faith said, not surprising anyone. Everyone knew she was tired of training. She wanted action.

"We've got them cornered in a max-security prison!" she continued, standing up. "It's perfect. We go in with all guns blazing, middle of the night."

"That's a terrible idea," Meredith said, turning to the whiteboard. "Sit down."

Faith looked at Clooger, then Dylan, then Hawk, searching for support. None of them would make eye contact.

"Give me the location," she said to Hawk. "I'll do it myself."

Meredith tried again: "Sit down, Faith."

"Give me the location!" Faith shouted.

A chilling moment of silence enveloped the room as Meredith turned back to the four of them, her cool sapphire eyes boring into Faith. "Yes, by all means, give it to her. Give Faith Daniels the location. She'll find it on her own anyway. And then she'll race right over there and save the world, all by herself. Never mind that there are three second pulses within that compound, and one of them is an Intel. Forget that each and every one of them has vastly more experience controlling their pulse, let alone their emotions, than she does."

"At least I'm willing to do it," Faith said, not backing down one inch. "Which is more than I can say for you."

Meredith took a deep breath and pointed her nose at the floor. When she looked up, there was fire in her eyes.

"Here's the reality of your situation, just so there's no

confusion. I run this show. *Me*. And I'm making the call. We are not going out there like a bunch of rabid dogs. You want revenge? I'll get you your revenge. But you're going to do this my way, or we're not doing it at all."

"I don't understand why we're—"

"Because you would be destroyed, that's why!" Meredith exploded. Her eyes fell on everyone in the room, all in their turn, and she thought of all those years with Gretchen and Andre, before Dylan was born. She lowered her voice. "I wish it wasn't so, but it is. They're not like us, and not just because they've trained longer. They'll do whatever it takes to change the direction this world is going in. Innocent people don't matter to them. They're collateral damage, nothing more."

"If they're willing to kill anybody to get what they want, isn't that all the more reason to take them out now?" Faith pushed. Dylan touched her hand, hoping he could get Faith to temper down, but Faith pulled her hand away. "And while we're at it, do you even know what they want? Because I sure don't."

"I do."

They'd all heard this before. Meredith knew things no one else did, and she would keep it that way no matter how much pressure was applied.

"Enlighten us, then. Tell us the score. You want to lead, then lead. Otherwise get the hell out of the way and let the second pulses finish the job."

Dylan had long struggled to feel close to his mom, but he hated seeing her lacerated like this. No single pulse, least of all his mother, could stand not being a second. But if she was wounded by Faith's words, she didn't show it.

"It's a supermax," Hawk said. He, too, wanted to cool the room if he could. "Florence ADX. It's intense, actually. Back when it was operating, ADX was the ultimate security prison full of the most dangerous criminals. Moussaoui was there, the guy who helped orchestrate 9/11, along with tons of other Al-Qaeda operatives. The Unabomber, Terry Nichols—he did the Oklahoma City bombing—drug lords and gang leaders. I'm telling you; this was *the* hotel you stayed in if you were a serious criminal."

"Obviously they're not being subtle about who they're comfortable associating with," Dylan said.

Hawk kept at it: "The location gives them good coverage. Florence is zeroed, so it's isolated. But the facility itself is also made to keep people inside, which in turn makes it hard to find out what's going on in there. They've got room to plan and train; obviously there are living quarters, kitchens, the works. It's pretty brilliant, actually. If you were planning on some serious criminal activity, this is a little bit like hiding in plain sight."

"And they're careful," Clooger said. His voice was low and rumbling, like the deep hum of a purring cat. "We were holed up for a couple days before going in, and we didn't see a single person. They don't come out unless they have to."

Meredith wrote the initials *ADX* on the whiteboard, along with a few other details from Hawk's location assessment. She'd pilfered a printer and some paper from a Staples down the road and had Hawk jack the signal in her Tablet so she could print photographs. Taking one of them out of a manila folder, she taped it to a corner of the whiteboard.

"This is Andre Quinn as of last night," Meredith said.

The photograph was green and dark, obviously taken at night with a special lens. Hawk had triple verified the image using photo recognition software, and he was 100 percent sure the photo was of Andre.

"So we know Andre is in there," Meredith said.

"And we know a few other details, too," Meredith continued. "Clooger and I consulted while Faith and Dylan were . . . what was it again?"

"Riding in a teacup," Hawk said. It was often difficult for Hawk not to provide an answer he knew, even if it meant a punch in the shoulder, which Faith delivered on cue.

"If you'd been here for the earlier briefing, you'd know the walls at ADX are upward of ten feet thick throughout the facility," Meredith said as she slowly paced back and forth. "More importantly, they're made of concrete, stone, and marble, substances we all know Dylan is susceptible to."

"You mean it's like his Kryptonite," Hawk said. He had recently taken to reading a lot of old comic books from a stall in the food court at the mall.

Meredith nodded tersely. "Throw enough concrete at Dylan Gilmore, and he's got real problems to deal with. Interesting they chose a place that's got more concrete than Hoover Dam."

Faith squirmed in her seat a little bit.

"They've also modified the security system," Meredith continued. "How does that work again, Hawk?"

"They've cracked the code on wavelength tracking, same as us. They appear to be using the same configuration I programmed into existing cell towers, which means they can sense a pulse from about fifteen hundred meters in any direction. If anyone flies near that place or tries to move an object telekinetically within a solid mile all the way around, they'd know about it."

"Why can't we shut it down?" Faith asked.

"Could," Clooger said. "But we'd need to knock out

the tower at the prison, which we're assuming would be a dead giveaway."

"So stealth is probably out of the question then—is that what you're saying?"

"Yeah, that's pretty much the deal," Hawk said. "We'd have to get in real close, like at night, and even then they'd know the second we went into action with any kind of pulse activity. I'm guessing alarms, machine-gun fire, possibly a heat-seeking missile."

"They've got rockets?" Dylan asked.

"Small ones but, yeah. They have rockets."

Meredith was making Faith look like an irrational fool, and everyone knew it. The enemy was holed up in a fortress as secure as Fort Knox. They had firepower, three second pulses, and isolation on their side.

A few more pieces of paper were pinned around the edges of the whiteboard—aerial views of the location—and then Meredith turned back to the group.

"Those people Hawk listed earlier, the criminals? Add them all up. What they did doesn't even come close to what Andre and the rest of the Quinns are capable of. You all know it's true."

"What are they planning to do?" Faith asked. "Why won't you just tell us?"

Meredith's face softened for the first time since she'd entered the room. If Dylan didn't know better, he'd have said her shoulders had even slumped ever so slightly.

"I can't tell you what they're planning to do," Meredith said. "Because I don't know."

It was a lie. Of course Meredith knew what Andre was planning, or at least thought she did. But no one in that room, certainly not three reckless teenagers, were ready for the truth.

"Based on recent events we know they have the resolve to kill in order to get what they want. And with three second pulses in Gretchen and the twins, they have ultimate power. They can destroy without being destroyed. And don't underestimate Andre. He may not be a second pulse, but he pulls the strings. He's the ringleader."

"What do we really know about him?" Hawk asked.

Meredith knew Andre better than Dylan, Faith, and Hawk could have imagined.

"He's come under the influence of some dangerous ideas," she said. "He's been poisoned by these ideas. And I have never known a man who could be so firm in his resolve once his mind is made up. They will do whatever he says, because that's what Andre Quinn causes people to do. They follow; he leads. And he's leading them and the rest of us over a cliff into oblivion."

"Great," Faith said.

"So what's the plan, then?" Dylan asked, narrowing the conversation to a bull's-eye. "What are you asking us to do?"

"Our task right now is to neutralize the twins," Meredith said coldly, her resolve returning. "That's the whole job."

"You mean kill them," Faith said. The words felt delicious in her mouth.

Even with all Faith's determination, Meredith wondered if this angry girl would have what it took when it came time to execute her enemies.

"But we have an advantage, and it's not the one you think it is. Of course they want us to know where they are. They'd love nothing more than to lure us into that prison and finish us off for good. We're the only things that stand in their way."

She had come to a hidden piece of information that had to be said.

"It's time," Clooger said, looking at Meredith as if he wished it wasn't so but knew that it was.

"Time for what?" Dylan asked. "What are you two not telling us?"

Meredith thought of the old song once more, of what it might feel like to have someone who loved her, who would wait for her no matter what. But that was the thinking of a young, naive woman, not a veteran of a long and heartless rebellion. The thought was gone almost as fast as it had arrived.

She wondered whether she should tell only Dylan the truth, not the whole group. That would have been fair. But for once in her life she was afraid, not of Andre or Gretchen or the twins. She was afraid of losing Dylan's love and respect. She couldn't do it alone.

"You're not going to like me."

"Mom, please. Just get it over with. How bad could it be?"

She looked him in the eye, because, in the end, she wasn't going to cower in the face of the only thing she'd ever really been afraid of.

And then she said it.

"Andre Quinn, the enemy of all that is good, is your father."

Chapter 5

October Road

Dylan looked at his mom and Clooger, and then he stood up and walked out of the room without saying a word. All eyes were on Meredith when the door closed behind him.

"You've got some explaining to do," Faith said, and, looking at Clooger, added, "What else aren't the adults in the room telling us?"

"That's all there is; and whether you like my methods or not, it's been planned this way for a long, long time. It's our way in."

"She's right," Clooger said. It was obvious he felt terrible about having kept the secret from them all, especially Dylan; but he also wasn't going to let Meredith take all the blame. "I've known since long before you and Hawk came into the picture. I could have said something, but I didn't."

"Why the hell not?" Faith asked. She wheeled around, facing Meredith, and seriously thought about putting both of them through a wall. "How come he gets to know and your own son doesn't?"

Calm down. These people are on your side, Faith thought. *Get a hold of yourself.* But her hands were shaking. She was barely keeping it together. "My parents pulled the same bullshit on me. I didn't know I was part of a rebellion until it was way too late. No one asked me."

Hawk was staring at his Tablet, doing whatever it was that he did that almost no one understood. It was his way of coping with confrontation.

"She's got a point," Hawk said without looking up. "If you're going to have us cleaning up your messes, you should at least be honest with us from the start. We probably would have said yes anyway."

Hawk wasn't exactly in the same boat as Faith or Dylan, but his parents were definitely caught up in the wreckage in their own twisted way. They, like he, were Intels. Their minds had been co-opted by Hotspur Chance himself a long time ago. He'd used them to advance the cause of the States, tapping into their brains as if they were nothing more than two supercomputers with processing power he could use as he needed it. No one ever discovered how Hotspur did this, but there was no doubt that he had figured out a way to use minds other than his own to process the most complex problems he wanted to solve. The trouble was, once he was done with them, they were never the same. All the Intels—hundreds of them in total—eventually turned in on themselves, their minds wandering in some unseen desert, searching for answers they would never find. Sometimes it took a year, other times it took decades; but it always ended in the same wandering madness. Hawk's parents had entered that phase of their journey, and they weren't coming back.

The difference for Hawk and Clara Quinn was that they were second generation, Intels by birth. They enjoyed the power of an evolved mind, but it was completely unknown if or when they, too, would devolve into madness.

Meredith looked at Clooger, and he knew, for once, he had to rescue her. It might never happen again, but it was happening right then.

"Sometimes we have withheld information, brought you along slowly. That was our call, and we made it. If you were in the military it wouldn't be any different.

You report to someone; you know some but not all the history; you bring the best you've got and hope it's enough."

He ran a hand over his noggin again, which was clearly becoming a habit he would have trouble breaking now that all those dreads were gone.

"Not a day goes by that Meredith and I don't wish we had second pulses or wish we were Intels. Good God, are you kidding me? If we could take care of this ourselves, we'd be the happiest people alive. But we can't, and that's a tough spot to be in: tough for me, tough for Meredith. We have to send you to do our job for us, because it's you three who were given the power we don't have. But make no mistake—*ever*: you do not have the good judgment to run this show. You don't get to call the plays. That's on us. And if you don't like the calls, there's the door. You can follow Dylan and make your own damn plan."

Faith and Hawk had never heard Clooger talk like this. It came straight out of nowhere, and it had the effect of shutting them up.

"You both know Dylan is as good as they come," Clooger went on. "But you didn't know him before. You two have only been in his life for what, six months? A year tops? He's come a long way."

"What's that supposed to mean?" Faith asked.

"He was angry, like you," Clooger said, staring at Faith with those fiercely independent eyes of his.

"Angrier," Meredith added.

Clooger leaned forward from where he was sitting.

"Believe it or not, you've settled him down," he said. "Don't ask me how, but you have. He can handle this now. At the beginning he was way too young. He wouldn't have understood. Then he figured out what he could do, and he had a hard time controlling it. He was as wild as a hurricane and twice as destructive."

Faith thought about how difficult it was for her to control her own outbursts. Wanting to throw a desk through a window was a daily temptation. She was in a relentless internal struggle, holding her power in check.

"The drifters took Meredith and Dylan in," Clooger said. "I was top dog. I ran the drifters. It was my call, not hers, not to tell anyone else."

"Dylan would have found a way to see his father," Meredith said, staring at the floor. "And that would have been a disaster."

"How so?" Hawk asked, snapping his Tablet to small and cradling it in his palm like a tiny bird.

"If you spent any real time with Andre Quinn, you'd know Dylan wouldn't have stood a chance if they'd met before he was ready. Andre is very persuasive."

It had defied logic, not telling Dylan; but Faith began

to see that in very real and important ways, it had made sense. And like any good secret, the longer one kept it, the harder it became to share it.

"Let's carry that forward," Clooger added. His eyes were still glued to Faith. "What kind of chance would we have—hell, what chance would *anyone* have—if Dylan was on the other side of this thing. We wouldn't even have you to count on, because it was Dylan who found you and trained you. We'd be a ragged bunch of single pulses, picked off one by one."

Meredith turned to the whiteboard and began writing with a dry-erase pen. "At this stage of the game a balance of power is our most useful weapon. Right now we have that balance, and they know it. They have three second pulses, but we have two—it's enough to give them pause."

"Pause from what?" Hawk asked. "If you expect us to trust you, you're going to have to start giving us more information."

Meredith didn't answer. She moved away from the board and let the words she'd written speak for themselves.

Protect the States at all cost. They will soon be under siege.

"So they want to do what? Destroy the world?" Faith asked. "But it doesn't make any sense. Why?"

"That's a question for which we currently lack an answer," Meredith responded in a cold, monotone voice. And on this score, even Clooger wasn't sure if she was telling the whole truth.

"Then how do you know they even want to destroy anything?" Faith asked.

"They did plan to kill the president," Hawk said. "Until Clara Quinn went rogue."

He was immediately sorry he'd drawn attention to Clara and what she'd done to Faith's best friend. Putting that information in front of Faith was like waving a red sheet in front of a rodeo bull.

"Really?" Faith said, feeling the sting of regret all over again, followed by the expected welling up of hate for Clara Quinn in her chest.

Meredith took a long breath and felt her fingers grip the pen tighter and tighter. She wanted it to explode in her hand, for the ink to spill down her palm like blood.

"I know because I was in the desert with Hotspur Chance and the rest, and I'm the only one who can make that claim. Nobody else in this room spent years with Andre and Gretchen. Only me."

How Meredith wished she had a second pulse at that moment. She'd wanted it all her life, and it was fine that Dylan had gotten it. But Faith Daniels? It nearly killed her to rely on someone who was, in her view, foolish and ungrateful and unpredictable.

"This inquisition is over," Meredith said, glaring down at Faith and Hawk. "We need Dylan, and we need both of you. I'm sorry it had to happen this way, but Dylan is an adult. He'll get over it. He'll understand."

As if he'd been listening at the door, just waiting for his mom to call him back in, Dylan reappeared. He left the door ajar, stared at Meredith, clenched and unclenched his fists. Meredith and Dylan stared at each other as if each were trying to read the other's mind.

"I'm sorry," Meredith finally said, which were two words no one in the room had ever heard her say. "I should have told you alone, not like this."

Dylan flinched, the muscles laced across the backs of his arms tensing. He nodded, almost imperceptibly, because somewhere deep inside himself, in the most secret parts of who he was, he had always known. Now that he'd been told the enemy was his own flesh and blood, he was surprised to find that it hadn't changed anything. The enemy was still the enemy, and his mom had done precisely what he expected her to do given the circumstances. She was, predictably, protecting him in the only way she knew how. Meredith may not have been the kindest mother around, but she had been right to tell him just then and not a moment sooner.

His eyes darted to the whiteboard for a split second.

Protect the States at all cost. They will soon be under siege.

When Dylan spoke, it was with a sense of finality and of knowing what was coming.

"What's the plan?"

Hawk breathed an audible sigh of relief, and Faith reached out her hand from where she sat on the couch. Dylan reached out and held on to it, and they shared a silent understanding as they looked into each other's eyes. The pathway to this moment wasn't what either of them would have asked for, but it didn't change the fact that finally, after all the training and hiding out, they were about to engage.

Time to even the score.

Fifteen minutes later, the core members of the drifters rebellion—Faith, Dylan, Hawk, Meredith, and Clooger—were now in a position to do something they'd been waiting on for far too long.

They were ready to fight.

"We'll be back, count on it," Dylan said. He was standing alone with his mom in the giant warehouse, thinking about how badly Faith had left things with her parents and how much she had regretted it. Faith's parents had died before she could reconcile with them; and no matter how angry he got with his own mom, he wasn't going to let that happen to them. It was selfish in a way, a sort of self-preservation. He wouldn't risk having regrets for the rest of his life. It wasn't worth it. Whatever problems there were between him and his mom, he wanted them put to rest, just in case. So he said a little bit more before leaving her standing there in front of the assembled rebellion.

"You were right not to tell me. I wasn't ready."

"I know," Meredith said.

Dylan pulled her close into a hug, something he hadn't done in years, and she slowly brought her hands up around his shoulders.

"But I'm ready now," Dylan said.

Meredith smiled weakly and forced herself to hold back the tears she would later cry alone, after he was gone. Dylan pulled away and had the distinct sense that she did not want to let go. That, for Dylan, was enough. He knew. In her own unusual way, she had loved him always.

The small army of single-pulse drifters, including the big Samoan, Semana, were lined up in a row in the center of the warehouse. Behind them, Hawk and Faith and Clooger stood before the vehicle that would carry them to their destination.

"Where are they going?" Semana asked Meredith as they walked past. All seven of the single-pulse drifters were curious about what was going on, but only Semana had the nerve to ask Meredith outright. Of course she didn't answer. Instead she walked up to Clooger and kissed him on the lips, touched his face, looked a little bit confused by the missing beard.

"You said no more secrets, right?" Meredith said. "This is what no more secrets looks like. Deal with it."

"Saw that coming a mile away," Hawk whispered to Faith.

"Sure you did." Faith nudged Hawk on the shoulder, nearly knocking him over. He was still a scrawny guy, even with the protein bars he'd been devouring and the push-ups he'd been doing.

Clooger pulled Meredith away from the rest of the group. "You're sure we shouldn't tell them the rest?"

"What would be the point? They wouldn't understand, and it wouldn't further the mission. They know exactly as much as they need to know. Nothing more, nothing less."

Clooger nodded, though there was a part of him that didn't understand at all. He let it pass, touched her on the cheek, and turned away.

"Shotgun," Hawk said, already opening the door of a vehicle that looked an awful lot like a Humvee.

"We can really get there in six hours?" Dylan asked Hawk as he climbed into the backseat next to Faith.

"This thing is nuclear. Trust me, we'll be fine."

The windows were down, and Faith jumped a little bit as Meredith came up close and put her hand on the door. The two of them looked at each other, a sort of stare-down, and Dylan touched Faith's hand on the seat next to him. She liked the way it felt, liked the fact the she was going away with him, away from Meredith.

"Don't do anything stupid," Meredith said. "Stick to the plan, and everything will play out the way we discussed."

"I'm just a pawn in this thing," Faith said, which was exactly the kind of sarcasm that worried Meredith. "Whatever you say."

As the modified Humvee pulled forward and the garage door opened slowly, the drifters sent them off with a cheer. Night had arrived outside, but Clooger didn't turn on the headlights; he just rolled slowly out into the darkness. Glory flew across the warehouse and landed in front of the vehicle so Clooger had to stop. All the drifters were single pulses, but Glory rarely used her telekinetic power in front of others. Of course she walked to Faith's window, no one else's. Faith seemed to be the target of all the advice on departure, and she couldn't decide if this made her feel extra appreciated or really pissed off.

"You remember what I said." Glory, like Meredith,

was not one to mince words. "Revenge ain't gonna get you nowhere. You do this because you have to, not because you want to."

Faith wanted to say *Are you crazy? Killing the Quinns is the only thing I want.* But she didn't. Instead she smiled winsomely, pulled Glory into a hug through the window, and let her go.

"I'll keep an eye on your parents, like I always do," Grace said to Hawk. "They'll be comfortable. They'll be looked after."

Hawk tried not to think of his parents, who hadn't spoken or acknowledged his presence in months. They'd already suffered the curse of the Intels. He could hope only for the mercy of passing now—that his parents would drift into death without pain or regret.

Glory flew away, glancing alternately at Faith and Hawk, until the garage door closed and she was gone.

When they were cleanly away from the training facility and out on the open road, Clooger tapped a series of commands on the Tablet-enhanced dashboard, then took his hands off the steering wheel.

"So listen," Hawk said, turning around to address Faith and Dylan. There was nothing like explaining new inventions for taking his mind off his worries. "The autopilot on this monster doesn't take passengers into consideration. If it senses something up ahead, like a broken-down car or a tree or whatever, it will maintain the fastest speed possible in order to avoid the hazard while also cutting the least amount of time off our excursion. Same holds true for tight turns."

Faith leaned forward in her seat and looked at the dashboard, where a Tablet was duct-taped on four sides with wires pouring out like licorice whips.

"We're doing 154 miles per hour," Faith said. "That can't be safe."

Hawk put his hand up defiantly. "Faith, please. We're not even close to top speed yet. This thing might look like a Humvee, but it's not. It's a HumGee."

"He likes to invent things," Clooger said. "And name them."

"When the Apocalypse is over, we're going to want these patents. Gold mine, trust me." Hawk turned back to Faith and Dylan in the backseat. "We're not really on the ground at all; it only seems like we are. Gyro-tech floats the wheels, so it's a little like a glider but not quite."

"That's why he calls it a HumGee," Clooger said. "Because we're gliding. But trust me; you'll still feel some bumps and curves. We're only an inch off the ground."

They were approaching a turn with a sign that indi-cated 45 miles per hour, not that anyone could see it in the darkness without headlights on; and the HumGee slowed abruptly to about 130, taking the turn at a velocity that lifted the two right tires a foot off the ground. Faith ended up in Dylan's lap.

"Seat belts are a must in this thing," Hawk said. "Sorry, I should have mentioned that."

The HumGee was as silent as a whisper, which only made the turns and the sharp jerks of the steering wheel more jarring.

"Me and Clooger retrofitted everything," Hawk said. "Wheels, tires, engine, electronics. She's smooth, but she's a beast. We can go up the side of a mountain if we need to. But out here, top speed is 240. Nice, right?"

"Are we really in that big of a rush?" Dylan said, pulling on his seat belt, which came down over his shoulder. The seat belt, the speed, and the fact that no one was holding on to the steering wheel made Dylan feel as if he were heading into a demolition derby.

"The less time we're out here, the better," Clooger said. "And don't even think about using a pulse. The closer we get, the more careful we need to be. No pulsing. Get used to it." Clooger paused and swiped the Tablet screen, which switched to a page showing miles to go (682) and time to arrival at current speed (3.6 hours). "Wake me in an hour; I'm bushed."

Faith and Dylan didn't believe sleep was even

remotely possible in this kind of ride, but Hawk had seen Clooger do it.

"He could snore right through a drag race," Hawk said. "And trust me. He snores."

They arrived on a long, straight stretch of highway, and Hawk let them know that the next hour would be fast and smooth.

"We can do 220 plus out here, really pile up the miles."

Clooger was asleep, snoring softly, and it gave the three of them a chance to talk in private.

"October road," Faith said as they angled slightly up on the pavement. They were heading toward Mammoth, a pass that would have been bursting with orange and yellow and green as fall approached. "This would have been a really nice drive during the day."

"You'll like Colorado," Hawk said. "It's beautiful up there. If it wasn't for the skunks, the wolves, and those a-holes the Quinns, I'd seriously think about relocating."

Dylan was brooding in the corner, staring out into the endless darkness as Faith leaned in close against his leather jacket. She loved the way it smelled and how it felt slick against her cheek. Sometimes she wore the jacket, which hung heavy over her shoulders. She was always surprised at how big it was on her, how it smelled so perfectly like Dylan.

"How are you holding up?" Faith asked.

"Yeah, how's it hangin', bro?" Hawk added. "This is going to be intense. Mostly for you."

Dylan shrugged and didn't speak, but they wouldn't stop staring at him. "All in all, I think it's a pretty good plan. I go in, act like I'm switching sides, and pretend that I think Meredith is a lunatic and a liar."

"That part is believable," Faith said, and then she felt like a bully for saying it. "I mean, if you don't know her like we know her. That's all I'm saying."

Dylan kept going: "I do all the recon I possibly can while you guys hold tight in the forest outside town."

"And if things go pear shaped?" Hawk asked.

"Pear shaped? What's pear shaped?" Faith asked. She moved her arm down and held Dylan's hand in the darkness, wishing they were alone in the backseat at one of those old drive-in movie places.

"Pear shaped. You know, sideways. Code red. In trouble."

"Can we stop talking about fruit? It's making me hungry," Dylan said.

Hawk held out a protein bar, got no takers, and unwrapped it for himself.

"Meredith said you had a communication device figured out," Dylan said.

Hawk set the half-eaten protein bar on the dash-board and started digging around in his backpack. "Move over, Faith, I'm coming in."

Hawk climbed over the seat, legs flailing, and forced his way in between Faith and Dylan.

"You need a car seat?" Dylan asked. He loved giving Hawk a hard time.

"Logically speaking, a car seat would be a bonus right now. But I'm fine, thanks."

Hawk's Tablet was in the small, handheld size, and he snapped it large. Soft light bathed the backseat of the HumGee, and Hawk looked up at Dylan and Faith. They were both taller and bigger.

"You should buckle up again," he said to Faith. "This straightaway isn't going to last forever."

"Is there a reason why you need to plague the back-seat? We were having a pretty good time back here without you."

Hawk didn't answer. Instead he opened a small, black box he'd brought with him and took out several items: a tube of clear gel, a set of long-nosed pliers, and what looked like a modified earring piercer.

"What the hell are you planning to do with those, Dr. Frankenstein?" Dylan asked.

The HumGee turned on a wide, sloping stretch of road, and Hawk's half-eaten protein bar slid along the dashboard, bouncing against the window and into Clooger's lap.

"I'll never see that thing again."

They were all bunched up together on Dylan's side in the backseat, like three aside on a roller coaster cutting hard to the right, when the road straightened out again and they all sat upright.

"I need to install sound rings on both of you, like this one."

Hawk moved a swath of hair away from his ear and revealed an earring. It was a black circle, not quite the size of a dime, and about half of the middle was hollowed out.

"That's a mighty big hole you've got there," Dylan said, trying to imagine what it would feel like to have a space that big stretched into the flesh of his earlobe.

"Usually you'd keep on inserting bigger metal bars so the hole widens slowly. But we don't have that kind of time. We have to do what usually takes a few months all at once."

"Huh?" Dylan said. He had a second pulse, but that didn't mean he couldn't feel pain if he let it in. This was going to hurt like hell. Faith, on the other hand, seemed mildly intrigued by the idea of what it might feel like having a pencil-sized hole punched into her skin.

Hawk continued: "I've been working on this thing

for weeks, just wrapped it up this morning. Meredith thought it would be best if I didn't mention it until we were on the road."

"Wait, how do you know if it even works?" Faith asked.

Hawk fiddled with the pliers and made a few adjustments on his Tablet without answering.

"So you're going to skewer us with that thing, and it *might* work?" Dylan asked. He knew this reaction from Hawk. He'd seen it before.

"It'll work. I'm practically sure. And it's worth it; trust me," Hawk said. "If we have these installed out in the field, we can talk with one another. All you have to do is cover the hole with your thumb and finger. In theory that will open up a connection between everyone who has a sound ring. No one else can hear us, but we can hear one another. Cool, right?"

"In theory?" Dylan asked.

Hawk had the first application prepared and ready to roll. "Undetectable, not on the Tablet grid. It uses old cell towers and outdated satellites instead. Who wants to go first?"

"I will," Faith said, pulling her long blond hair into a ponytail. Her drifters tattoo, the one with the ragged hawk on a limb, appeared at the nape of her neck.

"Stop staring and start drilling," Faith said. Hawk was definitely gawking. He'd never stopped thinking

Faith was gorgeous; and her neck was, in his opinion, first-rate. Also, she smelled fantastic.

Dylan almost said *I'll go first*, but he'd never had his ears pierced and Faith had. He at least wanted to see how it was done before getting stabbed.

Hawk foraged around in the black box and came up with two sides of an earring just like the one he was wearing, only this one was sparkled with blue and green, which was a perfect match for Faith's eyes. He held a penlight in his mouth, pointing the shaft of light at the two parts of the sound ring.

"Are those wires?" Dylan asked. Exposed silver tendrils as thin as strands of hair were rolled up inside.

"Yeah, and a circuit board. She's small, but she's powerful."

"I like that it's a she. We need more girl power on this mission," Faith said.

Hawk didn't answer as he loaded the two sides of the sound ring into the piercer, which Faith got a better look at for the first time. The center of the piercer was loaded with a pin that looked like a railroad spike.

"Umm . . . . ," Faith said.

"Not to worry; just smear some of this on your earlobe, and it'll loosen things right up." Hawk was barely paying attention as he held out the tube of clear gel.

Faith applied the gel and felt her skin tingle and numb, and then Hawk held out a length of cloth.

"There's maybe going to be a little blood."

"A little?" Faith asked as she took the cloth and Hawk moved in for the kill. She put up a hand and began softening her second-pulse shield. When she was ready, she nodded and Hawk leaned in, pliers in hand. It happened very quickly and without any warning, and Dylan was surprised when the profanities didn't wake up Clooger. Faith could curse like a sailor when she wanted to.

"Oh, my God, that hurts!" Faith said. Blood was dripping down the corner of the sound ring, but not as much as Hawk had thought there might be.

"Put some more gel on there, Tinker Bell. You're going to be fine."

Faith rubbed more gel on the wound and tried not to think about how it felt as if someone had cut off the bottom half of her earlobe with a pair of toenail clippers.

"You'll want to put some of that gel inside your ear, too. Smear it all over, just to be safe."

"Why would I do that?"

Hawk didn't know how else to say it, so he just came right out with the truth.

"A wire is about to uncoil from the inside of the sound ring. It's going to keep moving until it finds your eardrum, then it will stop. Not a big deal; it's superthin."

"So it's like a tapeworm. Oh. My. God."

"It's not going to eat your food, and it's not alive. It's a sound ring. It's cool. Trust me."

Faith couldn't help thinking there was something alive and sharp moving toward her brain. She felt something prick under her skin and began rubbing the gel all over her ear as fast as she could. The ear tingled, but the inside wasn't numb. It felt exactly like what it was: a needle moving along the cartilage of her ear, back into her head, behind her eardrum. She buckled over, shaking her head back and forth, and her long pony-tail slapped Hawk in the face like a horse's tail. When she sat up, the procedure complete, she called Hawk a name that was quite a bit worse than a-hole.

"I deserved that," he said, pressing the sound ring on his own ear. He turned away from Faith, and in the smallest sound of a whisper, he asked her a question.

"Can you hear me?"

Faith couldn't believe her ears. Hawk's voice was crystal clear. It was as if he were crawling around inside her head, closer than close. Faith pressed her own sound ring, and a little bit of blood seeped out at the corner. Her ear stung, but not as badly as she thought it might, and she yelled her answer.

"It works!"

Hawk bolted upright and shook his head, startled

by the volume of Faith's voice.

"For future reference, these things are powerful. You can just talk at normal volume. Or whisper."

"Sorry about that!" Faith screamed. She was still holding her sound ring.

Hawk's eyes went wide as the sound of Faith's voice rang like a gong in his head, then he turned to Dylan.

"She's pretty pissed off."

"Ya think?"

Dylan, having watched the entire proceeding, had turned wide-eyed himself, all the blood drained from his face. But there was no way he was backing down. If Faith and Hawk could do it, so could he.

"Let's get it over with. Give me the gel."

Several high-pitched screams, a harrowingly sharp turn on the highway, and a little bit of blood later, Dylan was wired up. His sound ring was white, but Dylan's hair was wavy and long, covering up any sign that he was hooked into the system.

"Even if it's exposed, I doubt anyone will think anything of it," Hawk explained. "It's an earring, simple as that."

"You're sexy when you scream like a girl," Faith whispered as quietly as she could, holding her sound ring between her thumb and finger. The message was meant for Dylan.

"I can hear you when you talk like that," Hawk said, pressing his own sound ring. Faith was starting to understand how the system worked.

"So if I press my sound ring and say something, everyone else that has a sound ring hears it?"

"Exactly," Hawk said. "And if you don't press it and we're far away from one another, no one else with a sound ring hears what you're saying. We're all connected; but to be heard, you have to press in. Unfortunately, I haven't figured out a way to turn the voices off in your head. That part you're stuck with. If one of us presses in and talks, you're going to hear it."

"So if I don't want you two hearing what I'm saying, I shouldn't press in?" Faith asked. She wanted to be sure she had this right, because she could already imagine some awkward scenarios, such as the one at Six Flags on the trampoline, where she definitely would *not* want to be heard by anyone other than Dylan.

"That's right," Hawk said. "Don't pinch your sound ring and talk unless you want to be heard. Keep it to the important stuff, like, for example, if you're surrounded by bears and forest trolls, that's a good time to press in."

There was no Dylan frequency, no Hawk or Faith frequency. They were all jacked into the same phone line.

"This is going to be awkward," Faith said. "And less fun than I was hoping."

"Just don't use it for some kind of audio make-out session and we'll be fine," Hawk said. "Actually . . ."

"Hawk, shut up," Dylan said. His ear was bleeding more than Faith's, which was turning his white sound ring the color of a fresh-picked cherry.

"Only one more victim and we're good to go," Hawk said.

They all looked into the front seat, where Clooger's shaved chin was resting on his chest.

"He's a little sensitive," Hawk said. "Better we get it done while he's sleeping."

"What, him?" Faith laughed. "No way. He's tough as nails."

Based on recent intel in the field, Hawk was positive this was not the case. Hawk hadn't told either of them, but when they'd been out in the field the last time, Clooger had been stung by a late fall wasp. The poor guy just about blew a gasket. If Clooger wasn't running on some kind of battle-induced adrenaline, he could be a serious wimp.

Clooger had an unusually large earlobe. It hung from the side of his head like a wad of chewed bubble gum, and Hawk had a hard time getting the piercer in place. The HumGee slowed down just as he clamped down, dropping from 190 miles per hour to about 120 in a matter of seconds, and Hawk flew forward, dragging

Clooger by his ear right into the steering wheel.

That was when Clooger woke up; and when he did, it could be said that things did not go well. Hawk hadn't quite gotten the sound ring in place, so he clamped down even harder as Dylan grabbed Clooger by his bald head and yanked him back in the seat, holding him steady. Dylan was a strong guy who lifted weights constantly. His arms were, in the truest sense of the word, a pair of guns. But even Dylan wasn't strong enough to hold Clooger still as Hawk clamped down as hard as he could and really drove the nail-like pin through Clooger's ear. All manual operations for the HumGee had been re-engineered so that autopilot rendered them useless, which was a good thing, because Clooger had Hawk wrapped around the steering wheel like a pretzel in nothing flat.

Clooger's string of profanity sent Faith into peels of laughter as Dylan got a hand on each of Clooger's shoulders and pulled him back.

"Cloog," Dylan said. "Calm down. It's us—Hawk and Faith and Dylan—and that pain in your ear? It's about to get a little weird."

"Weird how?" Clooger asked, freezing in place. He knew Hawk well enough to understand that as bad is this was, it could actually get worse.

"Lube him up!" Faith yelled, still laughing.

Hawk squirted gel all over the side of Clooger's head,

which effectively numbed everything from his cranium to his mouth, because Hawk had a terrible aim. Clooger was practically drowning in numbing agent.

"I'm having a nightmare," Clooger said. "That's what this is. It's not real."

But it was real, and when the wire started moving toward his eardrum, Clooger went for the door. It was the one aspect of the HumGee's fail-safe system that Hawk had never quite gotten to; and before anyone could stop him, Clooger had his door open, trying to roll out onto the empty freeway. While Dylan was being pulled clean up over the front seat and Hawk was on the floorboard wrapped around Clooger's legs, Faith pressed her finger and thumb against her sound ring and spoke.

"Clooger, this is your captain speaking. We've reached a cruising speed of 212 miles per hour. If you jump out now, we'll need to change your name to Road Kill. Now stop acting like a lunatic and close the door."

She delivered the message in a calm, Captain Kirk voice that caught Clooger's attention. He closed the door.

"I'm losing my mind," he said, but his face was pretty well numbed up, so it came out something closer to "Imoozingmimed," which sent Faith into another fit of laughter. She'd unbuckled her safety belt and rolled down on the floor of the backseat.

Hawk bolted from the floor, where he'd gotten wedged between the gas pedal and the brake, and tapped out an instruction on the Tablet duct taped to the dashboard, and the HumGee slowed rapidly. A few seconds later, they were stopped.

"I think that went rather well," Hawk said, his hair disheveled and wild on top of his small head. He looked in the backseat. "Where's Faith?"

They all got out and explained the situation to Clooger as he tried to eat half a protein bar he'd found on the floor under the steering wheel. His face was quickly coming back online, but the food was still falling out of his mouth as fast as he could put it in. Once he understood what had happened and tried out the new gadgetry a few times, he was in a fine mood, even excited.

"I don't approve of your methods, but the tech is, as usual, very strong."

It was sloshy sounding, but Hawk understood him just fine.

"Thank you, Clooger. That means a lot. And thank you for not killing me."

"So now you'll know everything I know," Dylan said, stretching his arms over his head. He was feeling a little twang in his right shoulder from the struggle with Clooger. "If I get into any good intel, I'll fire away."

"Don't be too hasty with it," Hawk said. "If they see you clutching your ear and talking to yourself, they'll be smart enough to figure this out. Only use the sound ring if you're sure you can get away with it. And listen, everyone; this system isn't for goofing around. Everything you say when you press in we can all hear. Let's keep it serious when we're on the ring."

"Affirmative," Clooger said. His face was back; he was feeling good.

"You're talking that way again," Hawk reminded him, then turned to Faith and Dylan. "He goes all military commando in the field sometimes. It's weird."

"I like it," Faith admitted. "Very direct, straightforward. No confusion."

Clooger nodded. "Thank you, Faith. We're going to get along fine."

Everyone became quiet, looking up into the sky or off into the woods at the edge of the road. There was a chill in the air, the first signs of winter moving in. It was too dark to see Mammoth Mountain on the horizon line, but they could feel it. Mountains, the big ones, were like that. Like the ocean or the Grand Canyon, their massiveness felt like a weight in the air all around them.

It was late, running on midnight, and the stars were thick and layered across the open sky.

"I guess we're stuck with one another for real," Faith said. "I can't even get you three out of my head."

"Welcome to the madhouse," Dylan said, smiling as they all got into the HumGee and started off again.

An hour later they left the main road and headed into the wild, Faith and Dylan leaning close to each other in the backseat, stealing kisses as they moved quietly along forested dirt roads.

"I wish we were alone," Faith said as quietly and closely into Dylan's ear as she could.

Dylan was in a quiet mood, a little distant, as if he was already halfway gone to someplace she couldn't go.

"Where are you?" Faith asked quietly, closely.

She searched Dylan's eyes for where his mind had gone off to but found no answer. He looked out the window at the passing shadows, and Faith kissed the soft skin on his neck. Dylan pulled her close as the HumGee sped up, passing 220 miles per hour on a long expanse of open road.

Not long after that, on the far edge of an abandoned stretch of Colorado farmland, Clooger stopped the HumGee.

"Close enough. Let's get some sleep."

They had arrived within a few miles of the prison, and with Clooger snoring and Hawk curled up like a kitten at his side, Faith and Dylan held on to each other.

Sleep took them all in rapid succession; only Dylan stayed awake.

Faith knew before she'd opened her eyes at the coming of dawn that something had changed. She felt a lonely weight in her chest as her arm moved around, searching for the soft leather. The jacket was there, but the boy who owned it was not.

Dylan was gone.

part two

PRISON BOUND

Chapter 6

Hey, Dad, How's It Hangin'?

Before Gretchen was the wife of Andre Quinn, she was a devoted follower of Hotspur Chance, the father of the modern State movement. She had been at the top of her class at Harvard before choosing Stanford to work on a double PhD. It had been there, in the chemistry lab, where she had taken the same test Meredith had taken on her Tablet, the one that asked its participants to concentrate and move objects with their minds.

Two days later she stood before a table, summoned into the Arizona desert by Hotspur Chance himself. She was struck at once by the clearness of his eyes, the way he zeroed in on her as if no one else existed. He had an intelligent smile that made her want, more than any-thing, to please him. This was the rare breed of man who attracted her: older, ambitious, driven, and against all odds smarter than she was.

Unlike Meredith, Gretchen encountered a lot of trouble with the color red. No matter how hard she con-centrated on the apple, it didn't budge. Everything else moved under the power of her mind, which she found both intoxicating and mysterious. But the red apple might as well have been hammered through with a tent spike. Her thoughts, no matter how focused, had no effect on forbidden fruit. Gretchen's intuition told her she had badly failed to come out on the winning end of whatever game she was playing.

"You're a special one," Hotspur said, and she turned away, feeling as if he'd slapped her across the face with his sarcasm.

Her gaze drifted away from the table and landed on Chance's assistant. Andre Quinn was more like a lap-dog than a high-level insider, at least that's how she felt about him. He was always smiling at her, telling her to remain calm, everything would be fine.

I have PhDs in astrophysics and biology, she thought then. *You don't need to worry about me. Worry about your-self.*

A month later Gretchen had mastered red just fine

and moved up in Hotspur Chance's pecking order. She was his star student, the *one*, as he liked to say. No matter how much she prodded, he wouldn't reveal anything else about her unique condition.

Gretchen also discovered, to her surprise, that Andre Quinn was not only a match for her intellect; he was a lot smarter than she was. There was nothing she knew that he didn't understand in a deeper way. Psychology, biology, physics, literature—he was a genius nearly on the same level as Hotspur Chance himself. At first this had infuriated her, but over time she came to find Andre almost as enthralling as Chance.

Gretchen had fallen into a routine of playing chess in the early afternoon with Andre, moving the pieces with their minds as they talked about the States, Hotspur's plans, genome sequencing. Andre routinely went easy on her until she insisted he try his very hardest. The results were swift and merciless: Gretchen was no match for Andre's brilliance.

It was then that she discovered her second pulse, because losing badly, especially at an intellectually driven game, made Gretchen see red. She got up from the table, enraged with herself, and walked out of the room. The hallways at the compound were lined with slick, painted walls of concrete. She balled up a fist, unable to accept the fact that five years of postgraduate work had done nothing to make her the equal of a natural-born genius. When life was unfair, it was fine as long as it was to her advantage. When it was not, Gretchen could barely stand the unjust nature of the world around her.

She turned to the wall, reeled back, and punched as hard as she could. Midway through this event her brain was loath to remind her: *This is going to hurt. It's going to break your hand. You're a fool for doing this.* But Gretchen didn't care. She'd expected her hand to flare with pain on impact. She wanted to feel the sharp blow all the way up to her elbow. When it didn't happen, Gretchen only grew angrier. She punched again, harder this time, and, looking at her hand, felt confused and frustrated beyond anything she'd ever felt (because confusion was a feeling that had always sent her into a tailspin). She went into a full-fledged rage. She flung herself against the walls, back and forth, harder and harder, until the paint started to crack.

When she lay on the concrete floor, sobbing and out of breath, she heard footsteps clicking down the corridor. They were far away, or at least they seemed to be. When she opened her eyes and sat up, Hotspur was crouching at eye level.

"I told you. You're special. You're the first."

"The first what?" Gretchen asked. She was, surprisingly, still thinking about the sting of losing to Andre.

Hotspur reached out and took her hand, pressed his fingers against the soft inside of her wrist, and closed his eyes. Gretchen felt her breath catch as he pressed down, the touch of his hand catching on something hidden.

"You have a second pulse."

Hotspur beamed as Andre came into view; and, looking at the man who had defeated her in chess, she understood that she had bested Andre in something much more important. She had something—something big—that Andre would never have.

"The rage will settle down, but it will take some work," Hotspur said, standing as he raised her to her feet. "Come with me."

He had developed a visual stimulus he called a Wire Code. He was still experimenting with the technology, but he felt sure a Wire Code would speed the process of bringing her emotions under control. As they walked away, Hotspur holding her at the elbow as if she were a doddering old fool, Andre returned to the room with the chessboard. He flung the pieces off the table with his mind and wondered if he would ever come to find a second pulse of his own.

Time and effort would show him that the answer was no.

It was, in the simplest view of things, the reason why Gretchen found herself able to be with a man who was smarter than she was. The fact that Andre was an Intel began to bother her less and less. She could put him through a wall whenever she chose, and he would cease to exist. He could not do the same to her. This was a variety of unfairness she liked in the universe, the kind that fell in her favor. But the unfairness could work both ways, and this seemed to be an especially strong pattern in her relationship with Andre. He had absolutely no romantic interest in Gretchen. It was as if her second pulse was an emotional wall around her, one he had no interest in scaling or knocking down.

First it was the brains, now it was his heart. This man had a way of always making her feel inferior.

And then Meredith arrived on the scene, a strikingly beautiful, older, and vastly more confident mature woman. From the moment Andre walked into the room with her, his hand on the small of Meredith's back, Gretchen knew. No matter how useless this new creature was, no matter how stupid or weak, it wouldn't matter. By virtue of no great skill or intellect as far as Gretchen could see, Meredith was the master and commander of Andre's heart from the moment he'd laid eyes on her. And she never let Gretchen forget it. Seven or eight times a day, sometimes more, Gretchen would fantasize about slamming Meredith's stunning face into the tile floor of the lab. She had to be careful about these thoughts, because fantasy and reality were but a hair's length apart when you could move things with your mind.

Wire Codes at lights-out helped settle Gretchen down; but the next morning she'd wake up, see Andre and Meredith walking in the desert outside, and her hatred would bubble up again. What she wouldn't have given for a piece of space junk to fall from the sky and flatten the wicked witch who'd shown up in her domain.

Of course Meredith never reached her potential. She was clever, but no genius. She never showed any sign of a second pulse or, for that matter, much of an aptitude with a single pulse. The most she ever moved with her mind was a garbage can full of bricks. Or was it a car? No matter. It was inconsequential. In the end, possibly because she was such a catastrophic failure, Meredith abandoned them all.

This was a turn of events that pleased Gretchen very much.

"Go to him," Hotspur had said, and though Gretchen secretly desired Hotspur even more than Andre, she did see the logic in the precise timing of reuniting with her husband.

She was pregnant with twins almost immediately, the course of her life set like a block of cement.

She would have been wise to examine carefully all

that had happened. Could Meredith have been with child when she left? And if so, how might that child be a problem down the line? Could Meredith have been smarter, more powerful than she let on? Was she really so weak, this woman who held the key to Andre's heart?

But Gretchen never thought about any of those things. Instead, as her belly swelled with the weight of not one but two second pulses, all she ever thought about was the fact that she'd won.

Years later, with their plans altered and Hotspur gone, Gretchen never forgot what those early rages felt like. She missed the pure energy they gave her, a feeling that was harder and harder to come by. She hadn't used a Wire Code since Hotspur Chance was still in the picture, a long time ago. And besides, she'd never believed they'd moved the dial on her emotions. Wire Codes were a fun little diversion, but no synthetic mind drug was taking credit for work she'd done herself. Gretchen was in charge of her own emotions, always was, always would be. She did find it humorous that the technology had leaked out into the abandoned world of youth culture. *Let them have a little fun,* she concluded.

She looked across the training facility and saw Wade and Clara laughing, and felt her mind flare with the idea of knocking their heads together. Not that it would matter if she did. Her children were second pulses; she couldn't harm them, and they couldn't harm her. It was a balance of power that took care of itself.

Why couldn't they take things more seriously? They were, without question in Gretchen's mind, the two most gifted children in the world. But they were undisciplined and arrogant and, worst of all, blatantly disobedient.

"This isn't a track meet," she yelled across the facility. "Get serious."

Wade Quinn was sick and tired of living inside a maximum-security prison. It was eating away at his soul.

"What's the rush? We have exactly nothing else to do today, and this won't take nearly that long."

"Get in position," Gretchen said. "Maybe you have all day, but I don't."

Wade and Clara were restless; she knew that. She knew what boredom could do, how it could make you lazy and less alert. Training was the only way to keep them focused and ready.

Gretchen tapped out a connection on her Tablet and gave the order. "Move in."

She had two units of single pulses, one with eight and the other with ten members. One of the units was stationed in the gun turrets, keeping an eye on the outside world. The other unit advanced on Wade and Clara with an array of weaponry. They couldn't use bullets inside the training grounds: too much risk of single pulses killing themselves with ricocheting or wild shots. It had already happened twice, and Andre had put a strict rule in place: no more dead pulses, guns were off-limits. At first the unit of single pulses hated the new rule that required them to throw and not shoot, but they got used to it. And they were getting more and more creative as the weeks went by.

"Better get ready," one of them said. "We got new tricks."

Clara rolled her eyes—*Yeah, right;* these guys always had some new deception they were trying out, but it never amounted to a hill of beans in the end. There was nothing they could do that Wade and Clara couldn't deal with. She took a good look at her competition. Throwing stars, shot puts, crossbows, ropes, a flamethrower— these guys were loaded for a real confrontation.

"This could be fun," she said. "I'd like to get my hands on that flamethrower."

"Let's go up," Wade said. "I have a feeling they'll try the net again."

"You go ahead," she answered. "I'll stay in the lower levels."

Wade shrugged. He'd known she wouldn't be told

what to do. It wasn't in her DNA to follow *anyone*, let alone her twin brother.

Wade rose sharply in the air, reaching the high ceiling in a split second. Five of the ten single pulses rose right along with him while the rest moved like lightning and surrounded Clara from the ground. The first set of challenges came in: three eight-pound shot puts, a favorite weapon this unit leaned on. Clara braced herself, felt one of the metal balls glance off her temple and another land on her rib cage, knocking her off her feet.

"Throwing the weight around nicely today," Clara said. What she wanted to do but knew she could not was heave these balls of fury right back where they came from. She could kill four or five single pulses without batting an eye, but that was not what this training session was about. She was supposed to find an escape route, for both Wade and herself, at the far end of the training room.

Wade was being blasted with fire from three sides, darting in and out of the flames. He was laughing; but he also knew that if his clothes caught on fire, he might end up flying around buck naked, and that was an outcome he really wanted to avoid.

"Come on, boys, shoot straight or go home!" he yelled.

Wade and Clara were both backed up against a wall,

and that's when they saw that the entire situation had been nothing but an elaborate distraction. A section of ceiling spanning twenty feet across came loose and crushed them both, pinning them under a pile of concrete. A massive dust plume filled the air. When the debris settled, all ten single pulses were standing on the fallen expanse of concrete, weapons at the ready, waiting for their two victims to slither out from under the wreckage.

"Didn't see that coming, did ja?" one of them said. Unfortunately, the slab rose up in the air like a magic carpet; and before they could react, it was back up through the hole from which it had come, trapping all ten of them on the second story, which was closed off from the training room.

Wade and Clara held the ceiling where it belonged while they walked toward the exit. They may as well have been walking in slow motion; they had all the time in the world. When they approached Gretchen near the exit, they let the slab of ceiling free-fall and almost wished the single pulses had been wise enough to move. It was a twenty-foot drop that caught them all off guard, and only some of them started flying in time to miss the landing.

The flamethrower bounced free, and Clara yanked it through the air with her mind, trained it on Gretchen, and fired. But Gretchen was lightning fast, jumping up in the air and flipping once, landing on the opposite side of them both.

"I do like this weapon," Clara said. She looked at Wade and imagined burning the clothes off his body.

"Don't even think about it."

Gretchen took two steps toward her children. When it came to relations between first and second pulses, she was having many of the same challenges Meredith was. "They're no good to us if they're hurt. And you should appreciate them more. We're in this together."

Clara and Wade kept walking, barely acknowledging that Gretchen had spoken at all.

"Give them back their guns," Wade said. "At least then it was fun."

Gretchen was ready to unload on both of them when the sound of a frantic voice came from her Tablet. She pulled the Tablet out of her pocket.

"We're under attack!" the unit captain on watch yelled. "Incoming!"

Wade and Clara didn't wait for instructions. They were flying through the compound as fast as they could, heading for one of the exits. The place was full of security measures; and, reaching the first of several, they found themselves held back by a giant door that looked as if it belonged at the entrance of a bank vault.

"Let's take it down," Clara said.

"Yeah but—" Wade said.

"Now!" Clara said. She was crazy for some real action, and if it meant using their combined forces to escape from a maximum-security prison, then that's what they were going to do. She looked at Wade, who nodded, and the two of them put every ounce of mental energy into ripping an iron door out of a wall made of solid marble.

Clara and Wade had focused as much pure mental force on other things lately, but the door and the wall were like one immovable object. Clara shot a bead of fire across the hall, knowing it would have no effect, then dropped the flamethrower in disgust.

"What a useless piece of garbage."

"Come on, Clara!" Wade yelled. He thought he could hear the door start to bend under the pressure of their combined power. He could definitely hear something that sounded like a very heavy door being moved. Being an Intel and, by far, the smarter of the two, Clara figured out what was going on before Wade did. She stopped exerting any kind of force and turned around just in time to see Gretchen smiling as the security door at the other end of the short hallway they were in closed.

"Wade," Clara said.

His eyes were glued shut as he kept at it, fully immersed in the effort of moving an immovable object.

"Wade!" Clara yelled again.

This time Wade opened his eyes and shook his head back and forth a few times.

Gretchen's voice filled the room from speakers embedded in the ceiling, and behind her voice, Wade and Clara could hear first pulses cheering.

"You're in the most secure part of the entire supermax," she said. "The walls are impenetrable marble on the outside, with two feet of reinforced steel hidden behind that. The door you're trying to open, and the one I'm standing behind, are both solid iron, with retractable iron rods that insert into the walls. Those rods are seven inches around."

"Bitch," Clara said under her breath.

"Don't talk to your mother that way," Gretchen ordered. "Also, there's no food or water in there. You'll be dead in a few days."

Cheers went up again, because it was the first time a unit of single pulses had bested Wade and Clara.

"They're good," Wade said. "Real good."

Clara had to agree, even if it made her want to throw up.

"Good one, guys. Now let us out of here."

A new voice came through the speakers. It was

Andre Quinn, and he wasn't in a favorable mood.

"I think it will be best if you spend a few hours in there. It will give you a chance to think about how not to make the same mistake twice."

"No way am I doing that," Clara said. "Lesson learned. Just open the door."

"I'd prefer it if you didn't interrupt me when we're training," Gretchen said. She hated it when Andre randomly inserted himself into her work.

Andre didn't answer, in part because he was, possibly, more annoyed than Gretchen was. Prison life had brought out the general in her. Andre had taken to holing up in the warden's old office, thinking about what was to come. They were days away from going into serious action, and serious action always made Andre nervous.

"We have a situation up here," Andre's Tablet announced. It was the first-unit supervisor from one of the gun turrets. "A real one."

Andre tapped his Tablet and spoke directly to Gretchen.

"Let them out. Now."

"Already doing it," Gretchen said. "But it's going to take at least a minute or two to get them all the way out there. I'll go."

"No, don't," Andre said. "Get the twins and meet me at the east turret. Let's not overexpose until we know what's going on. I can be up there in thirty seconds."

Gretchen was the only other second pulse they had, but if Andre wanted her to wait, she would wait. It was his funeral if something went haywire outside her control.

Dylan was walking steadily toward the walls of the supermax prison, still fifty yards off in the middle of an empty field. It was daylight, so the skunks and other vermin were holed up, out of sight.

"This is a secure facility," Dylan heard the voice over a loudspeaker warn. "Stop where you are. Don't run and don't advance. Don't move."

It was the second time the warning had been given, and Dylan wasn't changing his course of action. He saw, far off to his left, an abandoned van parked on the side of a road that hadn't been used for years. He picked up the vehicle with his mind, raising it ten feet in the air, and sent it flying. Glass and wheels and doors exploded off the wall, along with chunks of concrete from the wall itself. He very nearly blew a hole in the prison, which was maybe a little more damage than he'd intended to do.

But it sent the appropriate message. Before Andre arrived at the east gun turret, the shooting had already begun. Dylan was under fire from four different locations, bullets pelting the earth in bursts of dust. He didn't change his pace or his expression when the first bullet bounced off his shoulder. He felt it push against his skin, nudging him softly backward, but it did nothing to slow his progress. Another bullet hit him in the leg, puncturing a hole in his jeans.

"We've got a second pulse out here!" someone yelled. They'd skipped the loudspeaker this time, but everyone inside the prison went into high gear.

"That's not possible," Gretchen said. She had the door open, which was on a one-minute delay, and Wade and Clara were pouring out into the interior of the prison.

"There's only one person that can be," Wade said, feeling the adrenaline rush of a serious fight about to happen.

Andre was at the east turret, binoculars in hand, staring Dylan down.

"Hit him with a few rockets," Andre said. "Let's slow him down."

Andre had heard about Dylan Gilmore, but the intel he could gather was sketchy at best. The extent of his knowledge was limited to four items:

Dylan was a second pulse possibly aligned with Meredith, possibly not. There was no way of knowing for sure, because Meredith hadn't been seen by anyone in years. He knew she was out there, that she had her own collection of single pulses aligned against him, but that was all.

Outside of Gretchen and the twins, Dylan was the

only other known second pulse in the world.

They had determined, in a previous encounter, that Dylan Gilmore's weakness was stone, concrete in particular. (Andre was comforted by the fact that the prison was made of a substance that could prove useful as a weapon, should things get out of hand.)

Dylan had saved a single pulse named Faith Daniels because, presumably, he was in love with her. This was a touchy situation with Andre's daughter, Clara, who had killed Faith's best friend out of spite, because Clara was in love with Dylan, too.

"Gretchen?" Andre said into a secure line.

"We're on our way; what's going on?"

"It's Dylan out here. Clara's going to be upset."

Gretchen couldn't believe her ears. Dylan Gilmore? What was he doing attacking their camp?

"What's going on?" Wade asked. They were running up a switchback set of stairs, heading for a door that would release them into a long hallway.

"Nothing your father can't handle," Gretchen said, though she and Wade both knew that wasn't true. He was a single pulse. He could easily be killed if things went off the rails in the prison yard.

Outside, three rockets were fired in quick succession, exploding within feet of Dylan. When the dust cleared, Dylan was still walking. He was twenty yards from the wall when he uprooted a telephone pole from which the wires had been cut, turned it sideways, and sent it flying through the air like an arrow shot from a bow. It hit the main doors of the prison, rocking the turret overhead.

"Take it easy, Dylan," Hawk said into his sound ring. Clooger and Faith were next to him, monitoring everything from a secure location on one of the hills outside the prison. "No need to get them too riled up."

"We're taking fire," Clara said, smiling as she felt the walls in the hallway tremble. "Finally, some action."

When Dylan was close enough to see Andre in the east gun turret, he smiled cunningly. Andre was staring at Dylan through binoculars, so he saw the look, which was the last glimpse of Dylan he had before watching him vanish. Dylan had gotten much better at launching into the sky, and before Andre knew what had happened, there was no sign of Dylan at all.

"Find him!" Andre shouted as Clara, Wade, and Gretchen emerged into the sunlight. The moment they were through the double doors, all three were flying, circling the compound as they scanned the sky for Dylan.

But they were looking in the wrong place, because the approaching enemy had already landed.

Andre felt Dylan's presence behind him and wondered how on earth this kid had moved from where he'd been to where he was with such speed and stealth.

Dylan slammed the gunner's head into the wall and watched him slide down into an unconscious position.

"That's going to be quite a headache in the morning," Andre said.

"Better than being dead."

"Fair enough," Andre said. "Are you going to kill me, too? Because if you are, I'd rather like to fall to my death. It's just a thing I have about flying. Maybe you could carry me into the sky and then force me into a free fall. We both hit the ground at once, but only you live. How would that be?"

Andre was trying to distract Dylan only long enough for someone to see him, so it came as a shock when Dylan did precisely what Andre said. Everyone outside was searching for Dylan, but no one was looking for Andre. Dylan wrapped an arm around Andre's chest, pulled him out of the gun turret, and flew them both along the east wall of the prison. Dylan could slam into a wall or the ground and it wouldn't do him any harm. But Andre didn't enjoy that kind of second-pulse protection. He'd be a goner on impact and he knew it.

"Another twenty feet, security entrance at your right," Hawk said into the sound ring. Only Dylan could hear the words, because they were sent directly inside his head, on the back side of his eardrum.

"You got keys to this place or what?" Dylan asked, landing at the door and letting go of Andre.

For Andre, there was no point in running or fly-ing away. Dylan could alter Andre's path and send him sideways into the prison wall. He was helpless alone with a second pulse, and he knew it.

"I hope you know what you're doing," Andre said, holding his hand against a palm reader on the heavy metal door.

"Let's assume I do," Dylan answered, shoving Andre through the door and down a narrow, dimly lit hall. "Any cells in this place?"

Of course there were plenty of cells. It was a prison.

Andre's Tablet, which was in its small size stuffed in a back pocket, was full of chatter.

Gretchen: Andre? Where are you? Answer!

Wade: Is this part of the training exercise? It is, isn't it?

Clara: Lame.

"Give me that thing," Dylan said, taking the Tablet as Andre held it out and shoving him down the hallway. "Find me a cell. Now."

Dylan activated the audio for all parties on Andre's Tablet.

"Colder," he said, smiling. "You're getting colder."

"Holy shit, that's him," Clara said. "Come out in the open, I'll show you how a real second pulse plays!"

"Check all the turrets; make sure he's not hiding under our noses," Gretchen said.

"Still cold," Dylan said. "You're on Antarctica."

Dylan gave Andre back his Tablet as they came to a security door, which Andre opened.

"Plenty of cells in here. It's D block, impossible to escape."

"I doubt that, but let's test out your theory," Dylan said.

They entered the space, which was eerily somber. Incandescent lights cast a pale yellow glow on flat walls. As they came to the first of many open cells, Dylan was glad to hear Faith's voice in his head.

"Check in when you can. Let me know you're okay, lover boy."

Andre stepped toward the cell.

"Where do you think you're going?" Dylan asked. "The cell is for me, not you."

Andre looked at Dylan inquisitively. Andre was a brilliant man, but none of this made sense. Why would his enemy lock *himself* away in the most secure prison cell in the world? It was the kind of place even Dylan Gilmore couldn't escape once the bars slammed shut.

"Be my guest," Andre said, playing along as he cautiously moved out of the way.

To his surprise, Dylan walked right into the cell and sat down on the poured concrete slab that was supposed to serve as a bed. Andre's eyes narrowed—*What kind of trick are you trying to play here?* He activated the cell door and watched it automatically slide shut with a grinding metal sound.

Dylan felt the cold weight of the walls all around him. For Dylan they were like walls of dynamite waiting to be lit and turned into the one thing that could break through his second pulse. It sent a cold chill through him as he glanced around the cell and imagined the walls blowing apart and sending shards of stone raining down on him. It would take a lot of flying concrete to end Dylan Gilmore, but if it were used as a weapon, this place had enough. But this was all part of Meredith's plan. *You'll have to willingly give up your power,* she had said. *It's the only way he might come to trust you in the end.*

Andre stared at his prisoner, mystified by how he'd managed to lock him up so easily. His Tablet was going crazy with voices, but Andre didn't respond to any of them. He was into something highly unusual here, and the voices were distracting him while he tried to puzzle it out. He muted the Tablet, looked through the metal bars at what he assumed to be the only other second pulse in the world besides his wife and the twins.

Dylan looked up from his position on the concrete bed and spoke.

"Hey, Dad, how's it hangin'?"

Chapter 7

Cell Block D

"I wish I could have been there to see Andre's face," Faith said. "That would have been priceless."

"Agreed," Hawk added, fumbling around in his backpack for a bottle of water. "I'm working on rev 2 of the sound ring. It's got a video feed."

"You'll have to change the name. Too bad. *Sound ring* has sizzle."

Hawk stopped rummaging around in his bag and gazed into nowhere, aware that he'd fumbled the ball on branding.

"I need a marketing manager."

They shared a smile, because they both knew no

one was ever going to buy a sound ring or a video sound ring or anything else Hawk came up with. They were part of a rebellion, outside the State's system, fending for themselves. They'd be lucky to stay alive, let alone launch a technological product into the mainstream.

They'd set up a makeshift camp within a ring of fir trees that gave them excellent cover. They were positioned on the side of a hill, covered in tall, green trees. It was a zeroed part of the world, and according to Hawk, the only other people within a hundred miles were a small group of outsiders about eighty miles due west and the adversaries hiding out in the prison. The camp was deliberately basic and consisted mostly of the camouflaged HumGee. A tarp covered the rig, under which sat three folding chairs, a box of protein bars and ramen noodles, and several gallons of water. But it was no ordinary tarp; it was another of Hawk's recent inventions: a canvas that reflected the surface all around it, blending in like a chameleon. Assuming they'd stay long enough to need sleep, they'd do that in the HumGee, one in the front and one in the back, while the third member would take watch on a rotation.

There was a wide boulder on the far end of the encampment with a flat surface. From there they could see past two trees and right out into the open. All three of them—Faith, Hawk, and Clooger—were stationed on the rock, watching the proceedings die down.

"I can't believe they fired rockets at Dylan," Faith said. "I guess they weren't as concerned about their cover as we thought."

"Once they discovered he was a second pulse, I think secrecy went out the window," Clooger said. He was peering through a set of high-power binoculars.

"Now what do we do?" Faith asked. Unlike Hawk and Clooger, she'd never been on a stakeout.

"Now we wait," Clooger said. "And we don't use a pulse of any kind."

"And we lay low," Hawk said. "There's a good chance they'll send out surveillance fliers, just to make sure Dylan arrived alone."

"Hopefully he's a good liar," Faith said, but the truth was, she had little doubt Dylan could pull it off.

"Won't matter," Hawk said. "I've run some calculations, and given the size of our location and the obscurity of our hideout, the odds of being found by a flyover are one in seven thousand six hundred and nine. We're fine."

"Good to know," Faith said. She had a surprising appreciation for geeky statistical data.

They'd been out in the field for only a few hours, but already Faith was wishing she could get into the action. Just knowing Clara Quinn was close enough to go after was making her crazy.

"I'm going for a walk," she said. "I'll ring if I cross paths with a skunk."

Clooger shivered at the thought of skunks, told her to be careful and stay out of any prison sight line, and went back to his binoculars.

The forest grew thicker and darker of shade as Faith walked. A wet morning fog hung in the trees, which dulled the sounds all around her. It wasn't like the air and the open space near the Six Flags, full of brown hills and abandoned buildings. The fog and the trees and the strong smell of the wild calmed Faith's nerves, but the combination also put her in a melancholy mood in which thoughts she didn't want to have came to the fore.

She didn't want to think about her parents, who were both dead and who hadn't been there when she needed them most. But she did.

She didn't want to think about her best friend, also dead. But she did.

She tried not to imagine the one she loved surrounded by all that concrete and all those second-pulse rivals inside the prison. But she did.

This, she concluded, was why she did not take walks in the quiet of the woods.

Later she would conclude that another reason not

to go walking in the deep end of a forest at the edge of a zeroed city were the packs of violently territorial wolves. They'd talked a lot about wolves, but standing alone in their domain was a different thing entirely.

They were stealth, these wolves, all seven of them. And they were in the habit of attacking all at once, of taking no chances. Faith hit the ground so fast it knocked the wind out of her. She couldn't be hurt by these beasts of the forest, but that didn't change the fact that she couldn't catch a breath, her lungs confused and fighting for air. A set of teeth were wrapped like barbed wire around her forearm, more at her legs. Yellow eyes, bared teeth, and snouts were all she could see as she stared up toward the sky, wishing she could breathe.

When she finally got some air, a full gulping monster of a breath, she exhaled; and like the big bad wolf, she blew the space around her into oblivion. All seven wolves blasted up in the air, careening off trees and tumbling end over end.

Faith was on her feet in a flash, taking in deep wells of air, feeling the rage inside her.

"That all you got?" she asked, a pair of yellow eyes staring her down, the lone wolf that hadn't been tossed aside.

"Faith," someone said. She wheeled around and found Clooger and Hawk approaching delicately. One of the wolves Faith had blown up in the air had landed to the left and behind Hawk and Clooger, and it was moving fast.

"You should have called," Faith said, wishing she didn't have to do what she was about to. Hawk didn't have a pulse at all, and Clooger was only a single. They were both in danger. She started to think about altering the wolf's path as Clooger held up a compact cross-bow and fired. The animal fell backward, the arrow having passed through its neck. This seemed to have the desired effect on what was left of the pack. They hobbled away, turning back every so often, until they vanished into the fog.

"What did I tell you about pulsing out here?" Clooger asked. He was not in a happy mood. "Was I not clear enough?"

"Sorry, I—"

"Save it," Clooger said, reloading his crossbow. "It's my fault for letting you come out here in the first place. Should have known better."

"Hey, that's not fair. I was just walking. I wasn't doing anything. Those things attacked me. What was I supposed to do?"

Clooger turned on her. "Do. Not. Pulse. Is that clear enough? If you blow our cover, what's going to happen to Hawk? Or me, for that matter? Or Dylan? It's not just about you, Faith. Keep a lid on it."

He started walking away, but Hawk waited for Faith. She brushed herself off, pulled back her hair.

"Sorry," she said.

Hawk shrugged: *No big deal.*

"Now what?" she asked as the two of them followed Clooger back to the HumGee.

Hawk kept glancing over his shoulder, alert and nervous.

"Now we break camp and find a different location. And fast."

"Did you feel that?" Wade asked. He knew the difference between a first and a second pulse. Both created a sort of tremor under the surface of his skin, like a sonar sense that told him how far away the source was. And a second pulse felt different from a first pulse. It was deeper, lower, like the absolute bottom of a boom on a DJ dance track.

"Feel what?" Clara asked. Only second pulses could feel a second pulse, and obviously Clara and Gretchen either hadn't been paying attention or didn't care.

"I felt a tremor. It was strong," Wade said.

"I felt it, too," Gretchen said without stopping to turn around. They were heading for the prison cells, searching for Andre. "It's this Dylan kid. Must be him."

Wade wasn't so sure. Either his body was confused by all the mayhem going on, or he'd felt a second pulse coming from the direction of the hills outside the prison. But that was impossible. Still, not sharing vital information with one another was a Quinn family tradition. The Quinns were not unlike the family of a king in a royal court so many years ago: everyone was vying for position, the king had a vital weakness, and the pathway to the crown was full of deceptions and secrets. He decided not to say anything.

In cell block D, Dylan looked around his new digs and wondered how long he might be staying. Considering the fact that, for Dylan, concrete was akin to Kryptonite, it was about the most inhospitable room he'd ever been in. The bed he was sitting on, concrete. The floor was made of stone. There was an immovable concrete stool and a concrete desk jutting out from the concrete wall. There was a toilet, sink, and water fountain combined into one weird metal unit, and a tall stone pillar in the middle of the room with a showerhead.

"Nice place you got here," Dylan said. "Very cozy."

Andre examined Dylan like a specimen in a cage, trying to piece together whether it was possible that this second pulse sitting four feet away was in fact his son.

"Wade and Clara and Gretchen are going to be here in, I'd guess, under a minute," Andre said. "Anything you want to say before they show up?"

Dylan had rehearsed this part with Meredith and hoped he'd get it right. He'd succeeded in getting a moment of one on one; now he had to use it to lay some groundwork.

"They're not going to like having me around," he began. "Clara and Wade will want to kill me, which they could do. I have a weakness when it comes to cinder blocks, stone, that sort of thing."

"It's your second-pulse weakness," Andre said. "We know about that."

"I'm sure I'll get the full interrogation soon enough," Dylan said. "All you really need to know? I'm Meredith's kid, we're not seeing eye to eye on things, and I'm looking for answers."

Andre didn't believe a word of what Dylan was saying. He wished it was true, but it was impossible.

"I'm afraid you're wrong about that. I haven't seen Meredith for over fifteen years. The last time I did, she wasn't pregnant."

"You sure about that?"

"Yes, I'm sure."

But standing there and rewinding the clock on his memories, he pondered if it was in fact possible. It was not a period of his life he liked to examine, and it crossed his mind that, really, he deliberately had not thought about it for a very long time. He had been in love, he now remembered, and it pierced his heart there in the hallway.

"Meredith and I, we—" He couldn't bring himself to finish the sentence out loud, but it ran through his mind like a runaway train. *We were in love; I'm sure of it. Or was it only me?* He remembered the feeling of her body next to his, the nights in the desert when all had gone quiet and it was only the two of them alone with the endless stars overhead. And now he knew for certain why he hadn't thought of these moments in all the years after: because she had left him and he had never felt that way since.

"You and my mom were together, weren't you?" Dylan asked. "Seventeen years ago. And then she left, and you never saw her again."

Andre pushed the old feelings aside and raised his hands to his face, covering his eyes as he took a deep, cleansing breath. Could he wipe the shadow of pain and regret from his face so easily? He hoped so.

"It's hard to imagine you and I are related in any way," Andre said.

But his Intel mind had reversed the clock, calculated the odds, examined the situation from every angle. Conclusion: it was possible Dylan was his son, even likely.

A door slammed at the farthest end of cell block D. They were coming.

"I came looking for you because I've got questions," Dylan said. "Not for them, for you. And I let you lock me in here so you'd trust me. Run a DNA test on me; I'm sure they have that kind of tech lying around this place. You'll see. Either Meredith was lying, or I'm your kid. I'm not here for anything other than answers. If she was lying, then I recommend you do your best to try to terminate me. Because if I'm not your kid, I'm going to do some real damage before I get out of here. That's a promise."

"Andre?" Gretchen's voice echoed down the hall. "What are you doing down here? Where is he?"

"Run the test, *Dad*," Dylan whispered. "Let's see what comes of it."

Clara, Wade, and Gretchen all arrived at about the same time. It was Clara who spotted Dylan first, her blond brows creasing forward in confusion.

"Holy shit, it really is you," she said.

"And Andre trapped the little bastard!" Wade clapped his hands together, which produced an ear-splitting echo in the hallway. Then he turned to his dad, confused.

"How'd you do that?"

"Doesn't matter," Gretchen said. "He could kill your father with one thought. Get him out of here, now."

"It's fine, really," Andre said. He couldn't stop thinking about Meredith, about the day she'd left. And then Wade calling him *Andre*. Wade and Clara had both gone from calling him Mr. Reichert, his cover at the high school, directly to Andre. Just a natural progression, further away from *Dad*. Sometimes it felt as if they weren't even his kids any longer.

"Your funeral," Gretchen said. "But you know as well as I do—just because he's in there doesn't make you safe."

"If he'd wanted to kill me he'd have already done it."

Andre hated being a single pulse, especially in the present company. He was an Intel, he was brilliant, but he was also by far the weakest among the five of them.

Andre looked at the twins. "Give us a minute, will you?"

"Why would we do that?" Clara didn't ask so much as make it clear there was no way they were leaving Andre alone with this guy. She hadn't taken her eyes off Dylan since discovering him in the cell, and it wasn't clear if this was because she didn't trust him or because she longed to be with him. It was complicated.

Dylan hadn't brought along anything, not a Tablet

or a backpack or even a jacket to protect him from the cold. Black T-shirt, jeans with bullet holes in them, boots. That was it. He pulled the pockets out of his jeans, held up his hands, turned in a full circle.

"Unless you count my underwear and my socks, you're looking at everything I brought in here with me."

Wade laughed, then used his mind to throw Dylan into a wall inside the cell. Dylan flexed his entire upper body before impact and aimed his arm and shoulder to take the blow. He'd trained for this, preparing like a football player who would be expected to take some big hits, but the impact nearly buckled him over with pain.

It's going to take a lot more than that, Dylan thought as he stared Wade down. The blow had gotten through Dylan's second pulse and would, in due time, leave a bruise on his right arm. How had he let Meredith talk him into this again?

"Your brain is the only weapon you need," Wade said. "What do you think we are, idiots?"

Dylan focused his mind on Wade, stared him down like the enemy he was, and thought about throwing him down the long hallway.

"Don't—"

Wade tried to speak, but it was too late. He tumbled twenty yards end over end and slammed into the cell block D security door.

"You guys about through, or should we settle in for the show?" Gretchen asked.

Wade was back in a flash, ready to slam Dylan against the cell walls until he was finished for good.

"I say we end him right now," Wade said. "He's the only reason we've been waiting for whatever this grand plan of yours is. We kill him now, and nothing's in our way."

Andre didn't know what to do. His family was right: Dylan was extremely dangerous. He could wipe out the entire single-pulse army they had if he got out, Andre included. But the nagging question remained: *Can Dylan Gilmore really be my son?*

"Don't touch him," Andre said. "Not yet. He's not going anywhere as long as we've got him locked inside this cage. I need to think about our options. Gretchen, assess damages and put the units on high alert. Clara, stay here; keep an eye on our prisoner."

Andre turned on his heels and started walking away.

"And don't let any single pulses down here, too dangerous," he said over his shoulder.

"If we're not terminating this loser, then you can fill me in on your plan later," Wade said. "I don't trust him. I'm checking the perimeter."

Andre had expected as much. Wade was always

looking for a reason to escape the supermax. Seventeen and holed up for months on end with his parents and his sister was wearing thin. Clara, for whatever reason, had taken to the secret training center more readily than Wade had. But then she had always been more focused than her brother, more willing to bide her time in order to get what she wanted.

"That's a good idea," Andre said as he stopped and looked back, seeing his chance to splinter the team long enough to do what he needed to. "Give it a good flyover, check for anything unusual. Go alone. Now's not the time to risk losing anyone."

Wade was already moving down the corridor before Andre finished talking, and Clara seemed perfectly happy to stay with Dylan and keep an eye on him. Her second pulse would protect her if anything went wrong. That left Gretchen, who was boring down on Andre with her machine-like eyes as she walked toward him.

"We should interrogate him," she said. "Find out what he knows. I can do that if you'd like."

"Gretchen, please. Give me some time to think about this. Go talk to the units, get them organized. Make sure they know not to come down here; keep them on high alert. But let me deal with this situation my way."

There was a hint of condescension in Andre's delivery, a tone that had come up before when sensitive information was being discussed. There had always been a certain pecking order to which they adhered, and Andre, while technically the weakest among them, had been second in command after Hotspur Chance all along. When Hotspur was gone, Andre took over the directives for which they'd fought. Gretchen had always maintained a suspicion that it was because Hotspur, too, was not a second pulse. He could orchestrate the re-organization of the entire planet, but there was nothing he could do that would give him the power he lacked. He trusted Andre the most, Gretchen thought, because Andre was vulnerable in a way that she was not.

"I don't like the way this is playing out," she said. "Something is off. I can feel it."

But she didn't protest any further; instead she followed Wade toward the door and decided she would find out soon enough what was really going on. All the Quinns, most of all Gretchen, were in the habit of lying and deceiving one another. It was in their blood.

And so they went, all in different directions, all with their own hidden agendas in mind.

Chapter 8

She's a Little Unpredictable, This Girl

Clara was only too happy to have Dylan to herself. She hated to admit it, but she'd been obsessed with Dylan Gilmore at Old Park Hill, their last high school. He was eye candy, with his thick, dark hair and muscular body, and he was confident. He had been a diversion she enjoyed, someone to occupy her thoughts as one boring day led to the next, and she waited. It wasn't until she killed Faith's best friend that Clara realized her feelings were, possibly, much more serious than she'd ever realized. Once she discovered Dylan was a second pulse her emotions had intensified even more.

"You know what's really interesting about the two

of us?" Clara asked, flashing a toothy smile. She had kept her blond hair cropped short, which added to her assassin's beauty: strong, focused, gorgeous.

Dylan was tempted to say *Well, the really interesting thing is that we have the same father*, but he didn't.

"Go on, try to guess," Clara said.

"I'm no good at reading minds," Dylan said.

"You're the only other second pulse in the world besides my crazy mother and Wade. We're equal that way. We're special."

Dylan wanted to tell Clara that no, there was another. *Her name is Faith, and she's going to kill you.* But as much fun as that would have been, it was not in the cards just yet. It was the biggest secret he had going for him. So he played along instead.

"Look, Clara, I'm here because I'm through with the drifters. You think your mom is crazy? You don't know crazy until you've spent some quality time with Meredith."

"How is she nuts? Tell me," Clara asked. She was genuinely curious if Dylan's situation was like her own: an egomaniacal, controlling mother.

"She's got a god complex," Dylan said. "And she's mean. And she won't tell me what her plan is. It's like being in a cult over there."

"Where's over there?" Clara asked, smiling through the bars.

"Why should I tell you that? What's in it for me?"

"So you do have an agenda then," Clara said, smiling slyly as she paced along the bars like a caged lion. "I could open the gate on this cage and see what comes of it. I could come in there. That might be fun for the both of us."

Dylan smiled faintly and held Clara's gaze. How far was he required to take this in order to stay undercover? He regretted how he'd let his mom talk him into this and tried to move the conversation in a different direction.

"I don't have an agenda that involves Meredith or a rebellion or any of that. I came here because I have questions. Questions I think only Andre can answer."

"I've got a question only *you* can answer," Clara said playfully. "How's Faith Daniels? Or is she already dead?"

The blood at the back of Dylan's head pushed forward, a great pressure of resentment against his eyes as he willed himself not to slam Clara's head into the bars. It would do no good anyway. She would only laugh, and unlike her, he was sitting in a room surrounded by the one thing that could kill him if she slammed his head into it enough times.

"So she is dead?" Clara asked. Her brother, Wade, had gone quiet about Faith in recent weeks, but for a while Faith had been all he'd talked about. Her parents didn't respond one way or the other—an ordinary single pulse, who cared? Well, *Clara* cared. Clara cared a great deal.

"I don't see her much," Dylan said. "But she's not dead. At least I don't think she is."

Clara was pleased to hear Dylan wasn't with Faith and surprisingly enthusiastic about the fact that Faith was alive. She fantasized about killing her quite often. Now, it would seem, her wish might come true. It was only a matter of when.

"Clara?"

It was Andre's voice in her Tablet. Clara answered as though hearing from Andre was the biggest bother in the world.

"Yes, Andre?"

"Pick up."

Clara took her Tablet out of her back pocket and held it to her ear.

"What?"

A pause as instructions were given, in which Dylan tried but failed to hear the voice on the other end.

"Can't he do it himself?" Clara asked, obviously displeased with whatever she was being asked to do.

"All right, all right—I'm going."

She snapped her Tablet large and input a few keystrokes, searching the screen for information Dylan couldn't see.

"Dumb ass," she said under her breath, then, looking at Dylan, added, "Be thankful you're an only child."

Dylan smiled, but not for the reason Clara intuited. If Meredith was telling the truth about Andre, Dylan had a couple of half siblings, one of whom was staring him in the face.

"Don't go anywhere, my helpless prisoner. I'll be back."

Dylan did feel helpless. He wasn't used to this feeling, and he didn't like it. A few seconds later Clara was gone, and he touched his sound ring, pressing in and listening for voices. He heard none.

"I'm in the prison, safe for now," Dylan whispered. He thought about saying that he'd been thrown around some but knew it would serve no purpose other than to worry Faith. "Wade, possibly Clara, scouting. Stay invisible."

A long pause ensued, then Hawk's voice was big and loud in Dylan's head. It sounded as if Hawk were using a bullhorn.

"Copy, bro," he said.

"Sounds like you're screaming. Take it down a notch," Dylan said.

"Right, inside voice. Just excited to hear you're okay," Hawk said, and the volume went down considerably. "We've moved camp, higher up into the wild. Camo'ed the HumGee, looks like a giant rock. Pretty cool. Faith, you there?"

"Yeah. Hey, Dylan, I miss you. Tell me you're okay. Oh, and I got attacked by wolves. I'm okay, but I have another ripped shirt."

Dylan could hear the smile in Faith's voice, and he smiled, too. But he didn't answer because he could hear footsteps approaching.

"You're okay, right?" Faith asked. They hadn't been apart in a long time, and it was already weighing on her.

"How's the prison food?" Hawk added, trying to lighten the mood. "I bet they have some grade-A slop in that place."

"I miss you," Faith said, in a rare moment of letting down her guard emotionally in front of Hawk.

Dylan couldn't answer Faith for fear of being seen or heard. The girl he loved was saying she missed him, and he couldn't reply. It was agonizing.

Faith, sounding slightly annoyed, kept speaking. "So when a girl says she misses you, that's when you say something nice. Or send flowers."

"He's obviously got someone within earshot," Clooger broke in. "Shut up, you two, and stay focused. Dylan can take care of himself. Faith, anything?"

Faith was glad her reddening cheeks couldn't be seen from where she was hiding. Talking this way in front of Hawk was one thing, but Clooger? She'd half forgotten he was even listening in.

"Nothing to see here," Faith said. "All clear."

Faith was positioned up in a tree, a hundred yards in front of the HumGee, keeping an eye out for anyone who might come near. She stared off toward the prison, which she couldn't see through all the branches. She'd set up in a bad spot, a useless spot, and began climbing down for a better vantage point. Not hearing Dylan's reply made her anxious. Whatever he was doing, he wasn't alone.

"I'd like to review our situation, if I may," Andre said. He had returned, alone and focused of mind, and Dylan stood up.

"I'm listening," Dylan said.

"You have come here, unannounced, and willingly allowed yourself to be taken prisoner. If your mission had been to terminate me, you would have already done it."

"Still could," Dylan said. They both knew Dylan was capable of ending Andre Quinn's life in the blink of an eye if he wanted to.

"True enough," Andre said. "And yet you choose not to. The only explanation is that you really do think you're my son and, that being the case, that we'll have some things to discuss. But you're assuming this is true based on information you've been given by Meredith, who I happen to know is both cruel and deceitful."

"You know her well," Dylan said, stepping closer to the bars. He could almost reach out and touch Andre from where he stood. "But what if I am your son? What then? Maybe the two of us could help each other. Maybe we could find some common ground."

"What kind of common ground are you suggesting?" Andre asked.

"I don't know exactly," Dylan conceded. "But if you're my dad, I'd imagine we could figure out a way to work together instead of against each other."

Andre didn't respond. He stared at Dylan, and they held each other's gaze. Andre broke the standoff: "Let's assume I give you a DNA test. I can do that with my Tablet right now in less than ten seconds. I won't even have to draw blood. What happens when you're wrong?"

"I won't be," Dylan said.

"But what if you are? What then? You're safer to us dead than alive, that's what. Switching sides late in the game will have been a miscalculation that will cost you your life."

"I'm not on anyone's side. I don't even know what I'm fighting for, not really."

"You expect me to believe that?"

"Give me the test," Dylan said, taking one more

step, which put their faces within a foot of each other. Dylan could see the resemblance to himself in the dark hair, the straight nose.

"If I'm not your kid, I swear I won't hurt you. That's all I have; but it's my word, and I mean it. I won't retaliate."

"Okay, let's assume you are my son. That presents other problems you haven't thought of. Wade and Clara won't be pleased. They're competitive enough as it is. A half brother? They'll want to kill you, and frankly, I'm not sure I can control them like I once did. Gretchen hates Meredith even more than I do. She'll hate you twice as much and trust you even less. You can't win with her. If by some miracle we are in fact related, they can never know. It must be our secret."

"Agreed."

There was a long pause as the two of them stared at each other from opposite sides of the prison bars. "Look directly into the white circle, nowhere else," Andre said. He held his Tablet at eye level. A beam of light moved across Dylan's face, landing squarely in his eye. Dylan did not blink or move as Andre watched the kaleidoscope of brown and gold hues dancing on the screen.

"Andre? Are you in your quarters? I'm coming over."

Gretchen was on the move as the light from the Tablet clicked off. Andre engaged the Tablet receiver.

"Not now, Gretchen, I'm thinking."

He tapped out a few commands, one to turn off the voice and GPS activation so he wouldn't have to deal with Gretchen, and the other to set the DNA reading for its second stage.

"Now you," Andre said, handing Dylan his Tablet. It was strange, in a way, that everyone carried the same devices around. Holding Andre's Tablet in its compact size made Dylan feel that they had, if nothing else, this modern thing in common.

Dylan pointed the light into Andre's eye. If anyone had seen Dylan's eye and Andre's eye in the light, side by side, they would have said they were from the same person. Flooded with light and up close, the colors and patterns were nearly identical.

The light went out, and Dylan handed the Tablet back through the bars.

"So, what's your test tell you?" Dylan asked.

Andre didn't answer right away. He stood for a long time, staring at the small screen. It seemed to Dylan that a mix of emotions passed over his face like clouds shattered with lightning. Finally, Andre spoke.

"We are, as you say, father and son."

Andre looked down at the floor, and there his gaze remained as the two stood in silence. He was processing some unexpected realities. How many times had he and Meredith slept together? It had been a love affair more of the heart and the mind than a physical passion. But she hadn't only turned against everything they believed in and worked for, she had taken his son from him, lied about it, and kept that lie for seventeen long years. Meredith's betrayal was so much greater than he had ever imagined. It was this that had made it such an unlikely event in Andre's mind. *What kind of woman does that to a man?*

When Andre finally did look up, it appeared to Dylan that his father had made up his mind about some things. He was nothing if not decisive.

"This is our secret; you understand? No one can know."

"Fine by me," Dylan said.

"Right now we need to get you out of that cell."

Andre unlocked the gate, and it automatically moved aside. "Let me do the talking."

"Agreed."

Dylan started to exit the cell, but Andre stepped in front of him, taking a long look at who he now knew to be his son.

"It's going to be okay," Dylan said. "We'll figure this out."

"You're very—" Andre stopped short, searching for the right word. *"Unexpected."*

He put a hand on Dylan's shoulder, slapped it down a couple of times. "Life is never what I predict it's going to be."

"Join the club."

The two of them smiled at each other and walked out of cell block D, toward Andre's quarters, as Dylan heard Faith say something into his sound ring.

"You guys, someone's walking up through the woods. We're not alone out here."

"Get out of there, Faith. You'll blow our cover."

Clooger couldn't believe their bad luck. Why had he allowed Faith to recon in the first place? He'd said no, she'd said whatever, and when he'd looked back she was gone. Sometimes second pulses were a wild card he hated having to deal with, more trouble than they were worth. They could be like star athletes who suddenly disregarded plays called on the court for no other reason than that they could get away with it. *Go ahead, bench me. See how that works out for you.*

They had all three gotten into the HumGee and moved it down an old forest service road another two miles into the woods. One of the advantages of having a rig that floated an inch or two off the ground: no tracks to follow. It was cleaner than walking, left no trace. A broad, overgrown trail led them to a narrow clearing, where they pulled in tight against the trees and re-covered the rig. With the journey behind them and the chameleon cover in place, the team was nearly untraceable.

That was when Faith had requested a post outside, farther down from where they'd been, so she could bird-dog any approaching walkers or fliers. Clooger had said no, but, looking back, his star athlete was already heading the other way. Now she was down the mountain somewhere, hiding out in a tree, probably contemplating the use of her pulse.

"She's not going to answer," Hawk said. "Too risky. If someone's nearby, she'll keep quiet."

He and Clooger had slid past an opening in the cover and gotten into the HumGee. The only thing that could possibly give them away was if someone stood on top of the chameleon cover and discovered there was a vehicle underneath. Hawk detected the slight odor of skunk in the tight quarters and wished he could get out and breathe some fresh mountain air.

"We should be ready for this to go seriously sideways," Clooger said.

"Pear shaped," Hawk said, nodding as he squinted one eye. "I get you."

"If they find Faith out there, the whole Andre army is coming down on us."

"And Dylan is screwed," Hawk added.

Clooger nodded. "Yeah. And Dylan is screwed."

"If they've sent single pulses in, she could fly out. They won't be able to tell her pulse from their own, not with the system they have in place."

Clooger wasn't so sure; it felt risky.

"We give her an inch, and she'll take a mile. The last thing we need is someone getting killed out there."

If they could have seen where Faith was—more than a mile down the forest service road and off into the trees—they would have been even more anxious. She'd come down from one tree and started walking toward another when she felt a pulse nearby. It was subtle—a tiny tremor under her skin—but it was there. She couldn't say how close for sure, but the feeling scared her. If she flew up into the nearest tree, there was a chance that whoever was out looking for them would feel it, so she'd made due with her limited climbing skills and found cover quickly. Her long arms and legs had helped in the effort; but all the same, she was only ten feet up in the branches when she heard movement in the trees about twenty yards to her right. A few seconds later she heard a similar sound, like someone landing on the ground, behind her.

They've found me.

Faith looked up and thought about going for it, just

pulsing into the sky and moving fast enough that they couldn't see her. Maybe they'd think it was one of their own search party. If she could get inside the HumGee, she'd be safely hidden. The problem was her position. Branches seemed to be everywhere, and any kind of flying escape wasn't going to be possible without making some noise. The closer these two got, the tougher it was going to be.

She decided to wait, even though her heart was racing as she strained to hear the slightest sound. She heard the caw of two crows overhead but otherwise nothing. If someone was searching for an intruder, the window for escaping on foot was narrowing with every second she waited. Faith crept down as quietly as she could, dropped to the ground, and began running.

Wade sensed movement. He was particularly gifted at tuning his mind in to the world around him, and he was nearly sure this was the general location where the second pulse he'd felt had come from. He turned in the direction of the sound and started moving, floating just above the ground. He saw someone dart between two tall firs in the distance and took chase, flying low and deflecting sagging branches as he went. He picked up speed and rounded the wide trunk of a tree, turning sharply. It was a blind corner, and coming to the other side, something or someone shoved him hard to the left.

He tumbled wildly, crashed into a tree, and stood up.

"What the hell?" he said, standing and brushing himself off. He felt someone land behind him, felt the pulse in his bones.

"Whoever you are, you'd better run," he said.

"You're hopeless."

Wade wheeled around and saw Clara leaning against a tree, looking about as smug as he'd ever seen her.

"Cavalry's here," she said.

Wade wanted to pick her up and throw her at the prison.

"I don't need your help. Go back home," he said, already assuming a position to leap up in the air and leave her behind.

"For starters, that block of rock down there isn't home. I think we both know that. And second, Andre said you asked for help, so here I am."

"Didn't ask, don't need," he said. "Get lost."

"Wait—you didn't call for help?" Clara asked. She leaned away from the tree, took a step toward her brother.

"Hell no. Why would I need help searching a forest for signs of life?"

"Because it's a big space and you're one guy?" Clara mocked, but she was also processing the way Intels do: *Why did Andre send me out here? Why does Wade want me to leave?*

"You're hoping she's out here, aren't you?" Clara asked. "You're imagining that if Dylan is down there, then she must be up here. You're even more pathetic than I thought."

"I said get lost," Wade warned. "There's a whole lot of trouble out here for both of us. You want a fight, I'll give you a real fight."

He was referring to all the trees. The prison wasn't safe for Wade and Clara just because it was isolated and secure; it was also devoid of nature. Their second-pulse weakness, the thing that could get them into real danger, was nature itself. Roots, trees, ivy, plants—these were the things that could weaken them, even kill them if they came in violent contact with too much.

"Are you challenging me to a brawl?" Clara asked. She would have loved nothing more than to uproot a tree and hit her brother across the face with it.

"I'm going to say this one more time," Wade said. He was starting to feel the rage coming. If this went on for much longer, he'd go ballistic. "Get lost. I don't need your help."

Clara knew the tone of voice. Her brother was close to blowing his stack, and when that happened, all bets were off. It was a fight she might lose, and that was unacceptable. And what was Andre doing sending her out here in the first place? The Quinn clan was acting even weirder than normal.

"Good luck finding your girl," she said, smiling derisively. "And if by some miracle that actually happens, make sure she stays away from Dylan. Unless you want her dead."

Faith was hiding nearby, her bare arms touching the rough bark of the tree she leaned against. She'd heard the entire exchange and had a few thoughts of her own. It took all her willpower not to go after Clara and show her just how powerful Faith Daniels really was. She could beat Clara out here; she was sure of it. She'd put her chiseled face in the dirt, pin her under the branches of a tree, wrap a length of ivy around her sorry neck.

"Faith, I know you can hear me," Clooger said as he pressed into the sound ring. "If you're thinking about getting into some kind of confrontation, don't. Dylan's in there. He'll have a hell of a time getting out if you go bat shit right now. It's not time yet. Just stay calm, stay hidden, get here as fast as you can. And don't pulse."

Hawk looked at his partner's bald head, then at the look of concern on his face.

"You think she'll listen?" Hawk wondered.

Neither of them knew it was Wade and Clara out there. If they had known, the only sane course of action would have been to run.

"Who knows. Maybe."

"She's a little unpredictable, this girl," Hawk

observed. "But she's no fool. And she's not going to put us in danger unless she has to. Take it easy, big guy."

For her part, Faith didn't need the distraction of voices in her head unless one of them was Dylan. She wished he'd send word that the undercover plan—of which Faith had never been supportive—had failed. She wished he was calling for her to come on in: "Let's finish these bastards off right here, right now."

It was while she was thinking that precise thought that she heard a voice.

"You might as well come out. I know you're there."

Damn, Faith thought. Wade Quinn knew. He knew someone was hiding nearby, someone with a pulse. She could fly away, but what would that solve? She'd gone and blown their cover, and not with just anyone, with Wade.

This is bad.

She took a deep breath and stepped out from behind the tree, hoping the plan they had in place for just such an event would work.

"Faith?" Wade asked. He couldn't believe his eyes and for an instant thought she might be a ghost or an aberration of his own mind. Could it really be Faith Daniels, all the way up here in the middle of nowhere?

He was also, despite whatever he was supposed to feel, happy to see her. The fight they'd had at Old Park

Hill so many months ago swept across his mind. He'd thought, rightly so, that she might be dead. He hadn't been the one to throw the object that slammed into the back of Faith's head, but he'd seen it fly. He'd known it had hit its mark by the way Clara reacted. She knew when her aim was true.

"I know this looks bad," Faith stammered. "But let me explain."

Wade put up a hand and walked toward her, halving the space between them.

"I'm just glad you're okay. I thought maybe, after that mess Dylan got you mixed up in back at Old Park Hill—I thought you might have been really hurt."

"I was," Faith said, feeling a little more thankful for Wade's concern than seemed like a good idea. He was every bit the tall, striking person he'd been at Old Park Hill. If anything, he was even more attractive since the last time they'd seen each other. He was more muscular in the shoulders and arms, his face more chiseled despite a soft hue of three days without shaving. She had to admit she'd missed seeing him, not precisely because she liked him, more for the simple pleasure of gazing at a damn good-looking boy. "I didn't wake up for a while."

"How long?" He kept inching closer, which was making Faith nervous. If he tried to kill her, she'd have to reveal her second pulse; and that really wasn't an option at this stage of the game.

"About two weeks, I guess. That's what they tell me. I don't remember exactly."

"Well, I'm sorry," Wade said, clenching his jaw. He ran a hand through his blond hair, looked off into the woods with those sky-blue eyes. "He should never have brought you into this. It's not your problem."

"Well, it is now. I guess," Faith said. Stepping closer, trying to stay calm. "I owe him my life. Clara could have finished me off, but he protected me. It's why I followed him out here."

"Followed him from where?" Wade asked, the calculating, competitive part of his personality escaping for a moment. "No, wait—don't answer that. I don't need to know. In fact, it's probably better I don't know."

Wade was close enough to touch Faith if he'd wanted to, and for the first time, he seemed genuinely vulnerable and confused.

"Why did he come here, Faith? Why did *you* come here?"

She hesitated, thought again about flying away, and then put out the bait she'd been told to if this situation came to pass.

"He left all upset about something I'm not supposed to even know about. It's serious, also weird."

"Weird how?"

"You wouldn't believe me if I told you."

"Try me."

Faith wavered. It was Meredith's idea to tell Wade about Andre and Dylan, not Faith's. In her opinion, if telling Wade was an option, it presented the best of all circumstances.

"Is he okay? Can you at least tell me that?"

"He's a second pulse. It's not like anyone in there can end him without a mountain of effort. Dylan can handle himself just fine. You need to stop worrying about him."

Wade couldn't stand the idea that Faith might still be with Dylan. It made him want to knock down some trees. This was exactly what Meredith had wanted—*distractions.*

"You can't tell him I told you," Faith said pleadingly. "And you can't tell anyone else. He wants to handle this his own way."

"Whatever it is, it's not going to matter. You shouldn't be wrapped up in any of this. It's not your responsibility. I'll make sure he's fine, I promise."

It was possibly the biggest lie Wade had ever told, since he was dead set on killing Dylan himself the first chance he got. But he was starting to imagine a life after whatever tasks they had to complete were over, and Faith represented something normal and attractive to him. She was tall and pretty, headstrong, smart. He hadn't been able to stop thinking about her during all those long nights trapped in the prison, training for something he didn't fully understand.

"I shouldn't have come here," Faith said. "It was a mistake."

"No, it wasn't," Wade said. "I'm glad you're here."

He wanted to reach out to her, touch her soft skin, pick her up and fly somewhere no one could find them.

"You're not going to believe it, but I think it's true," Faith said, drawing out the end like a long thread from a spool. "Meredith told Dylan who his dad is."

"And this is important why?" Wade asked. He wished he could turn off the sarcasm in his voice, but it crept out just the same.

Faith hated it when he used that tone, always had. Go ahead, hit him with the hammer. He deserves it.

"Andre is Dylan's dad. For real."

Wade threw back his head and laughed out loud, because he was sure this was some kind of joke and she was about to get to the real information she was holding back. But looking at Faith, he knew at least one thing: she definitely *thought* it was true.

"Come on, Faith. That's a little wild, don't you think? My dad is Dylan's dad? That doesn't even make sense."

Faith shrugged. "Whatever. I'm leaving."

She began to float slowly up in the air, and Wade grabbed her by the hips and pulled her down.

"Don't touch me!" she yelled. Wade backed off and held out his hands as if he were dealing with a cornered animal.

"I'm sorry, just—just don't go."

"And don't treat me like I'm stupid. It's *true*, Wade. Deal with it. Why else would Dylan desert the drifters camp? Why would he come here, uninvited, and basically give himself up? His mom has been lying to him his entire life. He's looking for answers from his dad— *your* dad—and I'm scared for him. I'm afraid he'll never come out of that place, not alive anyway."

"I'll make sure he does, I promise," Wade said, a repeat of the same huge lie, because if Dylan really was his half brother, he was even more sure he had to get rid of him. The last thing in the world Wade Quinn needed was a brother to compete with. That was *not* happening, no way.

"Let me go back, check things out, see where we stand," Wade said. "I won't tell anyone you told me. I won't say you're out here. Just don't leave, at least not yet."

Faith half smiled and kicked the ground in front of her feet. She knew how important it was to sell this deception, but looking up once more, she felt an unexplainable attraction to the person standing before her. What insane gene in her DNA made it so hard to resist Wade's pleading? She felt the worst kind of regret—in love with Dylan but drawn against her will to a guy who had lied to her, who was on the wrong side of whatever she was involved in. *Why couldn't you have looked like a troll and lived under a bridge and had the most horrible personality ever?*

She took a deep breath and gave her answer: "I did bring provisions for a few days. And I raided a sporting goods store on the edge of town, so I have a sleeping bag. I like it out here. It's peaceful."

Wade agreed, it *was* peaceful. In four months of training they hadn't let him out for so much as a walk in the woods. It made him angry. And looking at Faith, he wanted more than anything just to leave everything at the prison behind.

"Meet me right here, tomorrow night?" Wade asked. "That should give me time to recon this thing and give you a better idea of what's going on. But no kidding, you need to stay out of this, Faith. It's dangerous. And Clara can't know you're out here following Dylan around. If she gets a second chance, she'll go straight for the kill. As far as she's concerned, you're the enemy."

Faith's smile, which had barely existed to begin with, vanished.

"I hate her."

Wade felt his Tablet, which he had set to silent, buzz in his pocket. The situation he'd gotten himself into was risky. Clara could come back; anyone could show up. His Tablet GPS was live, and he hadn't moved in five minutes.

"That situation at the games—" Wade said.

"You mean the hammer Clara put through my best friend's head? That situation?"

She held out her bare arm so Wade could see the hammer and the chain and the ivy. And most of all, the *C* for *Clara*.

"Yeah, I mean that. I had nothing to do with it. She did that all on her own."

Faith ran a hand through her long hair, pulling it back behind her ear. It was a nervous habit she didn't even think about, and Wade saw the blue-and-green circle that matched her eyes.

"Cool earring."

Faith took a step backward, wishing she'd been more careful. Had the unusual earring aroused suspicion?

But she needn't have worried. Wade loved her hair and those delicate ears and the fact that she could look him almost in the eye because she was so tall. The tattoo worried him, but for Wade the earring was just jewelry, something he could compliment her on in order to win points.

"Don't do anything crazy," Wade said, taking a last look at the tattoo on her forearm. He'd known a lot of single pulses who thought they could take a punch. It was like a disease with them. They could move a car with their minds, but sometimes they couldn't accept the fact that the very same car was solid enough to bash in their brains.

"Don't ever forget you're a single pulse. You could get killed just flying around for the fun of it. And you wouldn't last five minutes with Clara. It's not fair, but it's true."

Faith was becoming more controlled in the face of second-pulse bravado. It was getting easier to keep the secret. Her day was coming soon enough, and when it did, the payoff would be even better. She could imagine the looks on Wade's and Clara's faces when they finally knew: *This girl is a second. She's as powerful as we are.* Hers was a secret that was getting better with time.

"I'm careful," Faith said. "And I don't have any interest in whatever crazy mess you're caught in. I'm worried for Dylan, so I followed him. End of story."

"Same place, an hour after dark, tomorrow," Wade said.

He smiled that confident smile of his, a smile that had the unexpected power to confuse Faith's emotions, and then he was gone.

"Well, that was weird," Faith said. She wished she

had Dylan's jacket, because there was a chill in the air and it was a long walk back to the HumGee, where she'd left it. Then again, the jacket would have only set Wade off.

She started walking, pressed the sound ring.

"Sorry about that, guys. Coast is clear now. We're fine."

"No one saw you?"

Faith hated to lie, but things were complicated enough without Clooger freaking out.

"All clear, no worries."

"Don't leave us hanging like that!" Clooger yelled. "I call, you answer. You can't go AWOL, Faith. Not even for five minutes."

"Sorry, I just . . ." *What to say, what to say?* "I thought there was someone out here, but I was wrong. I didn't think a lot of chatter was a great idea while I was figuring it out."

Silence, then a slightly chastened Clooger. "Fair enough. Get back here as quick as you can and we'll regroup."

"At least you're efficient," Hawk said. "Took you all of one day to nearly blow our cover. Impressive."

"I'll be there in fifteen if I keep moving; fix me some lunch?"

"Unwrapping you a protein bar now. Chocolate peanut butter. Yum."

Faith made a sour face. She hated protein bars, but she was starting to love the walks in the woods. Wolves and skunks and Wade Quinns aside, it really was peaceful. Maybe someday she and Dylan would live on a mountain, have nine kids, and throw boulders at each other for fun. For some reason she thought of Wade, too. It had been more confusing seeing him than she'd expected, as if he were a magnet and she were steel and it would take some effort not to get pulled in, not to get hurt.

She belonged with Dylan, and as long as he stayed alive, that hadn't changed just because Wade Quinn was back in the picture.

At least that's what she told herself as she made her way back to the shelter of the HumGee, feeling the weight of all the lies that had piled up in such a short span of time.

Chapter 9

Trust Me, Grandma

Andre's private office had previously belonged to the warden of the supermax prison. There were rows of old books, which Andre had taken to reading in the evenings. It was an interesting collection that skewed toward wars, criminal justice, and true crime. There was also a smattering of poetry, most of it obtuse and depressing. The warden's taste in such things had run in the direction of Emily Dickinson and T. S. Eliot. The room had a long, wooden desk and file cabinets that had never been unlocked. A dim beam of light pushed through thick yellow glass high on one wall.

"Since the power grid went down we use generators for heat and light, but we try not to overdo it," Andre said, rubbing his hands against the light chill in the room. "Plenty of gas, but only three generators and no one mechanically inclined enough to fix them if they go down. If we'd been born a hundred years ago, we'd be practically useless. The modern dilemma, no?"

"Why did Meredith leave?" Dylan asked. Their time together could be cut short for any number of reasons, and he needed to move things forward fast.

"Right, down to business. Just give me one moment, if you would."

Andre knew he had only minutes before Gretchen or Clara or a host of single pulses showed up at his office door. The warden's office was one of the most secure locations in the entire facility. He tapped a few buttons on the wall next to the entryway, and Dylan heard metal bars sliding and locks locking.

"They'd need a bomb to get in here, and I'm not even sure that would work."

He tapped out a system-wide message on his Tablet and hit SEND:

I've got him in my office. We're discussing his situation. Leave us alone.

It didn't really matter how they chose to respond. If they didn't believe him, they'd assume Dylan had him imprisoned against his will. Either way, they weren't going to attempt any kind of rescue mission. Gretchen was too smart for that.

"I wish I knew why your mother chose to leave," Andre said, sitting down where the warden used to sit, in a worn leather chair Andre had come to love. The desk seemed more like an aircraft carrier when Dylan sat down on the other side, a vast wooden expanse between the two of them.

"You'll have to do better than that," Dylan said. "Where were you? Let's start there."

"A lonely outpost in the desert with very few souls. But we had our work with Hotspur Chance. It was all that mattered."

"Must have been something else, working with the smartest guy in the world."

"It was," Andre said, looking wistfully at the notepad on his desk, a relic from a time when such things were considered useful. "Your mother was one of the last to join us. I picked her up at the airport; can you imagine? She *flew* in—on an airplane. Seems like a million years ago."

A paperweight made of clear glass sat on the desk. Andre touched the smooth surface, imagined the chaos building outside as he sat in a locked room with a second pulse who had the power to end him with a single thought.

"Maybe what you were working on made her uncomfortable," Dylan said. "Is that possible?"

Andre felt cornered by the question and didn't want to answer it. He'd thought this might be coming though—it was unavoidable.

"For a long time I thought she left because she'd lost interest in me, and I do think that was part of it. I'm no fool when it comes to love, but I never really knew how she felt. Your mother was difficult to draw out. Not unlike Gretchen, come to think of it. I have a way of choosing the difficult ones."

Dylan used his mind to pull the paperweight out from under Andre's hand, slide it across the expanse of the desk, and land in his hand. It was heavy. Heavy enough to kill with, for sure.

"What were you working on out there in the middle of nowhere? Meredith told me Hotspur Chance got interested in human biology and genetics. That true?"

"Of course it's true. Without him there would be no pulse at all, not the one I have, not the *two* you have."

"Why'd he do it?"

"Why indeed," Andre said, standing and going to the wall of books. He pulled out a well-read journal, fanned the pages, stopped. *"No problem can be solved by the same consciousness that caused it in the first place.* Strange how this warden fellow had the same interest in Einstein as

Hotspur Chance himself, don't you think?"

He turned to Dylan, like a professor engaging a student. If Andre had all his faculties about him, which was not exactly the case, he would have remembered that it was he himself, not some long-forgotten warden, who had placed the journal there.

"Hotspur Chance loved Einstein, and do you know why? Because, like Einstein, Hotspur didn't see anything the same way we did. He was not of the same mind. He understood what was required for our survival in ways we can never fully know."

"The States," Dylan said. "But what's that got to do with developing or discovering the pulse?"

"It's a fine line—developing or discovering—isn't it? Hotspur did both. He unlocked parts of us that no one else could, because he had to."

"Why?"

Andre wouldn't answer the question directly. "The first second pulse was Gretchen. Did you know that?"

Dylan could sense that he was right on the edge of discovering what Andre's intent was. Meredith had always known the plan was violent, but she'd never been able to uncover any specifics.

"Gretchen was the one who changed everything," Andre said. "She gave us something the States alone could not. She gave us power."

Andre put back the book, continuing to talk as he did so. "We come to it now, don't we? If you're not happy with my answers, you'll kill me and go back from where you came. Isn't that right? Like taking an important chess piece off the table, then falling back to plan your next move. I'm very much aware of the simple fact that fathers and sons are enemies as often as not."

"Don't go all Shakespearean on me. I think you want to do something different than what you're planning. I think you want this all to end peacefully. Maybe together we can make that happen. That's all I want."

Andre flashed the same toothy smile he'd once used on Dylan's mother when they'd first met. He'd smiled that way at Faith Daniels the day she showed up for her first day at Old Park Hill. It was a smile he hadn't had much use for in quite a while, and he was glad to break it out for a little practice.

"And what if my plans don't align with your plans? What then?"

"Then we're at an impasse," Dylan said. "And I'll do what I have to do."

Andre sat back down behind the giant desk. "I don't want you to take this the wrong way, but should you choose to kill me, you'll never leave this room alive. It's secure. *Very* secure. You can throw things all you want, but nothing is getting out of this room unless I say so. It's locked from the inside, and only I know the combination to open it again. There's no water. You'd be dead in a few days. My side wins in that equation—the only second-pulse threat, neutralized. They can go on without me.

"It's not complicated, not really. You and I don't know each other, so we don't trust each other. We'd both like to stay alive. I don't want your mother dead any more than you do—well, maybe you do want her dead, but I don't. I just don't want her getting in our way, and she's done far too much of it lately. So we are at a bit of a stalemate, but one I think can be overcome."

"I don't want to kill you. I just want to know what's going on. I've been lied to my whole life. I have trust issues."

"Understood, and very helpful. So I'm going to tell you something now, and it will be up to you after that. Gretchen would not approve, but I'm telling you any-way. Consider it my olive branch."

Dylan nodded. It was a tight situation, and Andre was difficult to read. And he was right. If this were a game of chess, Dylan was a more valuable piece than Andre.

"Hotspur Chance developed an entire plan for the States," Andre said. "It was very specific. There was no ambiguity whatsoever about what was to be done. In the making of the States his plans were followed, but then the politicians got involved. Not just here, but worldwide. They took control, pushed Chance aside, and started making very big mistakes. These States, specifically the two American States, are not what you think they are."

"What's that supposed to mean?" Dylan asked. Andre had his attention.

"You don't know a prison when you see one," Andre answered. "The States are nothing more than that—comfortable prisons. And these are not prisons that will solve the climate problem. They've long since gone away from those plans, because politicians care about only one thing: reelection."

Andre leaned back in his chair and let this information sink in.

"All we want to do is get things back on plan, nothing more. We're the good guys, Dylan. Unfortunately, getting things back on track will require some persuading. Gretchen, Clara, Wade—they are an elegant solution. You must see that. They are very powerful. They are indestructible. They are, shall we say, persuasive. Hotspur developed the second pulse for this purpose: to persuade. It's my job to see that it's carried out."

"What about me? I'm a second pulse."

Andre shook his head, a cloud of frustration masking his face.

"I advised him not to teach Meredith how to draw

out a second pulse, but he did it anyway. You wouldn't even *know* you were a second if Meredith hadn't meddled where she shouldn't have. For that matter, there would be no drifters, no first pulses at all outside the ones I control. Her resistance movement should never have come to pass, don't you see? It's an abomination, a theft. It's a betrayal."

Dylan knew this part already, but Meredith had a very different view of her actions. For her, she was the only hope of resisting something that could overpower the rest of the world. Once she knew how to find and develop a pulse in certain people, she knew she had to flee. She would have to strike a balance or die trying.

Andre smiled that big smile of his.

"That's going to need to be enough for now. If you're willing to stay on, do some training, I'll make sure the rest of the team invites you in. You found us at a very opportune time, really you did. We're very near a decisive move, and I would love for you to be a part of it."

Dylan didn't trust Andre, not even close, and yet it was complicated. How much did Dylan really know about the resistance he'd been involved in his whole life? There had never been any real information, only Meredith's insistence that *they* were on the good side. From Dylan's vantage point, he couldn't be sure who was right and who was wrong.

"Wade and Clara aren't going to like this," Dylan said. He needed more information, so he wanted to keep Andre talking.

"Clara likes you; I think you know that."

"It was weird before; it's weirder now."

Andre's dark brows, which were not quite as thick as Dylan's but close, furrowed.

"Good point."

Andre had already thought of this, Dylan and Clara having the same father, but it bloomed in his mind once more like a poisonous flower.

"We can't tell her, can't tell anyone. She does well when she can't have something she wants; it's a useful distraction. Humor her. So long as Wade doesn't know you're my son, he'll go along. Not happily, but he'll do as he's told."

"They're not going to like it either way."

"Just do the training; I'll deal with them. We've got something new I think you'll find interesting. And if you don't like where this is going, I won't stop you from leaving."

"You're serious?"

Andre's heart appeared to soften, his eyes going a little wider and less authoritative.

"You're my son. It's highly unexpected, but the test doesn't lie. We'll talk more. I'll tell you more. And if at any point you want to leave, fly away and don't come back. I won't let anyone follow you."

Andre looked at his Tablet, checking the time, and saw that he had a string of messages.

"They're scheduled to train in an hour. Let's keep up appearances, have you stay in the cell as before. I'll make sure you're safe and well fed."

Andre was harder to read than Dylan had expected. Maybe this was all a front for keeping Dylan off balance and under control. But if he could hang on for a couple of days, hopefully he'd have the information they needed. They could stop the Quinns from whatever they were plotting.

Dylan would have been wise to consider more carefully the man with whom he was dealing. Andre Quinn was a master of manipulation. Much of what Andre had just said was designed to keep Dylan in line. When the time came, Andre would do the same with Gretchen and the twins: he would twist and turn the facts and events in order to advance the plan. And why not? He'd been thinking like a dictator for as long as he could remember. Dylan was another piece to be played in just the right way, an important piece because he was a second pulse. He would use Dylan carefully and productively. He would play both sides of the situation—his family and his estranged son—to advance the plan.

It was good to be the king of information, the minister of truth. It was the kind of power Andre liked most of all.

Andre opened the door to the warden's chamber and found Wade, Clara, and Gretchen waiting for him. If he hadn't been standing there as the only single pulse, it might have erupted into World War III the second the door opened. He could see that possibility in Wade's and Clara's eyes. But he was vulnerable—they knew this—and it gave him the time he needed to force the issue.

"Dylan has decided to join our cause. It's my call, no one else's. I've interrogated him, given him the basics and no more. He has agreed to willingly stay in one of the cells."

Wade was thinking: *You want him around because he's your kid.*

Clara was thinking: *If Dylan is pulling one over on us, I'll drop a building on his sorry ass. If not, I could get used to looking into those dark eyes.*

Gretchen was thinking: *Andre has finally gone insane.*

"Now we know there are no more second pulses out there to hinder our progress," Andre said. "Take him to cell block D and bring him something to eat. I'll check in on him after the training session."

"He's *training* with us?" Wade's tone was just shy of yelling. "You can't be serious."

Andre switched topics without batting an eye.

"I take it we're all clear outside, as far as you could tell?"

"Clear, yeah," Wade said, looking at Andre like *What the hell is wrong with you?*

"I didn't see anything, either," Clara piped in. "But it's big out there. The forest goes on for a hundred miles. He could have brought people with him."

"I didn't," Dylan said.

Wade was almost willing to out Faith, but it crossed his mind that Dylan might be telling the truth. Maybe Faith hadn't told him she'd followed him on a suicide mission. Wade liked the idea that Dylan might not know.

Clara was smart enough to realize that when Andre made up his mind about something there was no point in arguing. He was nothing if not decisive. She leaned in, reached toward Dylan with one of her trim, muscular arms, and smiled mischievously at him.

"Come on, prisoner of war. I'll take you to your cell for some personalized interrogation tactics."

"Clara!" Gretchen said. "Act your age."

"Trust me, Grandma—I am."

Wade usually enjoyed a certain amount of giddy

pleasure whenever Clara treated Gretchen like a dish towel, but this was even more priceless than normal. Clara was hot for her half brother and didn't even know it, and that gave Wade a level of satisfaction he hadn't felt in quite a while. The fact that he knew this and she didn't was so enjoyable it solidified his resolve. He wouldn't be telling her or anyone else for as long as possible.

There was a lot of anger and pent-up frustration boiling over at the door of the warden's office, but the Quinns were as good at evading confrontation as they were at creating it. Clara grabbed Dylan by the arm and pulled him out of the room, and Gretchen walked into the warden's office. As soon as Dylan was gone, Gretchen let loose.

"You can't seriously believe he's switched sides? It's ludicrous!"

Andre and Gretchen hadn't been seeing eye to eye on a lot of things lately, but he couldn't do this alone. He needed her, even if he'd long since stopped loving her. Had he ever really loved Gretchen to begin with? Meredith had come back into his mind and his heart in a way that he hadn't allowed since she'd left. *That* had been real love and a real heartbreak. He remembered now how it had felt. Whatever this was with Gretchen, it was not the same.

He stepped closer and put one hand on each of her shoulders. "Gretchen, he's possibly the dumbest kid I've ever met. It's almost sad, really."

"What are you saying?"

Andre walked around to the other side of his desk, beaming.

"I'm saying he's foolish and confused. He's willingly locked himself in a cage he can't get out of, and he's the only second pulse they've got. Without Dylan Gilmore, nothing stands in our way. He and Meredith had a falling-out. A *big* one. Take it for what it is—a stroke of luck."

Andre looked at Wade, who was leaning against the railing of the door.

"We have to make him believe we're taking him in, so let him train, at least for today. And then we move, sooner than we originally planned. Stick to the story when you're near him—we're planning a move in about a month—same as always. And rough him up. Don't kill him, just hit him hard. Understood?"

Wade liked the sound of that. He could kill Dylan by accident in a serious training scenario. There was enough concrete standing around to pull it off.

"Something's not right," Gretchen said. "How did he know where we were?"

"They've got drifters. Those guys are like trained hound dogs; we know that. It was probably Clooger.

He's ex-military, hard-core tracker. And that kid they've got—Hawk—he might be an Intel. But, Gretchen, it doesn't matter. Dylan Gilmore is in a cell in a maximum-security prison. And I've got some ideas about how Dylan could actually make our plans even more bullet-proof. He could really help. Either way, there's nothing Meredith can do now. We've got her ace locked up."

Gretchen calculated all the various permutations at play. It wasn't like Meredith to blow it like this, but it was spectacularly pleasing to think of having gotten the best of her.

"Either way, we need to move fast," Gretchen said. "The enemy is among us; that's a risk. If Clooger knows where we are, so does Meredith. And who's to say they haven't found another second? It's not probable, but it is possible."

Andre didn't agree with the reasoning, but he liked the direction in which this was going.

"So we move things up. We go day after tomorrow."

"Whatever gets us out of this hellhole fastest. I'm in," Wade said from the doorway.

Gretchen turned to her son and felt he deserved a reward for all his patience and hard work.

"Let's show Dylan what a real training session looks like."

Chapter 10

Wanna Play Asteroids?

Dylan stood alone in the middle of the prison awaiting instructions. While he lingered there, wondering if the training would include being attacked from behind, he thought about the previous hour or so. Fending off Clara's advances might not have been the wisest move, but given the circumstances, he hadn't had a lot of options. Clara had been cooped up with her mom, her dad, her brother, and a bunch of way-too-old single pulses for more than a hundred days. She was, to put it mildly, in need of some affection. He could have at least humored her for a day or two, and he might have been able to do it, but Clara was always aggressive when the mood struck her. He knew they had the same dad, but she had no clue; and this had turned the private space of cell block D into an awkward place for Dylan pretty fast. Clara had pushed him into the cell and asked, in her most seductive tone, *How about I lock us in here and turn out the lights?*

There was a limit to Dylan's acting skills, and the demands had quickly outstripped his abilities. His lame response had been that he was tired and wanted to be alone. That was when she'd pinned him against the wall of the cell, her chest against his, and whispered things into his ear that were strictly taboo between a brother and a sister.

"I'm still with Faith," he'd blurted out, a pronouncement he regretted a split second later. Whatever advantage might have been gained from controlling Clara's feelings had been lost in an instant.

Clara had backed off slowly, as if a cowboy had roped her around the shoulders and begun gently pulling against her will. "Then what are you doing here?"

"She's not involved in this, not anymore. But we're together."

"And here I thought she was dead," Clara had said, a mean tone in her voice as she backed up into the hall outside. "I should have thrown that rock a little harder, I guess."

"You're not attractive when you talk like that."

Dylan had managed to dig himself into a deep hole in a hurry.

"Whatever you say, Dylan Gilmore. I'm going to expel all this pent-up energy one way or another," Clara had said, engaging the lock system and staring at him from the hall with those steely eyes of hers. "You had your chance."

Now that he was waiting alone in the training yard, all he could think about was whether he was going to survive the afternoon. He'd been too cautious to press his sound ring and speak inside the cell; there had been too much risk of being heard by some surveillance system to keep pressing into the sound ring. He imagined that the whole cell block was bugged and wired up to monitors—had to be. And then Wade had retrieved him, escorted him out into the light of day behind concrete walls, and left him there.

The sky over zeroed cities and towns was always filled with circling birds. Crows and vultures flew with free rein over everything they saw, the natural order of things having taken over in the outside world. It made him wonder if it had been like that a thousand years ago, before so many millions of people showed up. A black crow, big and cawing angrily, landed on the prison wall. It looked out over the edge where Dylan couldn't see and flew off as if something were coming that threatened to end its life if it had stayed where it was.

"Dylan, get ready." It was Hawk, talking into his sound ring. He was seeing something Dylan wasn't. "They've got some new tricks up their sleeves."

As Hawk said this, something started coming into view over the wall. It was still far-off, but whatever it was loomed large enough that Dylan could see it from a hundred yards off. He hadn't been told not to move, so he floated up in the air on the power of his thoughts for a better look.

"Is that a—?" Dylan started to say. Hawk hadn't heard him, but he finished Dylan's thought just the same.

"You've got three train cars headed your way from the east side. West side, three more."

Dylan turned swiftly and saw what Hawk was seeing from his vantage point on the faraway rolling hills. Wade was standing on top of the closest car with three men lined up behind him.

"They've figured out how to combine powers," Clooger said. He was obviously watching, too. "No way one pulse could lift something that big."

"Hey, Dylan!"

Dylan whirled around at the sound of the voice and

saw that the other bank of three train cars had moved in much faster than he'd imagined. Three more single pulses stood on top of the short train, one each to a car. Clara was standing in one of the open doorways waving a metal pole in her hand. The end held a ball of concrete, which gave it the appearance of a huge lollipop or a tetherball pole ripped from the ground.

All the single pulses from both trains flew up in the air at once, taking up positions around the edge of the prison wall. These were trained soldiers and mercenaries, guys with combat training who had no interest in rules or regulations. They lived for this stuff.

"How are you doing that?" Dylan yelled at Clara.

"What, you mean this?"

Clara leaped from the doorway, and the train car began spinning around like a colossal whirligig flung into the sky. It was a ferocious mess of sounds—crashes and thuds and bending steel—with that strange sense of things moving in slow motion, like an elephant or a giraffe loping across a desert. But there was no doubt—this train was *seriously* moving.

"Come on out here," Clara shouted. "Better if we don't destroy the place."

Wade was pushing forward at Dylan's back with his own set of cars, forcing him to move out over the open field that lay between the prison and the hillside.

The single pulses followed along on both sides of Dylan. They were ghostlike, emotionless and focused, moving like shadows out into the open of the field in uncannily slow motion.

"I don't like where this is going, Dylan."

Faith was on the sound ring now. It felt good to know she was watching from some hidden place far up in the woods outside the prison, that she was almost close enough to touch. A sense of athlete's pride welled up in his chest and he moved, liquid and fast, out past the edge of the prison. He couldn't deny wanting to impress Faith. Why not show her what he could really do? The trains didn't scare him, and Faith would love it if he could get in a few choice shots on Clara Quinn.

They want to train? Let's train.

Dylan took control of the pole in Clara's hand, whipping the concrete bottom into her head and sending her crashing into a train car. She careened wildly through the air and let go of the weapon, which Dylan fired through the air like a rocket. It brushed past his face and headed for Wade. Dylan controlled it like a heat-seeking missile, matching every move Wade made; but it missed its mark when Wade darted at the last second and instead slammed into the line of trains, sparks, and concrete blasting away like a Fourth of July firework.

"Dylan, be careful out there," Hawk said. He and

the rest of Dylan's team were using high-powered bin-oculars, zeroed in on the action from a higher vantage point a few miles away. "Even with you distracting them, they're keeping a hundred tons of metal up in the air."

Clara's three train cars halted abruptly in a line across the sky. The cars faced Dylan where he hovered thirty feet up in the sky. Wade's line had done the same behind him. Dylan was flanked in on both sides, and the remaining two directions were lined with three sin-gle pulses each.

"She's back, watch out," Clooger said.

There were doors on both sides of the middle car in Clara's line, and the door on the back ground open. The metal sliding door on Dylan's side was already open, so he saw Clara drift in, that steely look of determination he'd come to know so well on her face. She lifted her arms, and the tops of the other two train cars exploded up in the air, flying like oblong dinner plates across the sky and skidding into the field. She had a wicked smile on her face, as if she was about to share something that was going to be an awful lot of fun.

Dylan heard a sound from behind, where Wade had done the same thing—the tops of those trains had blown off as well.

"I have a bad feeling about this, Dylan," Faith said

into Dylan's sound ring. "Get out of there!"

All six single pulses flew straight back, as if dragons or monsters were about to emerge from the train cars and they didn't want to be anywhere near the carnage that was about to take place. The train cars faltered, as if unseen ground beneath them had started to give way, and then they steadied again. Out of the tops of Clara's train cars there came a hailstorm of boulders, slabs of concrete, chunks of cinder blocks. Rocks as big as garbage cans and blocks as small as toasters all flew in Dylan's direction at once. Wave after wave, an ocean of stone, coming in from both sides.

"Move, Dylan!" Faith yelled.

Dylan imagined she was having an almost impossible time staying put. He had to escape fast or she'd break cover and come to his rescue. He rolled into a ball, grabbing his sound ring as he did—"Don't you dare come out here. I love you. And I got this." Dylan began spinning around, a whirling globe of energy, forcing his every thought into deflecting the storm heading his way.

Debris bounced off Dylan, flying in every direction. From Hawk's vantage point it looked as if someone had dropped a bag of a thousand marbles onto a kitchen floor. Rocks were flying everywhere, and the blast zone was getting wider and wider. Dylan came out of his rolling, ball-of-thunder move and expertly dodged everything coming his way. But Clara and Wade kept firing, and they kept moving the trains in closer and closer, narrowing the playing field foot by foot. One of the train cars in Wade's line suddenly lost its footing, drawing the other two down with it into a crashing blast of dirt and metal.

Dylan took his first damage, a recliner-sized rock landing squarely on his back, which sent him flying toward Clara. He dodged and parried oncoming objects, catching a glimpse of Clara, who had taken up another weapon: a chain with a block of concrete for a tip. She was swinging it in a circle over her head, her target flying out of control in her direction.

"No way," Faith said.

"Faith, don't!" Clooger said.

Clara let the chain go, watched the ball of concrete fly toward its mark, and didn't sense what was happening around her. Her aim, as usual, was true, but she never saw the resulting blow that sent Dylan into the dirt below. The train cars wrapped around Clara like an accordion, enveloping her in metal.

Faith put every ounce of energy she had into those three train cars. She couldn't hold it aloft, but she could sure as hell give it one good throw. The cars flew through the storm of debris, rocks ricocheting in every direction, and carried Clara along for the ride. When the train cars hit the prison wall, the sound was like a bomb going off. A giant swath of wall broke free, breaking into a thousand pieces.

By the time Clara cleared herself from the mess, the field had gone quiet. All but one of the objects that had been thrown had fallen to earth, including Dylan. Wade held the last one aloft—a table-sized slab of thick concrete—a few feet off Dylan's body.

"I can't let this happen," Faith said. "I can't."

"Faith—" Clooger tried to stop her, but he didn't need to. Dylan hit that slab of stone with the power of his mind so hard and so fast it carried Wade a hundred yards up into the sky. The slab turned sharply, flipping Wade over, and dived for the ground.

"Don't do it, Dylan," Clooger said. "You'll only make him angrier."

Dylan couldn't help himself. He'd taken some damage, could feel the bruises forming on his arms and back already. They'd wanted to finish him, and Andre hadn't stopped them. He watched Wade trying to scramble out from under the sheet of stone as it neared the ground below. He was a fly caught under a swatter, about to be smashed.

The slab abruptly flew to the right, which made it look like a broken Frisbee spinning out of control, and Wade slowed down from about a thousand miles an hour to three hundred before slamming into the ground. The dust plumed fifty feet in every direction, and when it settled, Wade was already wobbling to his feet. He walked two or three steps, fell to his knees, and toppled over like a bag of potatoes.

Dylan gazed off into the hills, searching for signs of life.

"Sorry, pal. Couldn't let you hurt him any worse than that," Clooger said. He'd broken his own rule and used a pulse to slow down the slab. "Here comes trouble. Better get focused."

Gretchen had arrived on the scene. She'd flown in, landed, and was using one of her feet to roll Wade over on his back.

"Get up," she said.

She looked at the demolished wall of the prison and shook her head. When Dylan and Clara arrived at the same time from different directions, she didn't bother looking at either of them. Wade sat up and spit the dirt out of his mouth.

"Two injured first pulses," Gretchen said. "Useless to us now. Happy?"

"Hey, you're the one who told us to turn up the heat on this guy," Wade said. He stood, brushed off his pants, glared at Dylan.

"I didn't authorize you to put our help in harm's way," Gretchen snapped. "It's always the same with you two, going rogue—it's exhausting."

"They're useless anyway," Clara said. "Just get rid of them already."

"Not an option," Gretchen said. "We'll be holding up a lot more than a few train cars. Then you won't think they're so useless. You think you're the only ones who matter, so irreplaceable."

"Interesting that Dylan could have finished you off," Gretchen said, staring at Wade as if he really didn't measure up. "You're not as indestructible as you let on."

Whoa. This was shaky ground. Dylan knew both Wade's and Clara's second-pulse weakness, and they knew his. Both sides had been exploiting those weaknesses throughout the training session.

Clara stepped closer, staring down at Gretchen from her lofty six-foot-two height. She had that reckless look in her eye. This girl was about to do something monumentally stupid.

"How about we bring out the hoses for our next training session? Do some real damage."

Gretchen flashed a look at Dylan that lasted a split second and was gone. *There! Right there!* Dylan thought. Something was revealed that should not have been.

"Lay off, Clara," Wade said, giving her a look that

revealed all too much. *Mixed company, what the hell are you doing?*

"This training session is over," Gretchen said. She glared at Dylan. "Take him back to the cell, then come to Andre's office. We've got things to discuss. I'll have the single pulses sweep the field of debris."

Gretchen drifted up in the air, staring bullets at Clara before turning her attention to the gun turret in the prison yard. Dylan turned that way, too, and saw the shadow of a man—Andre—and wondered how many puppet strings his dad was pulling on.

Once Gretchen was gone, Clara shot Dylan a smile with a raised eyebrow. She'd told him something valuable there and wanted him to know it. But why?

Dylan's curiosity was seriously piqued. He was also wondering if he'd bruised a rib that ran beneath his right arm. He hated it when his second pulse was breached. It was the only time he felt vulnerable. The thought crossed his mind that it had been exactly the kind of situation that could end him for good.

An hour later Clara and Wade finally knew the plan.

There were days, many of them, when Clara wondered if she would be kept in the dark forever, lost in a haze of training and curiosity that would simply go on into eternity. Hadn't the secrets been there, in one form or another, her entire life? Always more training, never being told what it was all for or when it would all end. It had long felt like her purgatory, or worse, her hell, with only two people who could unlock the gates and set her free: Andre or Gretchen. Maybe that was why, when she was finally told what the plan was, it worked like a lever on a great machine in her Intel mind, setting a series of thoughts in motion.

It was possible that some of what Andre and Gretchen had told her was a lie, but it had felt like the truth. They'd brought her and Wade into the warden's office, sat them down, and spilled the beans. They took great pleasure in the unfolding of their long prepara-tion, the surprising details, the essential agenda. Wade had responded in the expected way: whooping like a linebacker set loose on a quarterback. *Let's do this thing!* But like all good Intels, Clara had calculated everything as if the plan itself was laid out flat on a table like a dia-gram, each naked element examined under the brutal power of her mind.

At long last Clara had been given the details for which she'd been waiting. Now it was just a matter of using them to her fullest advantage.

She saw herself as setting a series of bombs that would go off at different times and locations. The first of these involved Gretchen, who she hated almost as much as Faith Daniels. Clara felt, rightfully so, that her mother had never cared about her. Not from the moment Clara had been born. Gretchen had only ever seen Clara as competition, someone to be molded and, ultimately, ruled over. Knowing this was true at the very core of her being made it a lot easier to reveal Gretchen's weakness to Dylan. Now that she knew the entire plan, the next order of business was pitting her two most hated enemies against each other. She'd wondered how this was going to be possible until her twin brother unexpectedly provided the solution.

"There's no way Dylan has switched sides," Clara said as they walked away from the warden's office. "It's cool we have him locked up and all, but he's not with us. He's with her."

"Yeah, well, Meredith is tricky. Doesn't matter. Gretchen and Andre aren't buying it anyway. They're smarter than that."

"I'm not talking about Meredith. *God*, you're dense sometimes."

"Who, then?" Wade asked. He hated the way his sister was always making him feel inferior. So what if she got the smart gene out of the twin arrangement?

"Look, brother, I love you," Clara said. "But you have to stop crushing on Faith Daniels. It's pointless. She's in love with Dylan, always has been."

"You don't know what you're talking about. Besides, I'm not crushing on anyone. I'm focused on the plan, like you should be."

Clara stopped walking, which had the desired effect of getting Wade to stop, too. She didn't say anything.

"What?" Wade asked.

And that was when Clara had set off the first bomb.

"I know she's out there, Wade. I saw both of you, together. And you know what was really difficult to watch? How hard you're falling for this girl and how little she cares. From my vantage point overhead, it was obvious. She's not into you; she's into Dylan. He told me as much."

Wade didn't see the point in lying any longer. His sister knew. She'd stayed out there and seen them together. And yet he had come to hate it when she cornered him. What he really wanted to do, right at that moment, was punch her in the face.

He stepped in close.

"Stay out of my business."

Clara wasn't one to back down, especially when she had the upper hand. She had the annoying habit of smirking when she had someone where she wanted them, and this she did as she moved even closer, their faces nearly touching. "Our enemy is in the woods, watching our every move, waiting for us to make a mistake. I think that's everyone's business whether you like it or not."

Wade took one step back, at once furious and helpless.

"Did you tell anyone else?" he asked.

"No. Didn't figure you'd want me to. But it's pretty damn risky. How many more are out there?"

"Just her, that's it."

"You sure about that?"

Wade wasn't precisely sure about anything anymore, including how Faith felt about him.

"You remember that hairy son of a bitch, Clooger? He's out there," Clara said. "And so is your little Wire Code buddy, Hawk."

"No way."

Clara took out her Tablet, snapped it to its largest size, and cycled through a selection of photographs. She'd been doing plenty of recon of her own in the woods outside the prison and had taken the pictures to prove it. There were a series of photos from above of Wade and Clara, others of two figures standing by what appeared to be a giant boulder. She'd flown high above where any radar could detect her movement and used the digital hyperzoom feature on her Tablet. The resulting images were grainy, but there was no mistaking the big guy with the bald head or the kid standing next to him.

"That's not Clooger," Wade said, as if it mattered.

"Oh, it's him all right. He's lost the dreads and the beard, but it's definitely him. And there's no doubt the pip-squeak is Hawk. *That* head of hair is unmistakable."

Wade was livid. Not only had Faith lied to him big-time, Clara had come to him with information he should have found on his own.

"She lied to you about this," Clara said, snapping the Tablet back to its pocket size. "What makes you think she wouldn't lie about Dylan?"

Wade didn't want to believe it.

"She's using you, so let's use her back."

Wade wasn't completely convinced, but he wanted the ammo in case everything Clara was saying panned out. If Faith really was using him and the whole thing was a setup, he wanted to turn the tables.

"What are you thinking?" he asked.

And then she lit the fuse on the second bomb in her plan.

"No one uses us, least of all a single pulse who has no idea what she's doing. Tell her when we're leaving and where Gretchen is going. Then tell her Gretchen's weakness."

Wade didn't quite understand at first and then he did.

"You want Gretchen dead?"

Clara feigned surprise.

"Whatever gave you that idea?"

"She's our mother. That's a little much, don't you think?"

Clara rolled her eyes, but she could tell: her brother was taking the bait.

"Faith couldn't kill Gretchen in her wildest dreams. She's a single, Wade. It won't take much for Gretchen to finish her off. All I'm saying is, maybe she can get in a shot or two before our dear old mom puts her in her grave."

"Sometimes I think this is all a little too much fun for you."

"Do whatever you want. Just don't forget: when this thing is done, Gretchen will be one more step up the power ranking. You and me? Our situation only changes if we make it happen."

Wade thought about everything Clara had said as she moved past him, leaving him standing alone in the corridor outside the warden's office. Women angered him—his sister, his mother, and the girl with whom he thought he'd been in love. They were all of them in their own way trying to control him. They were like a long chain linked together and wrapped around his neck, synching tighter and tighter. He expected the deceit and gamesmanship from his sister and Gretchen, but

Faith? She'd totally lied to him. She wasn't alone; she was with that Neanderthal, Clooger, and that tiny jerk of a kid, Hawk. What did she see in these people? They were nothing compared to him. *Nothing!* And Dylan Gilmore? What a joke. Mostly he was hurt that Faith was using him. Wade Quinn hated feeling betrayed by someone he liked, which was why he liked basically no one.

"Someone's gonna pay," Wade said. "And it's not going to be me."

Clara, thinking only of her own endgame and how she'd gotten exactly what she wanted in the transaction, smiled. "That's the spirit."

"What's the deal, Officer John McClane?" Hawk asked. He was lying down on his stomach, binoculars in hand, watching as the single pulses started cleaning up the disaster zone in the field. "I thought we weren't intervening?"

"Who's John McClane?" Faith had no idea who Hawk was referring to as she noticed the sun dip below the tree line on the far side of the prison. A couple more hours until dark, then she'd have to sneak away and meet up with Wade again.

"Chrome-dome action hero?" Hawk said, pulling his head away from the binoculars and looking at Faith as if she had failed to pass the easiest pop culture quiz ever. "Die Hard movies with Bruce Willis. There were nine sequels. Come on, that character was a legend."

Faith registered no clue and no interest.

"It's on the retro station. And while you're there, check out *Avatar*. Good stuff."

"You're a weird kid, Hawk," Clooger said. "But I like you anyway."

"I can't tell you how much that means to me. But seriously, why'd you do it?"

"Because sometimes you have to choose between two lousy options and in doing so change your mind."

Hawk turned this over in his mind. "So you're saying the rules are the rules until someone breaks the rules, and then those rules become the rules."

Clooger slowly ran the formula through his head and nodded. "Yeah, that's what I'm saying. But it doesn't apply to you. Or Faith. Only me."

Faith found the conversation exhausting and not terribly entertaining, and decided to take a short nap in the HumGee. She hadn't slept nearly enough and felt it was her best shot at catching up.

Two hours later, the sun down and a chill in the air, Faith talked to the guys.

"Mind if I go for a walk? I'll be careful, and I won't go far."

Clooger looked up from his Tablet, which held a digital copy of *Moby-Dick* he'd been slowly plowing through for weeks, and eyed her warily.

"I'll go with you," he said.

"No way you guys are leaving me here alone," Hawk said. He didn't look up from his Tablet. "Let's all go."

"Really, you guys, I'd rather go alone. I need space to think."

"Plenty of room over there," Clooger said, pointing to a grassy section about ten feet away from the camouflaged HumGee. "We promise not to talk to you."

Hawk was deeply embedded in whatever he was doing on his Tablet, some hugely complicated problem well on its way to being solved, Faith imagined.

"Look, you guys, I enjoy hanging out and all, but a girl needs a little breathing room."

"What about the skunks?" Clooger asked. "And the potential search parties?"

"Yeah," Hawk asked without looking up. "What about it?"

Faith couldn't tell them about Wade. No way, not yet. It crossed her mind that this didn't make her much of a team player, but teams had never been her strong suit. She was more comfortable going it alone.

"You guys should be worried about genetically altered wolves, not me. I don't even know why you're sitting out here. They could be just past our field of vision, waiting to drag one of us away."

This got Hawk's attention, and he finally looked up. "I'm the smallest one. They'll take me for sure."

Hawk crawled a few feet toward the HumGee, lifted the cover, and disappeared underneath. Faith and Clooger heard the door open and shut.

"We should all get inside for the night," Clooger said. His head was cold, too, and inside the HumGee was warm. "It's the safest place."

"I don't need safe; I'm fine. And what if they make a break for it in the middle of the night? Then what? We wake up and the place is deserted, Dylan gone right along with them?"

Clooger had thought of this possibility plenty of times, but it wasn't something for which they hadn't built in contingencies.

"Hawk can track the sound rings. We're not going to lose Dylan."

"Do whatever you want," Faith said. "I'm going for a walk and taking a pee in the woods, and I'd rather not have company."

Clooger knew Faith well enough to wonder if she had bigger plans than she was saying. He ran through the options in his head: she wanted to sneak in and see Dylan, she thought she could get in close and figure something out on her own, she hoped to find Clara alone and fight her to the death. All bad ideas capable of blowing their cover and getting them killed.

"Promise me you won't do anything stupid," Clooger said.

"I won't do anything stupid. I promise."

She deemed her behavior risky, not brainless, and therefore didn't categorize her answer as a lie, strictly speaking.

"If I call, you answer," Clooger ordered.

"Deal," Faith agreed, something she knew she couldn't possibly adhere to if a call came in while she was locked in a conversation with Wade.

Clooger stood up and yawned, long and loud as if he was overdue for a bear-sized hibernation. Faith smiled—*Thank you, I needed this*—and turned to go. A few seconds later Clooger was sprawled out across the long, wide seat of the HumGee, staring at the ceiling. The far back end of the rig was where Faith would sleep, and Hawk was up front. Clooger closed his eyes, just to rest them for a moment, until Hawk leaned over the front seat and held out his Tablet.

"Wanna play Asteroids?"

Hawk had thought the training event earlier in the day had been a lot like the classic video arcade game.

"Is that what you've been 'working' on?" Clooger

asked without opening his eyes.

"Yeah, well, can't work all the time. Fries the circuits."

"Uh-huh."

Hawk could tell he was on his own with Asteroids. He'd been feeling the pressure of everything, the isolation of the woods, and video games at least took his mind off his worries, which were numerous. He'd calculated the amount of power it had taken to lift all those train cars and move them so precisely. It was a lot. If Andre and the Quinns were planning something really terrible, he wasn't sure Faith and Dylan would be enough firepower to stop them. He worried about his parents and, more accurately, his own fragile psyche. He had come to realize that all Intels were subject to the strong possibility of going insane. It might happen when he was fifteen, it might not happen until he was forty; but it was going to happen. It was an unpleasant thought, like death and disease, and it was shared by Andre and Clara. They both knew, too. It was only a matter of time with Intels.

He went back to his game, listening to the sound of Clooger's snoring. The big guy was louder when he was on his back, and the inside of the HumGee was like a cave where a big sound only got bigger.

"If a bear snores in the woods and no one is there to

hear it, is there really any sound?" Hawk asked himself, willing his mind to tune out the racket.

The trouble with emulators that ran retro games on Tablets was that they weren't native. They covered the Tablet operating system like the skin on an orange, sealing it off until the game was shut down. Of course Hawk knew this, but stress in the field could have a debilitating effect on even the smartest people in the world. He didn't care or didn't think of it or didn't think it mattered for ten or fifteen minutes.

Which was why he didn't see the alert happening in the operating system under the Asteroids game. A pulse had been detected; someone was flying in close.

By the time Hawk closed the game, Wade had already landed and Clooger was still snoring.

Chapter 11

Sasquatch

Dylan had his first important piece of information, and he felt it was now worth the risk to try to make contact with his team. He was alone, locked in his cell, sitting on the floor. He'd hunched over, as if sleeping, and held his finger and thumb to his ear. He hoped someone in the woods would hear him whisper and whatever surveillance the prison had would not.

His head bowed as low as it would go, arms folded across his knees, Dylan spoke.

"Gretchen's second-pulse weakness," he said, then stopped at the sound of distant footsteps coming toward him. "It's water—her weakness is water."

He had deduced this remarkably important piece of information from the scene that had played out in the field outside, and he felt convinced he was right. As the steps grew near, Hawk's voice filled his head.

"How do you know? Hey, buddy, you there?"

Hawk didn't get a reply and assumed correctly that Dylan was in mixed company. He tried Faith: "Faith, are you hearing this?"

Faith had also heard Dylan's voice deep inside her head, but she was standing in the woods with Wade Quinn. There was no way she could answer, but a tingle of excitement ran up her spine at the idea of knowing how to breach Gretchen's second pulse. She smiled unexpectedly, thinking about pulling Gretchen into a tank of water and watching her melt like the Wicked Witch of the West. Wade smiled back and quickened his pace toward her in the dark. Regardless of whether she had betrayed him, he couldn't have been happier to see her smiling at his return to the woods.

Hawk, on the other hand, wasn't too cheerful about what he was seeing in the HumGee. Clooger was in a deep sleep. Hawk thought about waking him but knew it would take some work. When Clooger slept, he *really* slept. The news about Gretchen was important, but it wasn't time sensitive, not really. He could let the gentle giant grab a little rest while the getting was good.

Hawk looked at his GPS positioning system and found Faith—the sound rings were wired up, even if her Tablet GPS was off-limits.

She's pretty far down the mountain.

He rummaged around inside a duffel bag they'd gotten from a mega sporting-goods store back in Valencia. He'd been interested in the fishing gear at that store, especially the expensive fly-fishing stuff, but it was all virtually useless where they were going. What they'd needed at the time, or at least *he* had needed, was protection. So they'd filled the duffel bag with an array of hunting knives, boxes of shells, and two shotguns.

The sawed-off shotgun was Clooger's weapon of choice because, as he had explained, it threw a very wide net. A normal shotgun blasted a cloud of buckshot that widened as it went. Sawing off the end of the gun made the blast zone even bigger.

"You might not kill what you're shooting," he'd explained. "But if you're at close range, you'll probably hit whatever you're aiming at. And that will give you enough time to get the hell out of whatever mess you've gotten yourself into without killing someone in the process."

Clooger had sawed off the ends of the guns and given Hawk about ten minutes of shooting lessons inside the store, where they'd aimed directly into the open expanse of the golf section. Hawk's first shot had knocked him clean off his feet and left his shoulder throbbing. Most of the buckshot had hit the ceiling, falling like hail into the store. It had also been loud enough to make Hawk's ears ring for an hour afterward. Clooger hadn't put an end to the lesson until Hawk heard the sound of tiny metal balls pinging off five irons, drivers, and putters. His aim wasn't much to write home about, but at least he was firing at eye level.

"It's earsplitting, so don't fire unless you have to."

"That won't be a problem," Hawk had said. They'd grabbed a bunch of hunting knives and called it good on weaponry.

Hawk filled his pockets with shotgun shells, loaded the barrel, and slammed it shut with a clang. He took two of the hunting knives, which were held in leather sheaths he could attach to his belt, one on each side. One more look over the seat at Clooger, who had, expectedly, slept through all the activity.

Hawk exited the HumGee and put on both buck knives, one on each side of his waist, and held the sawed-off shotgun in his right hand. He'd recently been streaming old Rambo movies on his Tablet and gotten just a little bit obsessed with the idea of going out into the wild and shooting at stuff. Maybe it was some pent-up aggression. He'd been feeling uptight about not having a second pulse, a first pulse, a girlfriend, a big brother, or parents who could actually pay attention to what he was saying. More and more he was bothered by the fact that he was not only the smallest guy in the room, he was also the weakest. Couldn't the universe have fated him to have a pulse instead of brains to burn? He often fell asleep thinking of all the mayhem he would cause if he could pick up cars and buses and slam them into each other.

"Armed and dangerous," he said, thinking primarily of the wolves he was sure were watching him from the shadows beyond the tree line. He held his Tablet, which was in its palm size, in his free hand and began walking, following Faith's GPS marker on the screen.

As he made his way through the trees, a thought crossed his mind: if he was to use the shotgun to protect himself, it might be heard a long way off, maybe as far away as the prison. And if that happened, well, who knew? Maybe they'd think it was one of the outsiders, just a random hunter trying to feed his family. But more likely he'd be giving away the fact that someone was up in the forest looking down at the prison.

He picked up his pace. If he could get to wherever Faith was, she could protect him from almost anything. It was slightly demoralizing, no doubt about it. Wasn't it the guy who was supposed to protect the girl? *Well,* he concluded, *the world is upside down. Who knows what's normal anymore?*

When he reached the halfway point—the place where the GPS marker for Clooger was just as far away as the one for Faith, he thought it was the right time to let Faith know he was coming out there to find her. He pressed his sound ring and used his small voice, just to make sure Clooger stayed asleep.

"Hey, Faith? It's me. It's Hawk. Look, I know you were angling for some alone time or whatever, but Clooger's snoring the doors off, and I really wanted to talk to you about this Gretchen thing. I'm heading your way. Looks like, ummm . . . looks like about five more minutes. Stay put."

Faith couldn't tell Hawk to turn around and go back to the HumGee because Wade was standing right in front of her. The only way Hawk would hear what she was saying was if she pressed her sound ring. And she sure couldn't have Hawk suddenly appear, walking down the side of a mountain totally unprotected. Wade might kill him on sight.

"I'm glad you came back," Wade said. He knew she'd deceived him, knew she was possibly trouble. But he couldn't help it. His heart wasn't listening to his head. "I wasn't sure you would."

Faith put her hands in her back pockets nervously.

"Well, I did. What's new with you?"

Wade laughed and shook his head. "Oh, the usual. You know, picking up train cars, stuff like that."

Faith figured she had two minutes tops before Hawk would be close enough to be seen or heard. That was assuming he wasn't running.

"I haven't flown in days," Faith said. "You know, don't want to be detected or anything. I miss it."

Wade moved in closer and felt his pulse quicken. "I have a transponder. They know it's me out here. As far as they're concerned, I'm just doing some recon. No big deal."

He put an arm on her waist, wrapped it all the way around, and pulled her close. He was taller than Dylan, so his hand rested not on her hip, but against her ribs. For some reason this sent an electric charge through Faith as her body responded to his touch.

They lifted off the ground, not like two ghosts, but two rockets, shooting a hundred feet up into the sky. Faith felt the power of Wade's forearms, the incredible force of his strength, and couldn't help wrapping her arms around him. He turned abruptly sideways and blasted through the sky. The farther they went, the fewer lights there were below, until there was nothing but darkness, a sea of empty space without stars or life.

"That should do it," he said.

"That should do what?" asked Faith. She was lying on her back in the air, staring up into his face. He was on top of her, weightless as he looked into her eyes.

"They can't track me this far out," Wade said. "Once in a while I tell the night watch guys to let me go."

His eyes followed the curve of her face down to her lips. He touched the side of her cheek, wanting to tilt her face toward his.

Hawk was in Faith's ear—*Where are you going? Faith? Hello?*

"Why are we up here?" asked Faith, tuning out the voice in her head.

Wade looked into her blue-green eyes, felt her softening.

"So no one can find us. We can be alone up here, just you and me and the stars and the moon."

Faith rolled slightly to the side, as if they were on a bed together, floating through time and space. She pulled in close.

"It's so high up. And a little cold, don't you think?"

God, how he wanted her, more than anything in his entire, overstructured life. For years he'd been told what to do for every hour of every day. The prison had only made things worse. He was being smothered alive by Gretchen and Clara and Andre.

"Wouldn't it be something if we just flew away and

never came back?" Wade asked, moving back on top of her and pulling her gently through the air, farther away from the prison. "Wherever it takes us, just go and see where it leads. The two of us."

"Wade, I—"

He kissed her, their cold lips touching in the chill air. He felt the warmth of her breath and wrapped his arms tighter around her. He remembered then what a fool he'd been at Old Park Hill. How soft her lips were against his own, how she'd felt in his arms. Wade wished he could hold this moment forever, drift into eternity holding Faith aloft in his arms.

"That, my friend, was an alarmingly good kiss," Faith said, breathless when he pulled back and looked into her eyes. "Tell me something?"

"Anything."

"Why do you want to leave so badly? What's going on that makes you hate it so much you'd leave everything behind without a second thought?"

"For starters my mom is the control freak to end all control freaks. And my sister is impossible. She has to be right about everything, she has to win one hundred percent of the time."

"Yeah, but I mean, what are they planning? You must not agree with it or you'd want to stay, right?"

Wade was starting to feel a devious chill of emotion

in the air. He knew the difference between girls who were enamored of him for real and those who were faking it for their own gain. He'd seen plenty of both over the years.

"Why does anyone want to leave the family they grow up in?" Wade asked. "You don't agree with their ideas. They drive you crazy with all their bullshit. It's a lot of reasons."

Faith smiled winsomely, but there was something in the look that felt to Wade that she was, maybe, putting on an act. It was hard to say.

"My parents wanted me to join their cause and become a drifter. But it wasn't my fight, you know? They weren't my plans, for *my* future. Same thing for you?"

"Why do you keep asking me the same question in a different way?" Wade asked.

"What do you mean?" Faith asked. "I'm interested in why you want to leave. I'm trying to understand."

Wade kissed her again, and this time he could tell she was having a harder time keeping up the ruse. She wasn't coaxing him closer, showing him that she wanted him as much as he wanted her. Either he'd turned her off with his defensive attitude, or she'd been trying to trick him into giving away their plans from the start.

When he pulled back, Faith wiped her bottom lip

with the back of her hand. "You okay?"

Wade let Faith go, pushing a few feet away into the night, and for a strange and unexpected instant Faith wished he would keep holding on to her. There was, at least in the unseen places of her heart, a space that felt vulnerable and liked the protection of another person. It wasn't Wade—or was it? It was the fact of another human being, the warmth of another body in a world so cold.

While Faith was navigating a tricky situation with Wade high overhead, the stupidity of Hawk's decision magnified in his brain. It grew from the size of a pea to a watermelon that threatened to burst his head open. He was an Intel, one of the brightest people on Earth, and he had done a wildly stupid thing. For a moment he didn't move at all. He simply stood in the woods and listened to the sounds of the night, hoping not to hear growling of one kind or another. He knew about cougars and had done the calculations. There were at least a dozen in these woods, give or take, and they were quiet as mice. If one of them was stalking Hawk, he wouldn't know it until it was way, way too late.

Hawk weighed his options, which included climbing a tree, screaming Clooger's name into his sound ring, or begging Faith to come back. He chose none of these options. Later, when he had real time to consider what had happened, he would unpack the decision in his mind, take it apart, try to examine it for clues to his decision-making process. He would come to understand that sometimes even an Intel succumbs to the mortal fear of being clawed to death by a giant cat.

Hawk pointed the sawed-off shotgun up the mountain and started running.

It wasn't until he was almost all the way back to the HumGee that he realized how incredibly out of breath he was. He'd never been an athlete of any kind, and the cold air burned his lungs as he gulped breath after icy breath. He stopped, bent over with his elbows on his knees, and tried to regain his composure.

It was then he saw something coming toward him. He'd watched a lot of Tablet shows lately, and he was especially fond of retro classics—it was his thing. *Freaks and Geeks, Family Guy, 30 Rock*—anything off-kilter and funny from fifty-year-old television provided him with some sort of unexpected comfort he'd needed. Very recently he'd stumbled onto a documentary about a Sasquatch, a half man half ape of the woods that stood about ten feet tall.

As he rose up and saw the outline of a beast coming toward him in the nearly pitch-black of the night, Hawk raised the sawed-off shotgun and pulled the trigger. The blast threw him backward, and he tumbled down the gentle slope of the forest, hoping his aim had been true and not straight up into the trees as he feared.

He heard a scream, then the sound of something heavy hitting the ground.

Hawk didn't move, choosing instead to play dead and hope that whatever was out there would leave him to rot with the fallen leaves. That was when his sound ring popped to life and a familiar voice entered his head.

"Hawk?" Clooger asked.

Hawk silently reached for his ear, pressed, whispered.

"Get out here, buddy! I'm in some trouble!"

"Hawk," Clooger said again. "You're a terrible shot. But you still got me."

Hawk was too happy about the fact that he was no longer alone in the forest to care that he'd shot Clooger in the face with a sawed-off shotgun. He stood and ran up the hill in the direction of the large shadow of a man sitting on the ground. When he got there, he threw his arms around Clooger and laughed.

"Oh, man, that was—wow—that was crazy!"

"Hawk?"

"I thought you were a Sasquatch!" Hawk laughed at his own ridiculous imagination. "Oh, my God, that was insane. Insane!"

Clooger stood up and took Hawk by the arm, hauling him up the mountain toward the HumGee. The shotgun blast had echoed through the trees, and Clooger had to get them hidden in case anyone showed up. When he had them both safely under the camouflage of the tarp and inside the HumGee, he cranked on a light and looked at Hawk.

"I think I got you in the forehead," Hawk said. "And right there."

Hawk pointed to Clooger's cheek, which had a nasty bruise forming around a red dot. There were two other such marks on Clooger's forehead, one of which was bleeding.

"Really sorry about that," Hawk said. "I don't know what I was thinking."

"This is why I don't take naps. Faith goes totally AWOL, and you shoot me."

"Yeah, I can see why you'd think twice about the whole sleep thing. It's risky. For sure."

Clooger rolled his eyes, pressed his sound ring.

"Faith, if you can hear me, check in."

No reply.

"What now?" Hawk asked.

Clooger leaned back on the seat, took a deep breath, and touched the abrasions on his forehead.

"Now we wait."

———

"I need to ask you something," Wade said. He and Faith had landed on the catwalk of an old water tower a few miles away from the prison, where they sat staring out into the empty space below. Second pulses felt the cold less than a normal person, but it was still a little chilly. Winter was coming; the nights were getting colder. He turned in Faith's direction, but she wouldn't look back. He loved the way her long hair fluttered in the light breeze and reached out and touched it. He wished things could be different.

"Are you alone out here?" Wade asked.

Faith hesitated, but only for a split second.

"You already asked me that, remember?"

"I remember."

He let the words hang in the air and watched Faith's feet dangle back and forth beneath them.

"I wouldn't blame you if you'd lied to me before, and you actually did bring someone with you," Wade said. He was still searching for a reason to believe, because landing firmly in Clara's camp put a bitter taste in his mouth, as if he'd just bitten into an unpeeled orange. "I mean, it's the middle of nowhere. You'd have to be head over heels for some guy to come all the way out here by yourself. It's dangerous."

Faith knew Clooger and Hawk wouldn't stand a chance against Wade if she told him the truth. They might not make it through the night alive. She turned to Wade, touched his hand gently.

"I came out here for Dylan, but now I'm not so sure."

Something about the way she said these words did more than just put Wade on alert. A red froth of jealously boiled up through his head. She was bald-faced lying to him, and not just about Hawk and Clooger. She was using her charm and beauty to deceive him even further. She was a so-so actor, especially when it came to matters of the heart.

"I need to tell you something," Wade said. He'd made his decision. There was no way he was letting Faith do this to him. She'd had her chance, and there were plenty of other fish in the sea. Pretty soon the work would be done, and he could get as many girls as he wanted. He was Wade Quinn. He'd never had any trouble scoring. "Things are going to start happening soon," he said.

"What kind of things?" Faith asked. She moved in a little closer, squeezed Wade's hand a little tighter.

"Keep an eye on Gretchen," Wade said, shaking his head as if he couldn't believe it. "What she does tomorrow will matter."

"What do you mean? Is she leaving?"

A long pause, and then Wade was looking her in the eye. "We all are."

Faith wanted to ask if they'd be taking Dylan with

them, but she worried it would set off Wade.

"I've never told anyone this before, and I sure as hell shouldn't be telling you," Wade said. He hemmed and hawed, as if a great internal struggle was under way. "She hates you, Faith. Gretchen really, really hates you. If for some reason you end up face-to-face with her, I want you to at least get in one good shot before it's over."

"Thanks for the vote of confidence."

"You're a single pulse. Is what it is. If you get into a situation with Gretchen or any other second pulse, you're pretty much a rag doll. There's no firepower you can wield that makes any difference, except one."

Wade gave Faith one more look, in which he tried to see all the way into her soul. Was there any chance she loved him? Any chance at all he wasn't playing the fool?

No. No chance.

It's true, Wade thought. *She's taking you for a ride, bro.*

"You know how Dylan has a weakness for rocks and stones, stuff like that?"

Faith hated how the Quinns knew Dylan's weakness, but they knew. There was no getting around it.

"Yeah, I know. It can break through his second pulse."

"I'm only telling you this so you can use it to get away if it comes up, nothing more. If things get crazy with Gretchen, throw water in her face and run like hell. It's your only chance."

This was verification. Dylan had said it, now Wade. Gretchen's second-pulse weakness was water. It was all she could do not to pick up the very water tower they sat on, carry it over the prison, and unleash a torrent of liquid to flood Gretchen's dead body into the field outside.

"Thank you for telling me that," Faith said, regaining her composure.

"No problem," Wade said. "Gretchen could use a bump or two once in a while, not that you're going to have the chance. You see her and you're alone, just run, fly, do whatever you can to get away. Speaking of which, I better get back. They'll be wondering where I went."

Faith was relieved. She wouldn't have to stay at the water tower and make out with someone she didn't want anything to do with—up in the sky had been enough. Whatever the team needed and all that, no problem. She had done it gladly, but there had to be some limits.

As they flew near the prison, their hands parted and Wade drifted away.

"One more thing," Wade called back. The last part of the trap to set, then it was just a matter of whether Faith would take the bait. "Gretchen is going to the Western State. That's where her task lies, and it's hers alone. She won't be with anyone else."

He also knew how headstrong Faith was, so he said something more as he turned to go. "This isn't your fight. Go on home, and maybe when this is all over with, I'll come find you."

Faith nodded and smiled and dived for the ground.

Not my fight? That's where you're wrong, Wade Quinn.

After hearing the sound of footsteps coming toward him, Dylan looked up and found Andre standing at the bars, carrying a wooden stool. He put the stool on the floor with a clang and sat down, staring at Dylan. A moment of silence passed between them in which Dylan thought maybe he had been caught. What would this man do, his own father, if he knew his son had deceived him?

"Getting any sleep?" Andre asked.

Why is he here? Dylan wondered. *Alone, unprotected?*

"Just resting my eyes," Dylan said as he stood. He felt a deep thud of pain in his rib cage. "Training around here is intense."

Andre shook his head.

"Did you really think going after Wade would help our situation? I thought you were smarter than that."

"They were throwing rocks at me. I thought it was the least I could do."

A brief but meaningful smile played at the edges of Andre's mouth.

"You were already on his bad side. Showing him up didn't help your cause. They shouldn't have gone after you so aggressively, but I had to see what you could take. You impressed me until you tried to kill my son. Brawn is fine. Brains are better."

Dylan didn't have an answer, so he let the accusation hang in the air. "How long are you going to keep me locked up in here?"

Andre shuffled his feet back and forth, stared at the concrete floor. "I appreciate you coming here. Seeing you has been . . . *unforeseen*, as you might imagine. I want to tell you something."

"So tell me," Dylan said. He was listening to Faith and Hawk, trying to figure out what was going on as they pressed into the sound rings, while pretending there were no voices in his head. It was challenging, to say the least.

"The world is about to change. I mean *really* change."

Dylan didn't want to sound too curious, but this sounded big.

"In what way?"

Andre couldn't help smiling more broadly as he thought about what was coming.

"The States are not taking the approach Hotspur Chance envisioned. Tomorrow begins a process of change, one I hope you'll appreciate. It's been a long time coming."

Andre stood and picked up the stool as if he was going to leave. Something told Dylan he might not have many more chances to talk with him privately. Dylan's mind drifted to Hawk, whom he had come to love like a little brother.

"What about Intels?"

"Intels?"

Andre hadn't come down to the cell block to talk about that.

"Why'd Hotspur develop Intels? I've got a friend who's one. If I ever see him again, I'd like to tell him why he is the way he is."

Andre thought for a moment, weighed the risk, and determined that there was none.

"The Intel project was created purely for processing power, nothing more. Technically speaking, they were and still are human computers. They have a part of Hotspur in them, a sliver of his DNA."

"So they're clones?" Dylan asked, hoping he was dead wrong.

"No, not clones. Recipients of some approximation of Hotspur's intellect. The first ones were more closely connected. He could control them more readily, put them on complex tasks without having to spend years explaining things to them. Anything left over, I mean, any offsprings beyond the originals, are considerably removed from the hosts, as it were. They're smart, but they're not off the charts, if that's what you're asking."

"Are you an Intel?"

"Why, yes, I am. In fact, I was the first."

Dylan took a moment to respond as he listened to the data coming in. *Faith is doing what? Has she gone crazy?*

"Some of them don't do so well when they get to be about your age. Wires get crossed, as it were. Others see no effects at all. It's random, I suppose. The older ones, like me, well . . . let's just say it can get complicated."

Andre's eyes dimmed and his lips became a thin, straight line. Of course he knew what could happen to an Intel's mind. He knew all too well.

"Your friend, he's farther down the line," Andre said. "He'll be fine, just like Clara. Tell him not to worry when you see him again."

Dylan felt the sincerity in Andre's tone. He also got the feeling that the subject of Intels was something difficult for his dad to talk about.

Andre started walking away, thinking about how he sometimes awoke in the warden's chamber as if from a dream. At times minutes had passed, or whole hours. It was happening to him, too. Like Hawk's parents, Andre was slowly shutting down.

He called back to Dylan the line he often repeated

over and over in his head like a funeral song.

"No problem can be solved by the same consciousness that caused it in the first place." Dylan sat on the cold stone floor of the cell and genuinely began to wonder if his father was going crazy.

Another thought entered his mind, one he hadn't allowed any room for in hours and hours because it was a thought that wasn't going to do him any good either way. It was the kind of thought that could trip him up if he wasn't careful, a thing good soldiers weren't supposed to stew on. He was doing what he was told, following instructions in a plan he didn't fully understand. But now as he felt the walls closing in and time compressing, he let this thought wash over him like a suffocating wave on the sea.

Maybe coming here wasn't such a good idea after all.

part three

STATE OF CHANCE

Chapter 12

Departing Is Such Sweet Sorrow

It was the night before a long-awaited plan would be put into action.

Faith, the one who had a secret that could turn the tide, thought of Gretchen and Clara Quinn. Everything else Faith might have contemplated was blotted out under an inky stain of Gretchen's and Clara's presence in her mind. There was no Dylan, no Hawk or Clooger. There was no murdered friend or lost parents or even thoughts of revenge against Wade. On this night, Faith ached with an all-consuming desire to astonish Gretchen Quinn, to dominate her and ultimately to destroy her. And when she finished with Gretchen, Clara would be next.

———

Clooger had a secret, too, one that only he and Hawk knew about. It was a secret that had the power to divide the team when it was revealed, and its revealing would be soon. It wasn't as priceless or valuable as Faith's second pulse, but it had a deceitful quality he worried about constantly. The secret was not that he and Meredith were much closer than anyone probably imagined; it was bigger than that. His thoughts drifted away from the secret to Faith Daniels, reckless and untamable, and he worried for the future of the world. Why was something so important given to someone so ill equipped? It was a conundrum he would never understand. It was he, not she, who should have a second pulse. Imagine what he could accomplish with such a thing? He thought of Faith's admission, that she'd seen Wade not once but twice. Unbelievable. And he wondered if the information she'd been given was part of a sophisticated cauldron of lies, a deception coming to a boil. He hoped it was not.

Hawk felt best when he was inside the HumGee, where two of his best friends in the world—Faith and Clooger— were lying awake, not speaking. Faith was in the far back, the soft glow of her Tablet bouncing off the ceiling. Clooger stared into space in the backseat. Hawk shared a secret with Clooger he wished he didn't have to carry, but there was nothing he could do about it. Soon enough, the secret would be no more, and he would be forgiven. He thought of his parents, his mom in particular on that night. She had been a good mom while it had lasted, always there to take care of him. The last year had been the hardest, and lately it was as if she no longer existed. He pulled up a picture of her on his Tablet, allowed himself a few brief moments of melancholy, and went back to work on a complicated and time-sensitive task Faith had given him. That was when he heard the voice in his head for the very first time. It was not a voice he recognized, and the message was confusing: *The day of my departure draws near.* And with the sound of the voice, he knew a sudden and terrible truth: the slow unwinding of his Intel mind had begun. At some point in the near or distant future, he might hear nothing *but* the voice.

Meredith knew more than most and a lot more than she was telling. She felt the planet coming apart that night, a tender tearing at the seams that would eventually split the world wide-open. She worried about her son and Clooger the most, and Hawk, too, for in his absence, Hawk's parents had both died within an hour of each other. They'd all known it was coming, but it was still a bad thing. Hawk needed to be told, and soon. Meredith tried not to think of Faith; it only put her in a sour mood. She tried to remember the old days, the old songs, the years in the desert when they thought they were saving the world.

Clara lay pleased in her bed, rolling a series of thoughts over in her head, examining each as if it were a rat on the dissection table. The next twenty-four hours would alter her situation either a little or a lot. She was determined that it would be more, not less. Could Faith weaken Gretchen just enough, catch her off guard and inflict a little damage? If so, Clara could finish her off. And the bonus, which was delicious to think about, was Faith Daniels. She'd be dead for sure, her death orchestrated by Clara and carried out by Gretchen. Did it get any better? She didn't think so.

Wade was in his own quarters, which had at one time been a series of four prison cells at the far end of E block. There was nothing homey about the setup: a bed, a weight room, a place to throw all his dirty laundry. He was on his seventy-fifth pull-up, his mind adrift in the searing pain across his shoulder blades. A powerhouse of muscles and bones, that's what he was. He was done feeling emotions, unless they were emotions that could get him what he wanted. When he finished his workout and sat on the stone slab that served as his bed, Faith's smile flashed in his memory, cutting like a knife into his heart. *Damn that girl.*

Gretchen felt a heightened alertness she hadn't experienced for many months. It surprised her, this feeling of clarity and calm that had left her slowly in the course of days and days of planning. Now, with the deed so close she could touch it, she thought of how different her life would be. How long she'd waited, patiently suffering incompetence piled like cordwood in every direction she turned. At last the thing would be done. She thought of her part and wished it could be different, but she knew it was the safest, best course of action. Her part would take her far, far away from the thing that had to be done. She would be blamed for nothing. She readied herself in the highly unlikely event of an encounter with a second pulse of whom she wasn't already aware. Mostly, she worried about Meredith. Maybe she had always been a second pulse but never said. Maybe she would be waiting, come morning. She had a way of showing up at the worst possible time.

Andre's mind, unlike all the others', wandered. He'd been having more and more problems lately, especially at night. The voice in his head was, at times, unrelenting. There were many instructions, many commands. The days weren't so bad; somehow the light gave him clarity and he could think again as he once had. Such brilliant thoughts! And so many of them, filed one on top of the other. He wondered now if it had been too many thoughts, too fast. He might have wanted to pace himself, spend more time relaxing, less time processing. But here he was, the day upon him and his mind falling to pieces. It was not the timing for which he had hoped.

And Dylan. He was alone and thinking, too.

He had never needed much sleep, not even as a small child. A memory of sitting on a bed in a room at the age of two or three was rolling around in his thoughts. He was having a long conversation with a stuffed animal that had seen better days. It was a gray rabbit with matted fur and a missing ear, although strictly speaking, the ear wasn't entirely gone from the scene. Dylan had kept it under his pillow or, if he was wearing pants, in a pocket. Looking back on such memories, Dylan was surprised by what an old soul he'd been. How was it that he could sit up and hold long conversations in the middle of the night with a one-eared rabbit while his mother slept in the bed next to his?

Years later he was still in the habit of sleeping at odd hours or not sleeping at all, a valuable trait when he found himself training Faith while she slept. All those months at the bedroom window watching her like a phantom, the glass a fragile barrier between two worlds. How often had he thought about the moment when there would be nothing left to separate them from each other? When he could reach out and touch not only her mind, but her whole body as well?

He was sitting in the cell at the prison thinking about those long nights when he watched Faith float around the room on the power of his mind. In his hand he held the tattered ruins of the rabbit ear, rubbing the stubble of fur that remained between his fingers. He'd managed to keep it hidden away all those years. Early morning was dawning outside, but he'd already been awake for hours, thinking about Faith and Clooger and Hawk, about Meredith. What he wanted to do was call Faith on the sound ring—just to hear her voice would be a comfort—but instead he sat, cross-legged and stooped over, and felt the floor move under his feet.

It began as a soft, frothing sort of rumble deep underground, like the birth of a fissure cracking across the earth. A tremor.

This can't be good, Dylan thought, standing up and stuffing the rabbit ear into his pocket. He held on to the bars of the cell, glancing back and forth down the murky hallway, and wished he could be set free.

Faith was the first to hear the earsplitting sound of cinder and rebar and earth struggling against one another. Dawn was barely upon the woods, but her vantage point was high on the hill. Whatever was happening down below in the prison yard, she was in a position to see it if she exited the HumGee and flew just above the tree line. She went to rouse Clooger and found that he was already gone. She should have known—there was no snoring—but she was even more surprised to find that Hawk was missing also. For a brief moment she was terrified by the idea that Wade and Clara had come in the night and taken them while she slept. She rolled over into the backseat, pulled the handle on the door, and kicked the door open.

Outside, she found the camouflage tarp missing and began to think she was in a dream. Where were they? Where was the tarp? Why was the earth under her feet rumbling?

Faith burst up in the air, sick and tired of holding back her power and panicked at the idea of losing her friends. When she cleared the tree line she found Hawk sitting on Clooger's shoulders, the two of them staring off toward the prison.

"You're all right!" Faith said.

Clooger and Hawk didn't answer; they were slack jawed and staring out across the trees. The sound out in the open air was even louder: a grinding of stone and metal, a thunderous explosion of fire.

The entire prison was being lifted out of the ground. The basement floors were ripped free as the whole structure rose up in the air. Three figures were flying overhead in the sky like flies over a corpse, moving and weaving for position: Wade, Clara, and Gretchen.

"That's impossible," Faith said. It was as big as a Walmart, and the entire thing had been lifted off the ground. Gas pipes, ripped in two, exploded in bursts of orange and yellow. The flames made it look as if the prison were some kind of oblong rocket, launching into the sky on its way to outer space. Chunks of metal and rebar and piping fell from the underbelly of the prison. A section of basement, which had been carried up with the rest, broke free and crashed into the ground below. Before Faith knew it, the entire formation was at eye level and moving up in the air at a steady clip, rocks and roots and chunks of debris tailing its departure. It halted abruptly, shaking the last of the big stuff free from its undercarriage, and then it started moving toward the woods.

"Dylan?" Faith said, holding her sound ring. "Dylan,

please—just tell me you're okay."

A pause, then he was there, and they could all hear him: "Still in the cell, but I think we're moving. Can you see what's going on out there?"

"The whole prison is airborne!" Faith said.

"That's impossible," Dylan said. "No way they can lift that much."

"Apparently it is possible, because it's happening," Hawk explained.

The prison was nearly over their heads, and Clooger, with Hawk on his shoulders, began moving slowly below the tree line. "Better get down."

Faith followed, but they remained right at the top edge of the green-tipped firs, holding steady. As it passed over, the prison reminded Faith of Darth Vader's ship coming ominously into view. It cast a massive shadow, blotting out the morning sun as it moved silently across their field of vision. Random pieces of metal and stone and clumps of dirt fell like rain as Clooger and Faith dodged this way and that. The sound of wreckage hitting the HumGee below tinged into the open air of the woods like a broken church bell.

"That's a few million pounds flying through the air," Hawk said. He was as surprised as anyone, because his calculations put the event somewhere between completely ridiculous and totally impossible.

Clooger took his sound ring between his fingers and spoke. The situation had turned highly unpredictable and out of his control. It was time to let the secret he and Hawk had shared be known whether he liked it or not.

"Mother ship, engage," he said.

Faith glanced back and forth between Clooger and the prison moving through the air.

"Who are you talking to?"

"Mother ship, engage!" Clooger yelled the command this time, something they weren't supposed to do to one another unless they had to. Everyone else contained in the ring of sound—Faith, Dylan, and Hawk—they were all subjected to the siren sound of Clooger's voice at high volume, bouncing off the walls of their heads.

"Take it down a notch, big guy," Hawk said from his perch on Clooger's shoulders. "Just give her a second."

Faith knew who was coming online before the voice crackled to life in her ear. She was, to put it mildly, not pleased.

"Give me status," Meredith said. "Everyone else, stay quiet and don't do anything unpredictable. Clooger, report."

Faith floated to within a foot of Hawk and glared at him. "You could have at least told me she had a sound ring. Really?"

Hawk shifted his slight shoulders up then down and refused to make eye contact. He was not a big fan of confrontation in any form. "Just following orders."

Faith tried to remember all the things she'd said that Meredith might have heard. But what did it really matter? Meredith was in charge and had been all along. Faith wasn't as free of her control as she'd hoped.

"They've raised the prison," Clooger reported, dodging to the left as a shard of metal flopped through the trees like a dead bird. "The *entire* prison. It appears headed in the general direction of the Western State."

"Everyone, listen carefully," Meredith said. "No going rogue. I mean it. Faith, especially you. This is no time to take matters into your own hands."

Faith seethed under the thumb of this woman who wanted to control her. *Just you wait,* she thought. *I've got plans of my own whether you like it or not.*

"Dylan, they're going to let you out eventually. When they do, signal us with three sharp coughs in a row. Sample."

The sound rings went dead for two seconds and then Dylan delivered three short coughs.

"Good," Meredith continued. "Hawk, as soon as he's out, start doing recon for an escape plan. Clooger, you and Faith follow but stay low. My guess is they'll take the prison up to the cloud line where it's harder to detect, possibly higher than that. Were they wearing protective gear?"

Faith was at once surprised Meredith wasn't more shocked that a prison was flying through the air and disappointed in herself for not getting out binoculars for a closer look at the enemies as they passed over. The massive underside of the complex cleared their position, and Clooger took up his own high-power binoculars, training them on the figures darting back and forth over the prison structure.

"Copy that," he said. "Full-body suits, helmets. Looks like gloves, too."

"Get ready for it to really move," Meredith said.

"Oh, it's really moving; didn't we mention that?" Faith said sarcastically. She looked at Hawk for a smile among "enlisted personnel" but found that he was gazing up into the sky.

"Whoa," he said, and, looking up, Faith watched the prison rise higher in air as if it had hit the bottom of a bungee cord. It was racing higher and higher. Within seconds it was nothing more than a dot in the sky, moving to the east.

"Are you tracking it, Hawk?" Meredith asked.

"Yeah, I got it. Hard to miss something that big. No . . . wait. It's gone!"

"As I suspected," Meredith said. "They're using a

hybrid of the State's virtual-wall system. Hold, take no action until I give the order."

The second Meredith said the words Hawk knew exactly what she was talking about. Hawk spoke without pressing his sound ring.

"It's a reverse signal. The States won't know it's coming."

"What are you saying?" Faith had no idea what Hawk was talking about.

"The technology used for the energy wall around the States has been discovered and reassembled."

"Again, no idea what you're saying. Speak English."

Hawk was typing and swiping furiously on his Tablet while he talked. His response was every bit as rapid-fire. "Think of the wall as a virus—these guys captured it, examined it, decoded it. They know how to hide from it."

"And they know how to get around it," Clooger said.

Meredith had gone quiet as the entire conversation took place outside the sound rings. No one was pressing in. She couldn't hear what they were saying, but for whatever reason she wasn't giving them orders or asking them questions.

Faith took her sound ring between her finger and thumb.

"You need to alert them that this thing is coming,"

she said. "Hello? Meredith?!"

Nothing.

"Where the hell did she go?" Faith said. "If we lose visual we may never find them again. I'm going."

Faith burst up in the air, flying fast and high into the sky, until she heard the voices in her head, first Hawk then Clooger.

"I have them! I have a signal."

"Faith, get back here! Now!"

Faith stopped a few hundred feet over the tree line, looking back and forth between the ground and a prison that was rapidly getting smaller and smaller in the distance. Another minute and it would be gone entirely.

"I've got Dylan's sound ring," Hawk said excitedly. "I've got it! As long as they don't throw him overboard, we have a signal. We're good."

"Faith?" Meredith was back. "If you go you're on your own. You'll get no support from us. Understand?"

Faith hated feeling controlled, shackled to a plan and a person she didn't like and didn't trust. She wanted— no, *needed*—to retaliate for what they'd done to Liz. It was as if the very blood coursing through her veins was filled with a poison and the only antidote was revenge. It would start with Gretchen, then Clara. Those two, that would do it. She didn't need to kill them all, just those two. Then she'd be okay.

"Faith," Meredith said. "I know what you're doing. You're thinking about getting even. Your odds are better if you stay with us, I promise."

"Prove it," Faith said.

They were wasting valuable time, but Faith wasn't moving one way or the other without some assurances.

For a moment it was a silent standoff. Clooger stared up at Faith like an angry sergeant. To him she was a soldier disobeying a direct order. He was furious, the dome of his shaved head turning a mottled shade of pink. Hawk snapped his Tablet small and held it in the air, searching for something.

"I promise you, Faith," Meredith finally said. "If an opportunity arises to end Gretchen or Clara, I'll put you on the front line. That's the best I can offer."

Faith didn't think it was much, but she also had a serious problem. She needed Hawk on this, needed him badly. There was something she needed him to do without telling anyone else. Without that something, she wasn't ready to go it alone.

"Understood," Faith said, slowly lowering toward the trees as the prison turned into a small black dot in the distant sky above. "I just hope we all make it out of this in one piece."

"Agreed."

When Faith arrived next to Clooger and Hawk, they

descended down through the trees and landed next to the HumGee. Clooger took one look at Faith, fast and serious, and after that he wouldn't look at her again. He was disappointed in her, she could tell. He loved the chain of command, and she'd been breaking it all along. He had no respect for that kind of attitude. *I understand,* she thought. *But it doesn't change anything. And I'm not sorry.*

"I'm leaving in the next twenty minutes," Meredith said. "First I'll make contact with both States, prepare them for what might be coming. It's delicate; let me handle it. I'll bring everyone we have, all the single pulses."

"Sound rings are all calibrated," Hawk said. "I can track everyone."

"What's the sight distance for something that size?" Meredith asked.

Hawk started mumbling, but Faith could hear him.

"S equals $sqrt(2rh+h^2)$ where s equals line of sight distance, r equals radius of sphere, h equals height viewed from . . . There are some factors here that aren't perfect, but I think we're talking about three miles, give or take."

"So we can see the prison up to three miles away?" Clooger asked.

"About that, yeah, assuming there're no obstructions

like clouds or haze. And that's looking up. You guys can't go horizontal with the target if they get too high. Way too cold up there even with the bullets."

Hawk was referring to one of his other inventions, a piece of equipment that was about to come into play in a big way.

"That's why they're wearing protective temperature gear," Clooger said.

"The bullet gear will get you high enough," Meredith said.

"And they'll take you to around a thousand miles per hour, but I can't imagine they're planning to go anywhere near that fast," Hawk said. He tapped several commands out on his screen. "Then again, they're speeding up, already past three hundred. Slowing that thing down is going to be a trick. It's also going to be throwing a path of serious debris. Definitely stay back."

"Clooger, you and Faith follow at a distance of two miles," Meredith said. "You'll be able to see them, but they won't be able to see you. They shouldn't be able to track you that far away with all the garbage trailing, but be prepared in case they can. You may need to run."

"I won't need to run," Faith said.

Faith didn't actually love the idea of killing a bunch of single pulses just because they weren't on her side, but if she was pushed into it, she would. Her vengeance was focused on Gretchen and Clara like a two-pronged laser beam, and it suddenly struck her that this had not always been the case. Her rage had, for a very long time, been even more narrowly focused on Clara alone. Clara had sent the hammer flying, no one else. That there were now two she hated enough to kill had seeped into her system without warning.

Meredith didn't respond to Faith's bravado. "Hawk, you're our eyes and ears, our command center. Stay in the HumGee until this is over, keep us connected, look for escape routes, relay information."

Hawk didn't love the idea of staying in the woods alone, especially if this thing went on into the night, but he wasn't about to complain.

"I'll make the call, then we're on the move," Meredith said. "We're a go."

Clooger got down on one knee and held Hawk by both shoulders. Hawk's flop of brown hair was hanging down over half his face, and Clooger pushed it aside. Clooger's face was as pale as ever, and the scars that marked his many missions stood out in pink lines along his cheeks and forehead. The two new pockmarks Hawk had added blended in just fine.

"Sorry about shooting you," Hawk said.

Clooger smiled. "You get out to pee and that's it, understood? Otherwise, stay in the HumGee."

"Done," Hawk said.

Clooger stood but still wouldn't look at Faith. He crossed to the tail end of the HumGee and opened the swinging door. Inside were the bullet suits, which none of them had expected to use. He pulled them out and started the process of assembling each.

"How fast does a bullet travel?" Faith asked.

Clooger had laid a metal cylinder, which was shaped something like the lasso in a rope, on the ground. It was wide enough for Clooger to step inside of.

"Depending on the weapon, a bullet can go over thirty thousand miles per hour," Hawk explained. "You won't be going that fast. How much training have you had in that thing?"

Clooger scratched his chin, which was rapidly filling with thick stubble. "I don't know, six flights? Top speed was six hundred."

"Let's hope you don't have to go any faster than that," Hawk advised. "You're one false move from dead. A lot of bad things can happen at that speed. Stay way off the ground."

Clooger stepped into the middle of the ring and pulled the Tablet out of his pocket.

"Let's get some distance between us," he said, looking at Faith for the first time in quite a while. "Safer that way."

Clooger swiped the screen on his Tablet, which was

in its pocket size, and tapped an icon. A few more taps and a shiny gray cone rose around him in the shape of a bullet, stretching in the same way his Tablet would if he snapped it large. The surface was frosted glass, hard as stone; and when it curved in at the top, it made a popping sound, sealing Clooger inside. The tail end provided ventilation, but otherwise Clooger was surrounded by a shield of impenetrable, smoke-colored glass.

"If you veer out of control, stay in the bullet," Hawk said. "It's your best chance."

"Thanks, little buddy."

A moment later he blasted from the ground like a missile, powering up through the trees and into the open air.

"You'll be okay?" Faith asked. She stepped closer, reached out a hand. They were good at holding hands, though it reminded Faith of things she didn't want to be reminded of. Hawk reached out, touched Faith. He was never one to miss a chance to touch the soft skin of a pretty girl's hand.

"I'll be fine, me and the skunks. No worries. Let's get Dylan back, you and me."

Faith handed Hawk a letter she'd written on an old piece of paper and looked at him more seriously than she ever had before.

"Do this for me. For both of us. And don't tell a soul. It's our secret."

"I'm good at keeping secrets," Hawk said sheepishly.

"So I've noticed."

And then she was wrapping herself in a bullet, preparing to leave.

A few seconds later she was gone and Hawk was alone in the woods.

No matter what Meredith or Clooger or even Dylan thought about where Faith belonged in the world, she knew her destiny lay elsewhere. They all, in one way or another, wanted to contain her. What they failed to realize was how fundamentally unsound the idea of containing Faith Daniels was. It might be possible after her work was through, but until then they were all fighting a losing battle. Maybe that's why, as she flew across the open sky at a clip of five hundred miles per hour, she was even bothered by the protective cocoon of the bullet shield around her. She wanted to punch it, kick it, smash it into a million pieces. She could see Clooger up ahead and to the left and found herself fantasizing about turning hard, accelerating, and smashing into him.

Girl, you're starting to worry me. Take it easy.

The bullet was a fantastic invention, dreamed up by Hawk after dissecting the chemistry of a Tablet that snapped from large to small. Whatever that material was, Hawk had figured out how to manufacture it, shape it, bend it to his intellectual will. The brilliance of the material, Hawk knew, lay in three aspects: its strength, its flexibility, and its uncanny ability to go rigid or pliable, depending on the need. The stuff, Hawk had discovered, was full of nano-bots: tiny computer cells that could be programmed and controlled. Once all the information was stored in Hawk's head, it was only a matter of time before he created something that would make single-person flight at very high speeds both possible and comfortable.

And boring.

An hour into the flight, the thrill of flying at eight hundred miles per hour started to wear thin. Faith had already done enough low-level acrobatics to make her feel seasick, turning the bullet by shifting her hips back and forth. She thought about taking out her Tablet and watching a show, but that seemed like a crazy idea, even for a second pulse who could crash and come out just fine. Not having anything else to do, she decided to call Clooger and see if she could patch things up.

"Hey, Cloog," she said, pressing her sound ring. The movement of her arm made the bullet slide into a slow, meandering spin. "I'm sorry I haven't followed every order exactly right. I'm not military like you. Conforming isn't natural."

She got no reply.

"I'm just saying, it's not that easy. But I'll try harder, promise."

She couldn't think of anything else to say; and knowing that Meredith, Dylan, and Hawk were listening, she couldn't bring herself to stoop any lower.

When he finally did speak, his voice was softer than she'd expected.

"Just be careful you don't get someone killed. Not all of us are as invincible as you are."

Clooger's words stung, but they also rang true. She could take a bullet; most of her friends could not.

"Understood," she said.

"Now that you two have made nice, I've got some new recon," Hawk said. "They're up to nine hundred miles per hour, which puts the Western State only an hour and sixteen minutes away. Better speed up; you're two point four miles back, and the gap is widening. Also, they've moved indoors. No one is driving that thing from above."

The situation was becoming more and more unbelievable. Not only were the Quinns moving an entire prison through the air, they were doing it from within the prison itself. And they had what amounted to a small city block moving at nearly a thousand miles per hour.

If Dylan could have seen the outside of the prison, he'd have discovered a facility stripped to its bones. Like a wall sandblasted of paint, the prison had shed everything that wasn't part of its core. Every light pole had been sheared off, all the pipes and wires ripped away, any sign of the earth it had sat on gone for good. What remained was a behemoth box of gray concrete and rebar. A foundation of stone, walls of marble and granite, a massive shell of a million pounds on a collision course with a population base of a hundred and fifty million people. At its current speed, it could rip through thirty or more towers in a row and another fifty in collateral damage, toppling a tenth of the supercity in one fatal blow.

But Dylan didn't know any of that because Dylan was sitting in his cell, wishing he could come up with a way out. He'd tried to apply his greatest mental strength to the bars, to bend them to his will, but they were monstrously thick. Moving objects from one place to another was one thing, bending solid iron was another. It wasn't in his catalog of pulse skills.

He knew the prison was moving; that much he could discern from the way it had felt lifting off the ground and the chatter on the sound rings. He couldn't say he'd been surprised to discover his mother had been listening to everything they said. But he did take some solace in knowing that she had heard only maybe 10 percent of everything that had been spoken since their departure. She could hear what they said only when someone on the sound ring network pressed in. Everything else was a mystery to her, and that, for some reason, pleased him. What had passed between Andre and him was theirs alone, no one else's.

After what felt like hours and hours, the door on the far end of the hallway opened, and a gust of wind blew down the hall. Cell block D was under the foundation of the prison, but it was also *part* of the foundation. The structure that remained could have been flipped upside down, the once-underground cell blocks moved to the top, and it would have held together. It was all of a piece: a single, massive mold. When the door shut, the air pressure changed, and Dylan's ears popped. It was not a pleasant feeling.

Gretchen stood outside the bars. She was an unexpected visitor and one with a second pulse. He wouldn't be able to push her around even if he wanted to.

She came into view wearing a black jumpsuit that, he hated to admit, looked cool from a distance. As she came nearer, she brushed her short hair with a hand, then removed a pair of black gloves and slapped them against her palm.

"It's a fine day for this," she said. "Hardly any head-wind at all. We're making good time."

"So we're moving, then? I had a feeling."

Gretchen smiled unexpectedly. She was at her best when the pistons of a plan were firing on all cylinders in her mind.

"We've got a little ways to go. Hopefully this crate holds together."

She allowed herself the shortest of all possible laughs, which sounded like a bark from a small dog, and began pacing slowly back and forth in front of the cell.

"Dylan, why did you come here?" she asked.

Dylan didn't hesitate.

"Because Meredith and I didn't see eye to eye."

"Sticking to your story?"

"It's not a story. It's the truth. But I have to say, I'm starting to think it was a bad idea. I didn't think I'd be spending so much time in a jail cell."

"Well, it is a prison. One should expect to spend some time locked up. Especially when they're in the habit of lying."

"I'm not lying."

Gretchen stopped pacing and faced the bars of the cell. She took the required number of steps forward in order to have her face practically touching the metal.

"I know you're lying, but it doesn't matter. Whatever small bits of information you've gleaned during this failed expedition aren't going to matter in a few hours. The world is going to be a very different place before you know it. Better choose whose side you're *really* on, Dylan Gilmore. Time is short."

Dylan was a lot harder to rattle than that. He went on the offensive.

"Andre trusts me. And he's in charge, not you."

Gretchen turned her head sideways, like a bird examining a hole from which a worm was almost sure to emerge any second.

"Maybe you *have* flipped," she said, and then, shaking her head as if it didn't matter one way or the other, added, "I'm not going to see you again, not for a few days anyway. If you're still here when I return, well, we'll see about your future. But this is good-bye, for now."

She began to walk away, then turned back.

"I almost forgot the whole reason I came down here," she said. "Silly me."

She turned on him, firing that icy-cold stare down the hall and through the bars.

"I'm going to kill your girlfriend," she said. "I wanted you to be the first to know."

Dylan wanted to hold character and fire back with

a wad of attitude that said *Girlfriend? I haven't got any girlfriend.* But the way she looked at him and the unexpected message she'd delivered left no doubt on Dylan's face. He was rattled.

"That's what I thought," Gretchen said. She was on the move again, opening the slab metal door as the wind dived down the corridor and hit Dylan in the face.

"I hope you've enjoyed your stay," she said, slamming the door behind her.

Of course Clara had told Gretchen about Faith hiding out in the woods. It was another of her carefully calibrated bombs set to go off very, very soon. It had been a pleasant bonus informing Gretchen that Wade, hopeless romantic that he was, had known she was out there all along and hadn't bothered to tell anyone. Clara was a team player; she knew better. Of course she'd never keep anything that important from her own mother.

Had it been Gretchen's idea or Clara's, a showdown between the two of them? Clara knew it had been her own, but she was subtle to the point of sublime. As far as Gretchen knew, it had been Gretchen's idea to lure Faith into a little one-on-one over the Western State. Was she that angry? Was she reckless enough to fall for it? *Oh yes,* Clara had discovered, *I think she's both of those things.*

Poor Gretchen. Poor, stupid Gretchen.

She'd even thanked Clara for letting her do the deed, knowing Clara had long nurtured a seething hatred of Faith Daniels.

"Let me take care of this for you," Clara had said, touching her mother on the shoulder softly, as if there was even a chance the two of them were close. "You stay focused on the task at hand."

But Gretchen was going to take on some water. Her ship was going to see some damage. She'd easily kill Faith in the end, but not without cost. And then Clara would swoop in and finish the job.

The orchestration was precise and lethal, just the way Clara liked it.

Chapter 13

Buckshot and Fishtail

"Faith, be extra careful. Gretchen knows you're out there, or I think she knows. Sounds like she's coming for you."

Hawk was reading Faith's letter when he heard Dylan's voice, low and quiet through the sound ring. The letter was very specific, also cleverly designed to deliver a mighty blow of guilt.

"I'll be ready," Faith replied, which was followed by Meredith telling her not to do anything "off the plan."

"You guys are within an hour of the Western State," Hawk relayed. "Better prepare for them to slow down."

"And be ready for incoming fire," Meredith said. "If the Western State gets a visual, they won't hesitate to attack."

"Wait, what?" Faith said. "You can't let them do that! Dylan is in there."

A pause on the line, then Dylan was back.

"Don't worry about me. I'm a second pulse, remember? Consider it a prison break."

Faith wasn't so sure. "You're in what amounts to a stone coffin. If it hits the ground and you're under it, you could get really hurt. Or killed."

"I'll be fine. You just worry about yourself. I don't know how this is going down, but one way or another, Gretchen is coming for you. Be ready. I've already talked too much, not that anyone is paying attention."

Faith wanted to shout how much she loved him, how much she missed seeing him. But if she pressed in and told Dylan these things, Clooger and Hawk and Dylan's mom would hear every word. That made the whole situation feel about as romantic as a family reunion.

Oh, to hell with it, she thought.

"Remember before, when you told me you loved me in the Looney Bin and I hesitated or whatever—"

"Wait, what's a Looney Bin?" Hawk pressed in. "Translate."

"Zip it, Hawk," Clooger pressed in.

Faith closed her eyes and shook her head. She was losing her nerve.

"It's okay, Faith," Dylan said.

"No. It's not okay. It's not, and it wasn't."

She let go of the sound ring, loneliness gripping her chest like a vise. Then she was back. "I miss you. And I'm yours, just you, nobody else. I love you, Dylan. I do."

Hawk pressed in: "This is intense."

Clooger pressed in: *"Hawk!"*

A long pause transpired in which no one spoke, and then Dylan said the right words at the right time to lift not just Faith, but the whole team.

"Let's play our part the best we can. We can make a difference here. All of us. And, Faith, nothing is going to stop me from finding my way back. Count on it."

Dylan went quiet after that; everyone did. Hawk reread the letter. There was no pleading or deal making in Faith's request. She knew as well as he did that there was no score to keep in a friendship like theirs. They did what the other needed, no matter what.

Hawk didn't understand why Faith wanted what she did, but he hadn't been able to see how he could ignore the request. And he couldn't tell Meredith, either. And so it was that two hours before the prison reached the Western State, Hawk had tapped out some commands on his Tablet, bouncing a signal through cell towers and satellite systems in a random, untraceable order. Finding his target, he had sent out the instructions, which were precise and to the point and timely.

Hawk had officially gone rogue.

—▬—

Clooger barely fit inside his bullet tube, and a half hour later he had an itch, on his right knee. He tried to reach down and scratch it, but the distance between his fingers and his kneecap required some bending. Either the leg had to come up or the shoulders had to arc down or both. He chose both, thinking a little alteration from each end of his body was less likely to send him into a tailspin. He was wrong about this, and found himself unexpectedly spinning in a circle that looked like a poorly thrown football. When he finally got things back under control, he was disappointed to find that his knee still itched, having not been scratched, and that the prison was moving in a different direction.

"Faith, you seeing this?"

"Yeah, I see it. What's with the drop and roll?"

Clooger didn't bother elaborating on the itch and the scratch that hadn't followed as he watched the prison rise in altitude. It was heading into the clouds on a steep trajectory.

"You still got it, Hawk?" Clooger asked.

"Totally, not a problem."

"Good, because we just lost visual."

Clooger made a second, slower attempt at the itch and felt his fingernail dig into skin. The relief was practically cosmic as he accelerated toward the Western State.

"Whoa there, Cloog," Hawk said. "Slow it down. Whatever military firepower they've got inside the States, and I can tell you it's a lot, they might not hesitate to use it if they see you coming. They can't see the prison. But they can see you."

"Head up into the clouds," Meredith said. She was flying over New Mexico with the single pulses, having completely avoided the path of the Western State. They'd flown directly across Arizona on a path toward the border of Texas. "They're not heading to the Western State anyway. At least not most of them."

"You sure about that?" Clooger asked. "They've been headed right for it this whole time."

A pregnant pause on the sound ring, then Meredith answered. "Yes, I'm sure."

The itch returned to Clooger's leg, and he thought: *Holy hell, how much longer to go inside this crazy thing?*

"Install a bathroom in the upgrade, will ya, Hawk?" Clooger asked.

"You got it," Hawk answered as he began calculating the ways in which he might actually pull it off.

Clooger headed for the cloud cover overhead just as the Western State came into clear view on the ground below. It was surprisingly slender, given the number of people it held. Unlike Los Angeles or New York, the States used every square inch of ground space and grew up at a much faster rate than out. It was true the States were always gobbling up more landmass, but with 150 million people packed into each one, they were a marvel of compact, utilitarian design. The buildings looked like drinking straws from so far out, piled in close together like a fist full of wheat stalks. Everything surrounding the Western State was flat and lush from Clooger's point of view, a valley of deep green and orange and yellow, the fall coming on fast. A ridge of mountains to the north was already covered in snow.

"See you when we get on the other side, Faith," Clooger said, entering the clouds as he chased down the prison.

No, you won't, Faith thought. She said the words to herself and no one else, because she saw what no one else saw. A tiny figure, moving out from under the clouds.

"Gretchen," Faith said. "You better run."

Faith and Gretchen were both traveling much slower now, around a hundred miles an hour, as they came within five miles of the Western State spires. Faith moved in within a hundred yards, came to a complete stop in the air, and used her Tablet to run some commands. The bullet suit rolled down toward her feet, her hands bunching it together at the bottom. She placed the resulting ring on a carabiner at her side, like Wonder Woman's rope.

When she looked up, Gretchen had stopped as well. She was staring at Faith Daniels like a lion at its prey, waiting to pounce.

"This is bad," Hawk said as he fumbled around in the front seat of the HumGee, searching blindly for a bottle of water. He'd lost Dylan's signal in the clouds, which meant he had no idea where the prison was. For all he knew it could have crash-landed into the Western State while he sat helplessly in the woods. He tried four or five more connection points, running tracers between outer-space satellites and old cell towers, but he was getting nothing. Faith he could see, and Meredith, who was rapidly approaching the Texas border on her way to who knew where. She wasn't telling and no one was asking, not yet anyway.

"I need a better signal," Hawk said, staring through the windshield into the tall trees shooting up all around him.

He opened the door and without thought or emotion walked about ten paces to a slightly more open patch of blue, holding his Tablet in its large size up over his head. The voice that had surprised him earlier returned out of the blue, only this time it was longer, more interesting:

A black hole with a mass of one ton would have the same luminosity as the sun. The level of gamma radiation emitted from such a black hole would contaminate not one but two entire States in a matter of seconds. There is untapped power in luminosity. Examine.

Hawk shook his head. The voice was clear and crisp, like someone on the sound ring. He was suddenly very curious about black holes and the power of luminosity and wanted to examine the problem immediately. He shook his head, afraid of what was happening to him. It had started this way with his parents: a voice that had slowly drawn them down into madness.

I heard that voice again today, asking me the most interesting questions, his mother used to say, often when she was turning out the light and bidding him good night. *It's the strangest thing.*

What was it: a year, eighteen months? How long after that did his parents really go downhill? How long would it be before Hawk experienced the same fate?

He probably would have thought about the voice in his head and the potential doom in his near future had it not been for the growling sound behind him. He turned, very slowly, still holding the Tablet over his head and still getting no signal. The wolves were back, teeth bared and dripping saliva as they observed easy prey.

Hawk's eyes darted in the direction of the Hum-Gee, though he didn't move his head even a quarter of an inch. The flat, wide vehicle was farther away than he'd hoped and not at the best angle. There were four wolves, pacing now, inching closer in a rocking pattern that could turn deadly at any moment.

I'm fast. Real fast, Hawk told himself. *Even Dylan says so.*

But he was glued to the forest floor, frozen with fear.

"How am I doing, Hawk?" Clooger piped in. "Can't see a thing up here, but my Tablet says due east. That right? Hawk?"

Something about hearing Clooger's voice startled Hawk into action, and before he knew it, he was running. Thank God he'd left the door to the HumGee ajar—opening it was one less thing to do when he got there. The wolves took chase instantaneously, coming at Hawk at a forty-five-degree angle, cutting the distance between them in huge strides.

Hawk wished he'd brought the sawed-off shotgun. What had he been thinking? Time slowed down, the whole scene taking place as if it were encased in a pool of thick syrup, holding everything in a liquid silence as the wolf at the front of the pack leaped, jaws open, for Hawk's ankle.

Hawk dived, time speeding back up as he hit the seat of the HumGee and slid into the door on the other side, cranking his head sideways and crumpling to the floor. The lead wolf tumbled to the left, making room for the next two wolves to stare directly into the Hum-Gee and take their first tentative steps inside. Both were ready to pounce when Hawk found the handle of the shotgun. He lifted it to his shoulder, pulled the trigger, and felt the power of the burst push him backward onto the floorboards. Buckshot bounced like tiny pinballs throughout the cabin of the rig, pelting him on the legs and arms. He'd missed, badly, but it had been enough to push the beasts back into the woods. Hawk lurched forward, grabbed the handle of the door, and yanked it shut just as a wolf jumped forward and crashed into the window, pushing the door all the way shut with its weight.

"Yeah! Yeah yeah yeah!" Hawk yelled. He laughed, despite the incredible stress of the moment, and examined one of his arms, where a red circle was blooming. There were seven or eight such marks, but he didn't care. He'd shot himself, sure, but he'd outrun a pack of wolves. It was a victory against a bigger, badder foe, a good sign on a day when just that kind of luck would be needed.

"Hawk?" Clooger called.

"Answer," Meredith added. "Give us a signal."

Hawk grabbed his sound ring and yelled louder than he'd intended to. The adrenaline was really pumping.

"Here! Lost the signal, but I'm on it. Give me five!"

"No need to scream," Clooger said. "I'm headed east, gotta be past the Western State by now. I'll dip out of the clouds, see what I see."

"Better wait, see if Hawk can grab a signal," Meredith said. "No reason to risk it."

"Faith, you there?" Clooger called. "Faith?"

And somehow he just knew, without thinking twice about it, that she'd deliberately gone off on her own. He was actually surprised when he heard her voice.

"I'm here, same direction as you."

Hawk, on the ground in the woods where the pack of wolves had moved off, should have called it in. Faith wasn't following Clooger; she was holding a few miles outside the Western State. But he didn't say anything, let it slide, did what she asked and stayed quiet.

He was too small to reach the pedals of the Hum-Gee without having his butt hang halfway off the seat and his chest pinned against the steering wheel, but that was going to have to be good enough. He needed to get the rig out in the open away from all the trees. He needed a real signal, and that was going to happen only if he hit the accelerator and drove down the side of the mountain.

There was no firing up the engine; it was nuclear. Put the HumGee in gear and it just *drove*. He pulled the gearshift down, slammed on the gas, and burst forward, fishtailing around a tree and hitting it with the rear end of the right side. The HumGee pulled hard to the left and hit a steep section of grass. Hawk was driving down the side of a mountain whether he liked it or not. His feet fumbled around for the brake but kept landing on the gas, shooting him forward in gasps and bursts. Trees were everywhere, and while he wasn't hitting any of them dead-on with the grille, he was grazing plenty, spinning sideways and nearly flipping over as he spun the wheel wildly back and forth. He was, to put it plainly, 100 percent out of control. His luck held though, and soon he exploded into the open expanse of the field that lay at the bottom of the hill. Here, without the trees to dodge and crash into sideways, he sped up, passing fifty miles per hour before finally finding the brake and stomping down with all his weight. The HumGee pitched right and slid into the open as Hawk held on to the steering wheel for dear life. When the monstrous rig came to a stop in a plume of dust, it was upright, on all four wheels. Hawk was banged up and bruised, but looking back up the hill at the path he'd taken, he threw open the door and rolled onto the ground, letting out a cry of victory.

It was, possibly, the greatest moment of his life, and no one had been there to see it.

"Where are the cameras when I need them!" he

yelled, laughing at himself. His hair was a wild mess on top of his head, and his muscles ached with buckshot and rollover wounds, but he was feeling pretty good, all in all. A few seconds later he had his Tablet in hand, and, more importantly, he had a strong signal.

The prison was back online, moving at a thousand miles an hour, heading for the Kansas state border.

Hawk climbed onto the hood of the smashed-up HumGee and sat down, running calculations.

"Meredith, copy?"

"Copy," she responded. "We've landed in Texas, regrouping for five."

"Listen, I don't know if you're aware of this or not, but the prison is headed straight for the Eastern State."

There was a slight pause, and then she answered.

"I know. I've always known."

"What's that supposed to mean?" Clooger asked. He was confused and frustrated. He had a terrible itch, and he had to pee. The whole operation appeared to be falling apart all around him.

"Clooger, head back to the Western State. Faith might need the help even if she's not willing to ask for it. I'll take the rest to the east."

"What's going on, Meredith?" Clooger asked. He'd stopped in midair and rolled the bullet suit down into a loop he held in one hand. Snapping it onto his belt, he scratched his knee like a dog with a pack of fleas.

He was bothered but not surprised by the dead air on the other end of the sound ring. Their relationship had always been complicated. Neither of them were second pulses, so they were both vulnerable. But it was much more than that. Meredith knew things she would never tell him. She was aware, on some unknown and mysterious level, of where this was all going. And she wasn't telling anyone, not even him, the whole truth. Theirs was a relationship built on secrets. It was a shaky foundation.

What did he really know? What was he sure of?

Meredith had a fight ahead of her; that much was true.

The stakes were high. How high, Clooger had no way of knowing.

He had loved her as successfully as he could: listening patiently, not pushing too hard, holding on.

Clooger was also realistic, always had been. His fight would lead directly under his feet, through the clouds, in the Western State. Her fight would happen somewhere else.

They were two people living in a world where not a thing could be counted on in the end, not even each other.

Chapter 14

Personally, I Like the Javelin

Gretchen was not the type who took chances with even the smallest details. She kept her fingernails trimmed to a precise shape and length, long enough to inflict damage in a cat fight but not so long that they got in the way of using her Tablet. This was a more exact calculation than those around her would have guessed. She wore her hair cropped short, not because it was easier to manage or brought out her gloriously high cheekbones. She kept it short purely for reasons of strategy. The only use long hair had in a fight to the death was getting in the way. It could be pulled, shut in a door, tangled in the gears of a machine. This was the way her mind worked: observe the risks, minimize them, complete the task at hand, repeat.

It was this kind of disciplined system of thought that made her even more invincible than the other second pulses wandering the face of the earth. It was also why she carried the darts, because one never knew for sure about the last second pulse.

Gretchen, like Meredith and Andre, had what she liked to call "special information." Only the three of them, no one else, knew certain things. And Gretchen, for reasons she liked to turn over in her mind on a regular rotation, knew the most. She knew two things no one else in the world knew, because Hotspur had told her before the end. Her and her alone.

There will be five. Five second pulses, he had told her. *No more, no less. It is ordained. Two will be twins, so really, in a sense, there will be four. One of these two is a doppelgänger, a black mirror, a balance.*

Gretchen had never liked the sound of that. She'd also seen it as a miscalculation. Wade and Clara were both evil brats without vision or control. As far as she was concerned, they only reflected each other's incompetence.

Hotspur also told her something else: *There may come a time when these humans I have engineered must go. Even you, Gretchen. One day you must go. Water, the living things of earth, stone, and titanium. These are the way in, the way through, the darts of death. Do you understand?*

She had understood perfectly. These were the elements that could kill a second pulse. And she knew the owner of all but one. Stone for Dylan, the living things of earth for Wade and Clara, water for herself. She could drink it, wash with it, touch it—but water was extremely dangerous for Gretchen. It had to be consumed in small doses. She never submerged herself in water, only showered, and even that burned after a few minutes. It was another reason, possibly the main reason, she kept her hair short. Long, wet hair burned her scalp and took too long to dry.

That left titanium, and the one who had never appeared. Somewhere, alone and hiding or unaware entirely, an unknown second pulse lurked. The last, the fifth, the most dangerous of them all. Dangerous because titanium wasn't just lying around everywhere. Rocks, trees, water—these things could be found and used as weapons with relative ease. But titanium, well, that was another matter. It wasn't the kind of thing one had quick and easy access to in the event of a real confrontation.

He'd chosen it for obvious reasons. For Hotspur Chance, titanium was the perfect element. He had torn it asunder, reorganized it, manipulated it into the clay of God. Titanium was the seed of it all: the Tablets, the

States, the first and second pulses. But for one second pulse, the one Gretchen could never find, it was the poison that killed.

This was why she carried the darts in sleeves along her belt: six of them, made entirely of titanium, with tips as sharp as needles and feathers of coated steel.

She hated the fact that Meredith had been given the ability to sense the second pulse.

A balance of power is required, Hotspur had said. *I know what I'm doing.*

It had turned out to be his greatest mistake, for not long after that Meredith was gone; one of the second pulses was alive and kicking in her belly. Hotspur had let that happen and more. If the fifth second pulse was going to be found, it was Meredith who would make the discovery.

All these things—the number of the second pulses, the killing elements, Meredith's sixth sense—all this information had been given to Gretchen and Gretchen alone. She thought of these many shards of knowledge and how they added up to a complete picture only she could see.

As she stared across the sky at Faith Daniels, Gretchen ran a perfectly manicured finger across the slick titanium of six darts. She drifted up, higher in the sky, much higher than the top of the tallest spire in the Western State, just below the ceiling of clouds. Of course Faith followed her ascent, but she held back, biding her time.

Poor little single pulse, Gretchen thought, staring across the open sky. *Your days have been numbered. We arrive at zero.*

She heard the sound of Clooger's sawed-off shotgun before she felt the metal buckshot pellets bouncing off her back. The impact pushed her softly forward, as if she'd been struck by a blast of Nerf balls. She turned on Clooger and found he was surprisingly close, only ten feet off, reloading.

"Shooting someone in the back," Gretchen said. "I didn't take you for a coward."

"Whatever gets the job done," Clooger said, and then he shot her dead-on in the face at point-blank range, peppering her with metal.

Gretchen's lungs filled with a great breath of air as her chest widened, and she floated slightly higher, her chin resting on her chest. When the breath released and her head came up, she was smiling. The shotgun flew out of Clooger's hand along with all the shells he had in his pockets. Gretchen loaded the barrel with two rounds, but when she looked up to fire, Clooger was gone. He'd flown up into the clouds above, hidden from view. Gretchen felt a presence behind her but didn't turn. Faith was at her back, close enough to kill with one shot.

"I'm the one you want," Faith said, slow and steady.

Faith couldn't see Gretchen's face until she turned, only a few feet away, and fired the shotgun. At the same moment, Clooger descended from above, knocking Gretchen into a tailspin as he spun her around and around and let go, flinging her toward the Western State below. The timing was such that Gretchen hadn't seen the way Faith moved right into the shotgun fire as if it were nothing more than a steady rain. Her second pulse was still, for the moment, a secret.

Gretchen turned on Clooger, her anger fully engaged now, and fired the second round in the chamber. As Clooger dodged to one side, a half-dozen pellets stung his left forearm. It hurt but didn't break skin through his layer of clothes, and as Gretchen reloaded, he dived headlong, down toward her.

"Clooger, don't!" Faith screamed, diving alongside in the same direction.

All Gretchen could think was how perfect this was going to be. Two rounds in the chambers, the barrel slapped shut. *I'll take them both,* bang bang. *This was almost too easy.*

Gretchen took aim as both of her targets came in fast. The blast zone would be at least ten feet wide; two shots in a row would finish them if they stayed the course. She fired both barrels empty in rapid succession at thirty-foot range. Using the power of her mind, Faith pushed Clooger wide, tumbling him end over end into the vastness of the sky above the Western State. The full force of both shots, hundreds of lead pellets, slammed into Faith at close range.

And she kept on coming without the slightest hesitation. Gretchen's expression changed from a gleeful rage to confused surprise. The idea that Faith Daniels could be the one, the last of the second pulses, was somehow beyond her ability to grasp in those first few seconds. It was a fact of the universe that couldn't be true.

Faith's fist, the hand that wore the tattoo of the hammer, struck Gretchen square in the face hard enough to rattle Gretchen's brain. Her second-pulse weakness wasn't a fist, but the punch was so full of power and vengeance that Gretchen felt it all the way down her spine.

Gretchen tumbled toward the tallest spires of the Western State, setting off the first of many alarms in the security center of the city. They were close enough now to attract attention, and bigger than the biggest birds that might fly through the airspace above the state. This set a standard drone protocol in motion, of which Clooger was the first to take notice. He pressed the sound ring.

"Hawk! Incoming!" he yelled. "This is going to get complicated fast."

"I'm on it," Hawk said. There were six attack drones heading into the sky, all designed first to provide high-definition visual, then strike if necessary. Hawk had prepared for this and knew he had only twenty, maybe thirty seconds. He'd already hacked into the military system and set up a daisy chain of commands that led from the security center to the drone video feeds. The States relied on visual to determine threats coming in from overhead and had never gone so far as to fire on a target. The drones, each of them shaped like a four-foot fighter jet, were extremely accurate at determining enemy fire. Inside the security center, Western State officials were unconcerned. They'd never seen any-thing but low-flying condors or the occasional mass of space junk falling to Earth. They were on strict orders not to shoot birds out of the sky, but space junk was like target practice, something they always hoped for. Western State security officials had an expectation, and it was Hawk's job to meet it.

"Hawk?" Clooger said. "You seeing this? We got six fliers, coming in hot."

Hawk didn't answer; he was too busy programming, his fingers flying across his Tablet. *Just a few more key-strokes,* Hawk thought.

Got it!

"Okay, you're clear," Hawk said. "At least for these six."

Inside the Western State all six drones were returning images of three huge condors, birds with wingspans of four feet that seemed to be participating in some kind of high-flying mating ritual.

Gretchen looked down into the mass of towering spires and calculated her options. There were very few weapons so high in the air, many more down below. And it had been her primary job to get down there anyway, to create some havoc, a diversion that would hold the attention of both States.

She dived, headfirst, like a bullet into the core of the Western State. Faith pressed her sound ring.

"Don't you dare follow me in, Clooger," she said. "I can handle this alone."

Clooger was having none of that, taking chase right behind Faith as all three of them plummeted to Earth. But in his desire to help Faith any way he could, he'd set off a second set of alarms in the security center. There were now three, not two, objects in the sky, and one was unidentified.

"Cover blown!" Hawk yelled. "Cover blown! Get ready for incoming fire!"

Six additional drones launched off the tops of Western State buildings, making a total of twelve. Gretchen took control of the nearest one with her mind, guiding it in Faith's direction. They were both below the line of the tallest buildings now, darting back and forth between them. Faith lost Gretchen around a corner and, clearing the edge, found a drone staring her in the face. It slammed into Faith's midsection, buckling her over like a rag doll, pushing her backward. She slammed into the edge of a building, the metal and glass flying, and punched out on the other side. The drone was a rocket-fueled beast that wouldn't let her go, so she turned it toward the ground and waited for the impact. Hundreds of stories down she went, faster and faster, slamming through encircled walking bridges that spanned buildings, knocking wide holes through frosted glass and steel. She turned toward the ground, straining against the power of the drone, and guided it through a maze of elevated walkways. When the drone hit the pavement, the impact was felt for a hundred yards in every direction, like a small earthquake rattling the Western State. The hole was deep, ten feet or more.

Gretchen flew in close, hovering overhead, a titanium dart at the ready.

Drones weren't programmed to fly this low; it was far too dangerous. There was an enemy at ground level, and the protocol was to change to ground forces, which were dispatched from the nearest military station. Armored vehicles, loaded with personnel and weaponry, were on the move.

Clooger had landed on a building, where he assumed

the position of a gargoyle, low and still. Clad in a black T-shirt and green camo pants, he held a knife with a six-inch blade in one hand as drones flew back and forth overhead, searching for him.

"Clooger, stay low," Hawk said. "Airspace is crawling with drones. Must be thirty of them now. They're on to us."

"Is there anything you can do? Any kind of diversion?"

"Working on it. Hold tight. If you go airborne, they've got you."

Clooger looked down over the edge of the building and saw the crisscross of white bridges clogging the space, the shadows of people moving inside behind frosted glass. The space between himself and the ground below looked like a thousand white arteries pumping shadowy blood.

He couldn't help himself. Staying put just wasn't an option. He dived for the ground, knife extended.

"Where is she?" Clooger asked Hawk, pressing the sound ring with his free hand as he dodged bridge after bridge.

Below, Gretchen waited. She could already hear the convoy of military heading her way from three different directions. Maybe she'd only imagined Faith was a second pulse, or maybe their little Intel friend,

Hawk, had developed some sort of shield against a certain level of violence. Faith was probably nothing but a mangled corpse, ten feet underground, never to be seen or heard from again. She'd done her job—the military was on high alert, and the Eastern State was distracted with the mayhem she was causing. Everyone would be pleased with her effort, and she wasn't finished yet. She planned to have quite a lot of fun wreaking havoc in the Western State before she was done. Why not enjoy herself a little? She'd earned it.

Clooger saw three things on his way down, darting between bridges and buildings: the military convoys, coming in from three directions; the impact hole from Faith's crash into the ground; and his target, Gretchen. All three convoys converged into action at once.

The front end of all three convoys was made up of large assault vehicles, with doors that opened from the side, pouring armed soldiers out into the open like ants out of a hill. Within seconds there were a hundred of them in position, pointing everything from rifles to rocket launchers directly at Gretchen. Faith was nothing if not theatrical. She waited until the whole world seemed to be watching before bursting out of the hole, tripling its size as she came. Gretchen backed up in the air, momentarily stunned, then raised her arm and fired a titanium dart as if it were blown from a cannon.

Faith turned sideways in the air, but the dart grazed her left arm, tearing into flesh. She screamed and lurched backward, stunned by the searing heat of pain. Blood began to flow as Gretchen took a second dart in hand. Someone was speaking through a bullhorn.

"Prepare to fire!" the voice said. There was a distinct feeling that whoever was in charge didn't know what else to say. There were people flying in the air. This was not in the playbook.

Gretchen was about to fire the second titanium dart when Clooger slammed into her from behind. He smashed the knife into her back, but it was like hitting a slab of marble with the tip of a sword. Gretchen turned on him, thrust the titanium dart into his arm, and pushed him away. She pulled the dart back—it was far too valuable a weapon to waste on a single pulse—and veered in the direction of Faith.

That was when the bullets started flying.

"Fire! Fire! Fire!" the commander shouted. The whole quad between the buildings erupted with sparks and reverberating sounds as Clooger, stabbed and bleeding, flew back up through the walkways toward the top of the building he'd come from.

"Things are getting pretty hairy down here," he said into his sound ring. "How's that escape plan coming?"

"Just about got it, really close," Hawk said. He'd

never worked so feverishly in his entire life. His brain was fizzing with data as he went around every firewall the Western State had and dug right into the brains of the drones themselves. The dreadful voice reared up in his head like a warhorse: *Plans proceeding as expected; it won't be long now. Fire! Fire! Fire!*

Hawk shook the voice free and kept programming as Clooger landed on top of the highest bridge, just below the line of buildings. He looked up and saw the blue sky above, looked down and saw the red blood pouring out onto his upper arm, dripping onto the white bridge. The shadows moved beneath him: people, running for their lives, trying to make sense of the brutality outside.

Down below, Faith was realizing something she hadn't expected.

She knows. She knows I'm a second, and she's got a weapon that can get through.

It was this thought that sent Faith flying out of the melee, around the first of many buildings. Gretchen took chase, the two of them leaving three military convoys scratching their heads and wondering what had just happened.

Faith hadn't expected the maze of bridges and buildings to be so difficult to navigate, and she bounced from turn to turn like a badly thrown bowling ball skidding across multiple lanes. Along the way she saw people walking outside along the pristine streets, staring up at her as if she were some sort of aberration, a ghost or a phantom from another dimension.

"Hawk!" she yelled, pressing her sound ring. She turned a corner around a building and felt as though she was going in a big circle. "Where's the field? Guide me in!"

This was the kind of distraction Hawk didn't need, and it was only made worse by the other voices that were pressing in all of a sudden.

Dylan: "Faith, get the hell out of there! Whatever you're doing, it's not worth it. Get to safety!"

Clooger: "Patching up a wound here, just about back in business."

Meredith: "Everyone stay calm and let Hawk focus. No more chatter! I mean it."

The line went dead, and Hawk switched to a split-screen view on his Tablet. On one side, the coded brain of a drone lay before him; on the other, Faith's position in the Western State, the location she needed to get to, and the route she had to take.

"Left around the next building, straight for seven buildings, right for three, you're there. Got it?"

"Got it!" Faith yelled, and she was moving faster, thirty feet up, darting between the endless web of bridges spanning the towers.

Gretchen gamely followed, doing her best to destroy as much as she could as she went. Faith was attempting to leave no trace; Gretchen had a stated goal of wrecking as much as she could. She flipped armored vehicles as she passed over them, threw white Western State vans into bridges, killed innocent bystanders with complete and utter disregard for human life.

"I'm doing you a favor," she said to herself as she watched a military truck slam into a plateglass window, crushing bystanders as it tumbled end over end.

Faith felt the wrenching regret for her decision to take Gretchen head-on and wished her plan had never included the Western State. Why couldn't she have lured her out into the abandoned world and done this? Out there they could have gone head to head for hours and no one would have been hurt. But she knew this was Gretchen's plan, too. She knew it would end up here, that it would be violent. She knew Gretchen was sent to do some terrible deed here, in the Western State. The collateral damage wasn't Faith's fault, but she felt the weight of guilt all the same.

I have to get her out in the open, she thought. *And fast.*

It was as she thought this very thing that Faith Daniels finally arrived in the place where her best friend had been murdered: the outdoor coliseum, the location of the Field Games. The grass was a bright green beneath her as she flew into the middle of the field. White stone columns, tall and thin, encircled the field, and behind them, the vast seating in row after rising row. It looked like something out of the Roman Empire, a beautiful expanse of white and green, the red ribbon of a track separating the two.

Faith glanced at her arm, crimson with blood from the slight wound, and felt a sudden burst of energy. She liked the pain and was glad to have it. It was she and Gretchen now, standing on the otherwise empty field, staring each other down.

"This is for you," Faith said, looking up into the cobalt sky and thinking only of Liz. She looked at her arm and saw the tattoo of the chain and the ivy, then looked at the palm of her hand and saw the hammer. All she wanted was to feel no more pain, and the only weapon against the deep chasm of sadness that held her was the hammer of justice served.

Faith saw the titanium dart heading her way as Gretchen moved in closer. A column of stone stood to Faith's right, and moving with sudden speed she avoided the weapon. But Gretchen was all business now. Killing Faith had become her complete and total focus. She moved with stunning speed, around the side of the column with another dart in hand. She rounded the corner and pulled to a stop as Faith backed up in midair, staring at Gretchen.

"I have you now," Gretchen said. "You can run, but there's no place to hide."

Faith nodded curtly, as if she understood but didn't really care one way or the other. Gretchen held the dart at the ready. One clean throw would do it. She was trying to decide whether to go for the head or the heart, savoring the moment. She was also enjoying the idea that she was taking this opportunity away from Clara. God, how she hated Clara's arrogance. She had a radio receiver of her own, though she'd been careful not to use it for security reasons. Now that she'd unleashed the Western State army and cornered Faith, she felt it didn't matter who knew where she was. And besides, she was invincible. Nothing could touch her.

"Connect CQ," she said, which automatically sent a signal to Clara's receiver, where Clara was soaring above the clouds in the prison.

"Everything going as planned?" Clara asked, her voice projecting out in the air as it sent waves of rage pumping through Faith's veins.

"Oh, I think it's going better than that," Gretchen said. "I wanted you to hear this. It's going to be something special."

"Whatever you say, Mother."

Faith could practically see Clara rolling her eyes with boredom.

"I didn't know my own weakness," Faith said. "I should thank you for pointing that out to me."

"Sorry I couldn't return the favor," Gretchen said.

Gretchen had put all the pieces in place. Her spoiled brat was on the line, listening in. She'd gotten Faith out in the open where there was no place to hide. She had the weapon that would finish her in hand. It was perfect.

Which was why, when she should have been more aware of everything happening around her, Gretchen was caught unaware. A mass of water was beginning to rise from directly below her, where Faith had carefully planned its arrival in a fifty-gallon drum. The barrel itself wasn't moving, only its contents. Fifty gallons of water, rising slowly and quietly up through the air, dripping like the tentacles of a poisonous jellyfish. Only now it was moving much faster on the power of Faith's thoughts, so fast that Gretchen had time only to glance down before it surrounded her body, rising to the level of her neck.

"I don't know if you're hearing this or not, Clara," Faith said. "But your mother is having a little bit of a moment here."

Gretchen was choking. It sounded like she'd swallowed a small potato that was now stuck in her windpipe.

"Cat got your tongue?" Clara asked, and Faith

couldn't be sure if Clara was kidding, not at all aware of how much trouble her mother was really in. Either way, Faith's work wasn't finished yet. She had enlisted the help of Liz's special somebody, the guy with the softest hands on Earth. Noah, the one who had been sitting next to Liz when the hammer came down, the one who had placed the barrel of water right under the column where Faith could find it. Faith looked across the long length of the green field and saw him standing alone.

"Time to go," Faith said and, raising her hands out in front of her, swept away Gretchen, encased in a prison of water. Faith followed closely behind as Gretchen descended toward the far end of the field, where Noah waited. In his soft hands, the hands that had caressed the one he loved, he held a javelin. One end of the javelin was stuck in the ground, the other end angled up in the air at forty-five degrees.

"Better say good-bye," Faith said.

Gretchen took a massive, gulping breath and found the strength to form words.

"Titanium. Her weakness is titanium!"

And with that she somehow managed to remove her hand from the watery prison that surrounded her and release the dart. It was, Faith would later recall, poetic in a way. She felt the piercing sting of the dart enter her side at the same moment Gretchen landed, back first, on the javelin. Coated with water as it slid into Gretchen's spine, it passed through her heart and out the other side. The water surrounding Gretchen like a clear cocoon turned a divine shade of pink in the morning sunlight, then clouded into an ugly swirl of red.

Faith let the water fall to the ground, but Gretchen stayed where she was, pinned to the field like a bug in an experiment. Faith would always remember this as a moment of sweet release, a letting go. If her vengeance was a cancer the size of a melon in the pit of her stomach, she'd just chopped it in half with a clean, violent slice. She felt lighter, less weighted down. She would also later discover that the biggest reason for this new lightness in her head was the blood quickly staining the side of her shirt. The dart had gone all the way through, burning like a hot knife as it passed. "Personally, I like the javelin. It's a good weapon, don't you think?" Faith said, a little weakly.

Noah didn't know *what* to think. He'd gone along with the plan because he owed it to Faith and Liz and Hawk, but now that he was standing there staring at the dead body of someone he didn't even know, he wasn't anything but scared shitless. He started backpedaling.

"You better get out of here, Faith," he said. "They're coming. You don't want to be here when they show up."

Noah started running at about the same moment

the signal on Gretchen's end popped and fizzled and faded away, the water finally having worked its way into the sealed casing of the device strapped to her belt.

Clara wasn't entirely sure what her mother had said, garbled as it was through a wall of water, but she was smart enough to record the conversation. The first four or five replays revealed the whole message, which was as clear as a bell but far, far away, as if being heard from behind many doors.

Her weakness is titanium.

"Thank you, Mom. That information is going to be helpful. And thank you, Faith. I couldn't stand the old bag any longer. You did me a solid. I won't forget."

"Clooger!" Hawk yelled. "You're clear! Go now! Go!"

"Any chance he could swing by and pick me up?" Faith asked. She was lying on the field, a red stain growing slowly wider at her side. Blood was pumping not through her but out of her as she stared up at Gretchen's terror-filled eyes. Faith half expected the body to reanimate, for Gretchen to pull the javelin from her own chest and begin laughing hideously.

Clooger didn't think twice. He was in real trouble and he knew it, but it sounded to him as if Faith wasn't doing much better. He was expendable; she was anything but. How she could have gotten herself really hurt he didn't know, but it didn't matter. He had to get her the hell out of the Western State, and fast. He looked up, saw nothing but blue sky, and went for it.

"Five buildings down, then a right," Hawk said. "Make it snappy; this diversion I've set in motion isn't going to last all day."

"Roger that," Clooger said, flying at breakneck speed between bridge spans, any one of which could have killed him on impact. He was giving it all he had, taking every risk he possibly could that wasn't completely out of control.

He was one, maybe two minutes from his destination when Faith and Dylan started talking on the sound ring.

"One down," Faith said, and then she got confused. Was it one down, one to go? Or one down, two to go? Two sounded weird, but she thought there were two: Clara and Wade. Or was it one?

"Are you okay?" Dylan asked. He was done worrying about who might hear him. The world outside was coming apart at the seams. "Tell me the truth."

"She throws a damn good uppercut," Faith said, the world of reality swirling like an eddy of water around her. "But I knocked her out. I took care of it."

Dylan could tell she was fading. Faith was in real trouble. He wanted to break out of his cell, fly to her side, take her out of the mess he'd gotten her into. How had he allowed himself to end up in such a helpless situation? Trapped in a prison, no way out, flying away from the one he loved when she needed him most.

"Don't leave me, Faith. I mean it. I'm not going to make it without you."

"Such a romantic," Faith said. "I always liked that about you."

"I'm sorry," Dylan said, trying to hold it together. "I'm really sorry."

She thought of the secret places that were theirs alone: the top of the old Nordstrom building, the Looney Bin. She started to cry, tears clouding her vision as the sky turned into milky sapphire liquid.

"I love you, Dylan," she said. "I only ever loved you. Come home."

Dylan got up and went to the bars of his cell. He took one in each hand and pulled, harder than he'd ever pulled before. He screamed with effort and frustration, and the bars gave way, inching apart. But it wasn't enough. He was in a maximum-security prison. The place was designed to hold the Hulk, and he wasn't getting out until someone let him out.

"I love you, too," he said, and felt his heart ripping in two at the thought of losing her. "I'm coming for you. Wait for me!"

Faith saw the frozen look of desperation on Gretchen's lifeless face and summoned the will for one more thought before passing out.

"I might have been wrong about this revenge business. It's not as great as I thought it would be."

Meredith had remained quiet throughout, listening as she crossed into Arkansas territory with the rest of the single pulses, but now she spoke.

"It never is."

Clooger couldn't believe his eyes when he arrived at the coliseum. Gretchen, one of only five second pulses, pinned like a bug with a javelin to the ground. It was at once horrifying and beautiful, the kind of vision he knew all too well from one too many days as a soldier. The joy of a good victory was always overshadowed by the overwhelming bleakness of death.

He saw the stain of blood surrounding Faith.

Clooger had played doc plenty of times in the field and knew he needed to get her medical attention, and fast.

"Hawk, find me a hospital," he said. He looked skyward and saw the crisscrossing trails of drones and the first of many explosions.

"Copy that," Hawk said, thinking for an instant how he, too, was beginning to sound like a stowaway on the *Starship Enterprise*. "Just get airborne. I've set the drones to attack each other, but that's not going to last much longer. They're going to override my hack. Matter of time."

Another explosion in the sky above as one drone blew up another and Clooger had Faith in his arms. She stirred momentarily, looked into his eyes.

"I'm scared."

"Don't be," Clooger said, the tone of his voice full of strength. "I have you."

Anyone who had come up against Clooger when he was in this kind of mood knew what it meant: proceed at your own risk. It didn't matter if you were a warrior or an army or a second pulse; you knew there would be hell to pay. You might kill him in the end, but there would be consequences for messing with this guy, and those consequences would be harsh.

A few seconds later Clooger was airborne, where he dodged and parried his way through a maelstrom of explosions and drone fire, flying away into the blue, carrying the most important cargo the free world had in its arsenal.

Chapter 15

Doctor Doom!

Dylan and Hawk kept up a heavy chatter on the sound ring as Clooger and Faith escaped the Western State by the skin of their teeth. The number of drones in the sky over the city had swelled to more than a hundred, exploding into one another all around them as Clooger raced for the outer edge of the city.

"How's she doing?" Dylan asked, but no sooner had he asked the question than the door of cell block D was thrown open and a blistering wind ripped down the corridor.

"She's out but breathing," Clooger said. "Hawk, get me to a hospital, now!"

"Stay the same course and keep pressure on the wound," Hawk said. "I've got a beeline on a hospital due west."

"Copy that. Let me know if anything follows me."

"You got it."

Dylan listened to the chatter without responding and stood holding on to the bars he'd bent a few inches apart as two men dressed in black-and-gray camo appeared.

"Don't give us any trouble," the larger of the two said. He had a set of pork chop sideburns and a thinning head of dirt-colored hair that was flying over his head like strands of cotton candy. "Boss wants you upstairs. Can I count on you not to kill both of us?"

Dylan could have already hurled them into the walls of the corridor, ending their lives in the process. They were nervous, aware of Dylan's power, acting as if they'd been given the worst assignment in the world.

"Take me to your leader," Dylan said, as if he were some sort of alien creature they'd been holding hostage.

Pork Chops looked at the other man and nodded, then took his Tablet out of a small side pocket on his pants.

"Cut him loose," he said into his Tablet. "We'll bring him up."

The wall of bars slid slowly open, and Dylan stepped

out into the hallway, taking the full brunt of the wind for the first time. It was like a blast of water out of a fire hose, steady and powerful, pushing all three of them away from the exit.

"Hit a hard headwind in the last hour," Pork Chops said. "Should be out of it shortly. We've started our descent."

Descent? Dylan thought. *We must have arrived . . . somewhere.*

Climbing the stairs outside cell block D was comically difficult, forcing them all to use their pulses to navigate. The door to Andre's office was closed when they moved past, and Dylan stopped.

The guard who wasn't Pork Chop said, "Not in there, come on," then shoved Dylan hard in the back.

"Really?" Dylan said, turning on him with a glare. The man should have wilted under Dylan's gaze, understanding in an instant what a foolish thing he'd done. But this guy was having none of it.

"That way," he said, shoving Dylan forward again. "And stop turning around or I'll Taser your ass."

Dylan couldn't believe his ears. What was with this guy?

"Better tell your partner to take it down a notch," Dylan said to Pork Chops. He began walking again, hitting another set of stairs that would lead him up to the main level. "Guy's got a serious attitude problem."

"Don't mind Stan," Pork Chops answered, standing at a door with his hand on the handle. "He's a little tired of being pushed around by second pulses. Just one of those days."

Pork Chop turned the handle on the door and pushed, letting a stream of sunlight into the gray landing. The wind had died down considerably, and Dylan had a feeling in his stomach that they were moving down at a rapid clip.

"Name's Paul," Pork Chop said. "Paul Sanders. Go on now, they're waiting for you."

The light source appeared to be somewhere above the door, out of Dylan's line of vision. Dylan leaned forward cautiously, and Stan Tasered him in the small part of his back. It didn't hurt, but it did send an electric shock through his system, making him jump forward far enough for Paul to slam the door and lock it from the outside.

"Good luck, amigo!" Paul laughed. "See you on the outside!"

Dylan was usually cool headed in times of stress, but the situation was unnerving. He'd just been Tasered by a disgruntled single pulse and locked in a space yet again. He was starting to feel like a rat in an experiment as he scaled the steps warily, searching for a way out.

He was staring at a ladder, and he knew where it led: to one of the gun turrets jutting out in the air like a tiny lighthouse.

"Looks like I'm headed to the eye of the beast," Dylan said, pinching his sound ring. "Not sure I'll be able to say much once I get up there."

"We're closing in on your location now," Meredith said. "I can see you."

Dylan was shocked as he held on to the ladder with one hand. "Then you know where we are?"

"I know, too," Hawk said. He'd been tracking the prison all along, but with everything else going on in the Western State, he hadn't said.

"You're approaching the Eastern State," Meredith said.

"If my calculations are correct, you'll get there a few minutes before Meredith," Hawk added. "You've slowed way down. You're starting a decline in altitude."

Dylan didn't know what to say. The Eastern State? It was all the way on the other side of the country! He shook his head, angry and confused.

"Thanks for keeping me in the loop, you guys. Really appreciate that. Anyway, I've been summoned. Signing off."

Dylan was feeling more and more like a pawn in someone else's game.

No order came from Meredith, no other information from Hawk. The line was dead. He knew Faith and Clooger were out there, too, but they felt farther away than they ever had. The Eastern State? Jeez. It might as well have been another planet, as Dylan started climbing the old-fashioned way, on rungs. Each time his hand touched metal he thought of how he and Faith had climbed or, more often, flown to the top of the Nordstrom building and spent time training. Those were good times, the Western State clouding the sky with soft light in the distance, the two of them alone in the quiet of the night.

At the top of the ladder lay a round hatch crossed with a metal bar. Dylan used his mind to move the bar and throw open the door. He felt as if he were climbing up and out of a submarine as his head cleared the opening. His shoulders were next, then he was all the way out, feeling the piercing sting of cold air on his face.

"Right on time," Andre said. He was standing alone, staring through a windowless opening. The entire space wasn't more than ten feet across, and the hole Dylan had just stepped through took up two feet in diameter. He slammed the iron door shut, leaving a perfectly flat surface where the hole had been. Dylan leaned out through a wide opening adjacent to the one Andre was looking through and took note of where he was.

Below, closer than he'd expected, lay the grandeur

of the Eastern State. From his unique vantage point, it was vast and beautiful. He was one of the only people in the world to have ever seen the Eastern State from where he stood, a thousand feet overhead. It was like looking down on a dense forest, the trees shorn clean and painted white. Buildings like tall, narrow trunks soared up in the air, connected by a million limbs of white. Or was it more like a vast bed of nails infested with a legion of spiders connecting millions of webs from nail to nail? Either way, looking down from high above, Dylan understood what a miracle the States really were.

"What's that old saying?" Andre asked. He took two strides across the gun turret and stood next to Dylan, staring out over the infinite mass of spires. "What man has wrought, let no god put asunder?"

"It's the other way around," Dylan said, not really thinking at all but merely trying to orient himself to the miraculous situation he was in. "What *God* has wrought, let no *man* put asunder."

Andre flinched at the idea.

"You can keep your god, I'll take the Marvel comics version. Doctor Doom."

"Are you being serious right now?" Dylan asked. He was genuinely unsure.

Andre laughed.

"Only trying to lighten your load. You're going to

need that. And for the record, Doctor Doom said it my way, and he did battle with the Fantastic Four, Spider-Man, the X-Men, *and* the Avengers. Pretty good company."

Dylan looked over his head for the first time and saw two figures.

"That would be Wade and Clara," Andre said. "But let's not worry about them just yet."

It struck Dylan all of a sudden that Andre's wife, Gretchen, was dead. He'd discerned that much from all the chatter on the sound ring. Gretchen Quinn, the ice queen, dead. A sense of moral obligation flooded his system. He was Andre's son; he should tell him the bad news. But as Andre kept talking, the urge passed as quickly as it had arrived, like a wave heading back to sea.

"I know this hasn't been the easiest introduction to each other, but it's a start. And we'll have a lot more time after today."

"Will we really?" Dylan asked. He glanced over his shoulder and thought he saw a flock of birds approaching from the distance. Or was it something else?

Andre cleared his throat and observed his son with ambivalence, then smiled with a forced sincerity.

"I have to say though, as complicated as this is, I'm glad you're here. Something important is about to happen. *Very* important. Seeing it with all my children here is more than I could have hoped for."

Andre pulled his Tablet out of a pocket with a shaking hand. The man was clearly freezing in the high altitude even with the protective gear. Dylan felt a vigorous chill, nothing terrible, and looked once again at the approaching flock of birds.

"I'm going to send him up in just a moment more," Andre said. At the same time, Dylan received a message from Meredith on the sound ring.

"We're not coming any closer until they move out," she said. "Do whatever they ask, Dylan. Just follow orders."

Dylan watched the flock of birds, which weren't birds at all, stop in midflight and hold its position.

"We've got visitors," Wade said. "Three o'clock."

Andre reeled to his left and saw the mass of single pulses forming on the edge of his sight. He turned back to Dylan.

"I had a feeling she would show up. She always does."

He observed Dylan with an evil eye, sizing him up.

"You've been in contact this entire time, haven't you?"

Dylan didn't answer.

"I don't know how you did it, but you're going to wish you hadn't done that. It's not going to be good for them."

"I didn't tell them to come," Dylan said, and then,

exasperated by all the secrets hovering around him, went on: "What's happening? What are you doing here? Why won't anyone tell me what's going on?!"

Andre smiled ruefully, as if he felt a little sorry for the young man standing before him.

"My dear boy, it's the beginning of the rest of the story. It's the start."

Dylan wanted to scream with frustration.

"Just remember one thing," Andre said, his enigmatic personality coming to flourish in the gun tower. "Home is not the place you go to. It's the place you leave. Not many people understand that, but in the end, it's the truth."

He took one last look at his son, then turned his eyes to the sky.

"I'm sending him up. Let's get the show on the road."

A few seconds passed in silence and then Dylan saw all Andre's single-pulse army exit the prison from every side like bees leaving a nest. Another second or two and then Dylan felt the air come out of his lungs as the full weight of the prison started to free-fall toward the Eastern State.

"Better get up there," Andre said, holding on for dear life. "You've got work to do!"

Dylan leaped from the turret, up in the air above the falling prison, and put the full force of his mind to work in an attempt to slow its descent. At its angle it was capable of taking out seven, maybe eight spires in the Eastern State. What would that be, two million people? Four million? More? He had no idea, only that it would be a catastrophe of untold proportions. At least it was coming in from the top and not the side, which could have toppled ten times that many buildings. The prison slowed, but not by much, as Clara and Wade drifted down, one on each side of Dylan.

"Don't force it," Wade said, smiling roguishly. His eyes began to flutter, and he raised an arm. Clara did the same, and the prison grinded quickly to a stop. It happened so fast Dylan wasn't prepared for it, and he couldn't correct his speed before slamming into the prison itself. He hit the east-side wall and bounced, the impact on stone crushing his ribs with pain. The Eastern State was harrowingly close now, the tops of the tallest buildings only a few hundred feet below as he buckled under the pain of the blow.

"Come on; we're in a rush here," Clara said. "Get back up. Try again."

There was a chatter of messages from Hawk and Clooger in his head, but he blocked out the voices and flew back up between Wade and Clara.

"That's a good boy," Clara said. "Now listen carefully. This is what we call a diversion. Understand?

Like Gretchen in the Western State. Di-ver-sion. Say it."

Dylan wasn't about to cow to Clara's condescending demands, until she lowered her arm, and the prison moved down another hundred feet and stopped.

"Say it. Di-ver-sion."

"Diversion! I get it," Dylan said, the pain in his ribs subsiding into a dull roar.

"Good," Wade jumped in. "We wouldn't want you feeling confused about your role here. What we need you to do is hold up this prison for as long as you can while we go do something more important."

"I can't hold it up alone!" Dylan yelled. "That's impossible."

"Oh, I think you can," Wade said. "It's a lot harder moving it. All you have to do is keep it here. We already did the hard work."

"Give it all you've got," Clara said. "Now."

Dylan was terrified she would let it fall again, and a million or more souls would be on his conscience. He focused his entire mind on the prison, blocking out everything else, including the voices in his head.

"Think of it mathematically," Clara said. "That's the trick. Don't be lazy. It's not about the whole damn thing. You have to break it down, piece by piece, room by room, wall by wall. Bring it all into your mind, one piece at a time, and you'll be able to hold it. Understand?"

Dylan thought of the cell he'd been in.

"How many cells are there?" he asked, eyes closed and utterly focused.

"Now you're thinking!" Wade said.

"One hundred seventeen cells," Clara said. "Four gun turrets, nine walls, eighteen offices, twelve corridors, a foundation."

Clara and Wade watched Dylan as his mind worked over each part of the prison, holding it up one section at a time.

"He hasn't got it all, but it's close enough, I bet," Clara said. She took out her Tablet and glanced at the screen. "We're late. Better go."

Wade nodded, and together he and Clara slowly let their minds wander away from the prison, one piece at a time. Dylan felt the weight of each thought as it left them, like a scale that was loading up with piles of gold, his side getting heavier, theirs getting lighter, until every fiber of his mind stretched under the pressure of the task.

When he opened his eyes they were gone.

He was holding up a million pounds of stone and steel with his mind, the vast power of its weight pulling against him, dragging him foot by grinding foot toward the tallest spires of the Eastern State.

Chapter 16

Universal Donor

Andre, Wade, and Clara slipped away, down into the maze of buildings, as their army of single pulses spanned out across the sky. The drones were already coming, but whoever commanded them appreciated the situation: an object heavy enough to inflict unspeakable damage was hanging by a thread above the city. Who knew what might cause it to come crashing to earth? What was even holding it up to begin with? Where had it come from? Special care was required. They couldn't fire on the object or any of the people who appeared to be flying over the Eastern State. It was all, every part of it, wildly out of protocol. No one had ever seen anything like it; there was no manual or experience to prepare them. Something about the world had gone haywire in a way that was unprecedented and dangerous. And so they proceeded gently, as if tiptoeing around a floating nuclear bomb and its guardians in the sky.

The air swarmed with drones, circling and watching, dodging one another as they photographed and examined. The data transmissions only confirmed a world gone berserk: the object floating in the sky was a prison that weighed more than a million pounds.

There were what appeared to be two opposing forces at a standoff in the sky, floating as if weightless, staring each other down.

And the unimaginable fact that a young man appeared to be somehow or other holding the prison aloft.

Transmissions were also coming in from commanders in the Western State, who reported a major breach of security, the destruction of several tube bridges, a body count of more than two hundred, and an unexplainable encounter with flying people.

All this taken as a whole would have been enough to distract anyone from a smaller, far less noticeable event taking place on the 354th floor of a certain building in the finance and government district of the Eastern State. But Andre needed to be absolutely sure the decoy was so big it would capture the attention of everyone who mattered.

"We knew they would come," Andre said into his Tablet. He was hovering outside a window, looking at the frosted white glass and imagining what lay behind it. Meredith, he knew, would never go down without a fight. He felt a strange comfort in knowing she somehow always knew when he was making a very large move. She'd made a mistake this time though. The stakes were too high. This time Meredith would have to pay the highest price.

He looked at Clara and Wade and wondered for an instant how it had all led to this. Then he held his Tablet close and gave the order. "Take them. Take them all."

The swarm of black-camo single pulses moved as one, all of them brandishing handguns or knives or throwing stars that had previously been hidden. Four of them carried Smith and Wesson Magnums: guns that kicked like a bull when fired. Andre and Gretchen had always preferred classic weapons of war, and the Magnum was as classic as they came. Knives were of the hunting variety, with wide blades extending six inches away from pearl handles. The throwing stars were razor sharp and as broad as a grapefruit, cut in the shape of gears with teeth for ripping.

Meredith's forces had plenty of weapons of their

own, which they carried inside their discarded bullet suits. She was more inclined to heavy artillery of the grenade and cannon varieties, and half her forces shouldered rocket launchers at the sight of incoming forces.

The battle was on.

Shots were fired first by Andre's men, great blasts of fury that rang through the sky and scrambled the coding inside more than one drone. Security forces watching from nearby buildings slung code as fast as they could, trying to bring the drones under control. They were hardwired to attack at the sound of gunfire, and Andre's men retreated to the prison, where they took shelter in the four gun turrets. One of them didn't make it out of the open war space before taking fire from a set of two drones. The single pulse turned, faced the oncoming assault, and emptied all six Magnum rounds, strafing fire across the bow of both drones as he spun in a circle. His body armor, in which both teams of single pulses were covered from head to toe, took the brunt. But soon he was surrounded by two more drones. He was out of ammo, and though he'd destroyed some serious machinery in the effort, a spray of bullets finished him off. The man fell toward the earth and was caught by the roof of a building a few hundred feet below.

Meredith held back, giving orders to *Fire! Fire! Fire!*

She didn't seem to care that half the effort was resulting in damage to the prison itself, sending shards of metal and debris falling toward the Eastern State. Drones were everywhere, filling the sky with rocket-fueled flames.

Meredith commanded her small army to surround the prison and fire at will. What resulted was an all-out war around and within the prison itself while Dylan, pestered by Hawk's voice and a hundred drones doing flybys, fought against the immense weight of the prison he held. The prison lurched fifty feet downward, sending Andre's army swarming into the sky like hornets. Dylan regained his mental footing, and the giant concrete structure pitched to the right, turning sideways like a badly thrown Frisbee.

Meredith's single pulses were falling out of the sky one after the other. Semana was hit dead in the chest with a bazooka-fired rocket; another fighter watched his body armor slice open at the hip as a throwing star ripped through flesh and bone. Skulls were breached by Magnum fire, bodies blown apart by grenades thrown. And Glory, wise old Glory—her chest was struck with a blade, and she tumbled and tumbled and tumbled.

Meredith hadn't expected it to be so bloody, so swift and cruel. But there was no calling for a retreat now. It was way too late for that. All her small army could do now was take out as many of Andre's soldiers as possible, a fight to the bitter end.

He's going to be even angrier when he finds out Gretchen is dead, Meredith thought.

She hated leaving her drifters, but there was no choice. She had to at least try to stop what was coming. Meredith let herself drift down and out of sight, under the line of spires, and made her way around many tall buildings to where she knew she would find Andre. When she came to the tall white spire for which she was looking and glanced up into the sky, she saw that the prison was inching its way downward directly over her head. Like a black cloud bursting with the weight of water, it shed chunks of metal and stone, ripped free by a fight that would not end. It was shockingly close now, less than a hundred feet from the top of the highest buildings.

Meredith turned toward the spire with a look that might have been described as two parts fierce and one part shell-shocked. A wide hole had been punched in the side of the building, behind which lay a red-carpeted hallway. As she stepped through the broken shards of glass, Meredith felt a wave of sadness, all the memories of struggle and sorrow crashing at once on the open wound of her soul. She'd been strong for such a long time, never flinching, never giving in. Listening to the symphony of violence and regret outside grow quieter with each step, she began to hum the old song once more.

Clooger and Faith arrived at an abandoned hospital outside Colorado Springs. The chill in the air on the flight had slowed Faith's breathing, and Clooger had stemmed the bleeding by wrapping his giant-sized hand around her side as they flew. All the doors were sealed tight, so Clooger picked up the nearest boulder he could find, throwing it through a metal door with his mind. The boulder, a good four feet in diameter, bounced down a darkened linoleum floor and came to rest against a hospital gurney. What lay in shadow was surprisingly pristine: a hospital that had been sealed off from the decaying world outside.

"How's it going?" Hawk asked, pressing into the sound ring. "I'm not getting anything from the East. It's gone quiet."

Hawk had been watching the signals flaring on his Tablet screen, unable to say for sure what was going on. If he had to guess, it was Armageddon. Whatever was happening, it wasn't good, and Dylan either wouldn't or couldn't answer his calls.

"There's a lot of blood loss, but no major organs hit," Clooger said as he examined Faith, shaking Hawk out of his thoughts. He'd laid her on the gurney, where he could get a good look at her, tearing the blood-soaked shirt from her torso. She wore a pink sports bra, stained red along the rim of elastic. "The wound is nearer the outside edge of her abdomen than I originally thought. I need to stitch her up good and get her a blood transfusion fast."

Hawk was happy to hear Clooger's voice, happier still that Faith had a fighting chance.

"Find the OR and look for a blood bag and a syringe. We need to convert at least a couple pints."

"Hawk, you sure about this?" Clooger asked. He used one hand to press the sound ring, the other to push the gurney down the hall, banging it into a set of swinging doors that led to a darkened wing of the hospital. He was becoming adept at using one hand to work and the other to communicate. It wasn't so different from being in the field during a war holding on to a two-way radio. A guy got used to it.

"It'll work," Hawk said. "But I need to send you some files. Get on a network and start extracting. I'll download while you work."

Clooger tapped out a few instructions on his Tablet, putting it into satellite search mode. It honed in on a signal as he rummaged around gathering supplies: a puncture, tubing, antibacterial liquid, surgical thread, needle, sponge. When he returned to the gurney, the files he needed were already downloaded and ready. A new icon had appeared on his screen.

"Do you have what you need to extract?" Hawk asked.

"Got it."

"Sew her up first," Hawk said. "That's job one."

Clooger splashed the wound with antibacterial liquid, and Faith sucked in a fast, harsh breath of air, her eyes going wide with shock.

"Oh, hell," Clooger said, pinching his sound ring. "She's awake!"

"That's probably not a good thing," Hawk said. "Faith, can you hear me?"

She nodded and looked into Clooger's eyes and tried to sit up. Clooger pushed her back down as he watched blood pump out of her body.

"Stay still, Faith. Really still."

"Faith, listen to me," Hawk said. "We need to stitch you up and get some blood in you. You're not feeling any pain, I gather?"

She slowly raised a hand to her ear, pressed the sound ring.

"Not a thing. I am a little light-headed though. And cold."

"Must be a second-pulse thing. Clooger, get sewing. Her body doesn't know the trouble it's in. Just stay still,

Faith. Moving is only going to make it worse."

Clooger went to work, stitching up the wound on the front first, then rolling her gently on her side and doing the same on the back.

"Dylan?" Faith asked, hoping to hear his voice on the other end. There was only dead air, and she began to sob quietly.

"Hey, hey—he's just busy, that's all," Clooger said. "Give him a little time. And also, you're all stitched up. Now you need blood. And I have plenty of that."

Clooger slapped his monstrous bicep four or five times, bringing a vein to the surface.

"We're ready," Clooger said. "Run the program?"

Hawk thought he'd perfected the process of changing blood types, but he couldn't be precisely sure.

"Yeah, run it. Lay the tube on the Tablet, let the blood flow between. You'll need to get your arm up in the air."

Clooger did as he was told, strapping the tube to his Tablet with four or five wraps of gauze. He pressed the icon and watched as the screen filled with a random assortment of flashing colors: bright green and blue and yellow, bursting like a strobe light. A wave of sound pierced his ears.

Clooger rose up in the air on the power of his mind. He stabbed the wide vacutainer needle into his vein and felt the blood start pumping out of his body. The tube turned red, filling until it reached the Tablet, then it seemed to back up for a beat before continuing on its path.

Clooger hovered down, right over Faith, and took the other end of the tube in hand. They didn't have a lot of time, and they needed to push in a lot of blood fast. He attached an equally wide vacutainer needle to the tubing and stared at Faith.

"This was where I would have woken you, but since you're already awake, I can skip the face slapping."

"I appreciate that."

Clooger smiled down at Faith.

"You have to let it in. Tell me when you're ready."

Faith had let things in before, but it was a rare event in her life. She'd done it twice with a similar object, only much narrower: the tattoo needles, which provided a sweet, stinging sensation. It was part of what she liked about getting tattoos. She could really feel them. And the sound ring, she'd let that in. Now, as it had been with those procedures, she needed to let down her guard, a mental process that required a surprising amount of focus. It wasn't easy throwing aside the armor of a second pulse. She had to work at it.

Clooger waited as Faith's body relaxed and all the tension drained out of her face like an android cycling down.

Ten seconds passed, then twenty, then she spoke. "Okay, I'm ready. Stab me with that thing."

Clooger plunged the broad needle into Faith's arm, and she sighed with pleasure. Maybe it was the loss of blood and how light-headed it had made her. Either way, she acted as if she were in a happy dream, smiling as the blood flowed into her.

"Better be O positive," Clooger said.

"If she's going to reject, it will happen in a few seconds; otherwise let it flow."

O positive wasn't like the A and B types of blood. Anyone could take O positive. But Clooger's blood was B and Faith's A. She'd reject his natural blood, and in her weakened state, it would more than likely push her into cardiac arrest. They needed to change Clooger's blood from B positive to O positive, and that was a serious trick of organic chemistry. Hawk had been experimenting with light and sound and their effects on blood type for months in a lab setting, but never in a high-stakes situation. Faith either had pulled her guard all the way down and let in a poison that would devastate her frail organs, or she was getting the one thing that could save her.

They waited, neither of them speaking, while blood poured out of Clooger, past the Tablet of flashing, colored lights and its high-pitched squeal, and down into Faith's arm.

A minute passed, and still Faith didn't move. The sound from the Tablet wailed like an ancient fax machine blaring into the operating room, and Clooger wished he could shield his ears.

She stirred, her fingers moving first, and then her eyes slowly opened.

"I feel good," Faith said. "*Really* good. That's some class-A juice you got there."

Clooger pressed his sound ring with his free hand.

"Nice job, Hawk. It's working."

Out in the middle of nowhere, with nothing to hear him but the wolves and the skunks, Hawk got pretty excited. He pumped his fist in the open air of the Hum-Gee, yelled a few times, shook his head. Even he was a little surprised it had worked. The process was a lot more delicate than he cared to admit.

"Congratulations, Cloog," Hawk said, pressing his sound ring. "You're a universal donor."

Faith and Clooger smiled at each other as the blood kept pouring down the tube. Clooger was feeling a slight tingling in his head, and he allowed himself to enjoy the victory. Faith Daniels, the most important weapon they had next to Dylan, was going to make it.

His happiness would last only a few seconds, but he'd come to expect this. Every war he'd ever been in was checkered with small miracles, and they were always like doves moving through a dark sky. They were surrounded by violence and destruction, pressed too quickly into memory by the constant surge of war. It was no different there in the operating room of an abandoned hospital in a zeroed city.

Meredith was back on the sound ring, telling everyone who remained to get ready.

Something terrible was about to enter the known world.

Chapter 17

Now You Must Run

"Flee if you can. Don't come back," Meredith said. "He is coming."

Clooger and Faith couldn't look into each other's eyes without feeling like cowards. It was just the way they were wired. They weren't where they were needed the most, not even close. Helplessness enveloped them both, but it didn't stop Faith from trying to understand.

"What do you mean? And where's Dylan? Dylan?!" asked Faith.

"Go," Meredith said, her voice quiet and oddly distant. "Run and don't look back."

Meredith wished she could talk to Dylan alone. Actually, she wished a lot of things as she came to a door that sat ajar at the end of a long hallway. She wished she'd never sent Dylan to the prison. She'd hoped Dylan would somehow magically turn Andre in another direction, but she'd been wrong. She wished there wasn't a prison hovering over the city; but it was there, and her only son's every effort was focused on keeping it aloft. Andre had made him useless—a fine trick, she had to admit—and her only other second pulse was a thousand miles away. At least her single pulses had put up a hell of a fight; for that she was thankful. They'd decimated Andre's numbers. It was something.

But the power of the resistance had been diminished now, and that was assuming Dylan and Faith would get out alive.

A hard wind of fatigue blew across her mind as she stared at the ornate, beautifully crafted door. She'd come the whole way now—into the Eastern State, up to the top of a looming skyscraper, and down the long hallway to the president's door. She'd passed by six or seven bodies on her way down the hall, stepping over them or altering her path in order to go around. Her regrets were many, too many to count, as she pressed her fingers against the wood, pushed, and stepped inside.

The room was large, with couches and tables where many a meeting had been conducted over the years. There were red velvet curtains on the walls and a wide, plateglass window looking out onto the Eastern State.

Three more bodies lay scattered on the floor. There must be something worth protecting behind that beautiful door.

Andre stood before her, his hands clasped behind his back, the same toothy grin on his face as all those years ago. Behind him stood Wade and Clara.

"It's been a long time. Too long, I think," Andre said. "I wish we could be seeing each other under better circumstances."

Meredith offered no explanation. "Don't do it, Andre. You're wrong about this. Very wrong."

Andre's welcoming smile vanished, anger clouding his face.

"You might have told me we had a son. You had no right to keep that from me."

He looked out the window, where the prison cast a shadow over everything. "He's remarkable. It took the twins months to learn that. But I knew the moment I saw him he was something special."

Wade was more often the target of Andre's barbs. It was rare for Andre to allude to such things about Clara, mostly because of how sensitive and unpredictable she could be. But now, even as they both stood on the other side of the room watching, he seemed less inclined to hold back anything.

"You don't have to do this," Meredith said. She was

on the verge of tears as Clara, suddenly aware of how dangerous the situation was, thrust her hand up in the air. Meredith flew backward into the solid mass of the door through which she'd entered. Her back hit first, then her head cracked the wood and she fell to the floor.

"Was that really necessary?" Andre asked.

"You're a single, or have you forgotten?" Clara said. "She could throw you through that window if she wanted to."

"She would never do that. Never."

Meredith was on all fours, shaking her head, coming to.

"I say we finish her," Wade said, stepping forward into the middle of the room. "Clara's right. It's not worth the risk."

Andre may not have been a second pulse, but he still maintained emotional control over both Wade and Clara. All he had to do was look at them in a certain way— *You will leave her alone*—and they backed off. As far as he knew, neither Wade nor Clara knew Dylan was their half brother. Of course, he was wrong about this. They both knew Meredith wasn't just anyone. But that was one of the curious facts of his life and that of many other geniuses: Andre used logic when navigating the nuances of relationships, a critical error he had never corrected.

"If you're not going to enter the codes, I will," Clara said.

She moved toward a Tablet that lay on the main table in the room, but Andre picked it up with his mind and pulled it through the air, where it landed in his outstretched hand.

"They're right, you know," Meredith said. "I could kill you."

"But you won't. It would serve no purpose." He lifted his chin in the direction of Wade and Clara. "They'll just do it for me, and what would be the fun in that?"

The Tablet was red, which meant it was government issue, connected to an array of important documents and codes within the central command of the Eastern State. Andre snapped the Tablet large and tapped in several commands. The curtains on the back wall parted, revealing an iron door that looked as if it belonged at the entrance of a bank vault. He tapped in several more codes, then took three long strides to a body lying on the floor, snapping the Tablet back to small as he went. He turned the man's head toward the ceiling and used his thumb to force his eyelid open. Placing the screen a few inches from the face, the man's retina was scanned. He tapped out several more commands, and the door, which to Meredith looked more and more like the entrance to Fort Knox, began to open.

There was a deadly silence in the room, as if the space were caught in a time before and a time after. Through the opening there came a man in a black shirt that covered his arms and circled his long neck. He had a sharp nose and a short crop of gray hair. His eyes, as blue and deep as an ocean, took stock of the room.

Hotspur Chance was no longer in the highest-security prison in the known world. His long wait was over.

He was out.

The first words he spoke were not aloud but inside his vast and complicated mind.

I am Hotspur Chance. I am free once more.

Hawk, the only Intel in the resistance, heard the voice in his head and knew what had happened before anyone else outside the room. These words were heard by Hawk because he was an Intel. Hotspur may not have been able to control Hawk's mind as he wished he could, but he could make him hear his voice. He'd been doing it for quite some time already. It was the voice Hawk had been hearing all along, not the voice of a dead man but of someone who was very much alive.

Hotspur looked at Wade, then Clara. "Where's your mother?"

Neither of them answered, Wade because he didn't know and Clara because she surely didn't want to be the one to tell.

"Gretchen is dead," Meredith said, not out of spite but simply because it was.

Hotspur feigned disbelief for the shadow of a

second. His mind veered through the various points of fact that made such a statement impossible. *Gretchen is a second pulse, she's careful, she's methodical. She's unkillable.* And yet, something about the way Meredith was looking at him broke through the veil of his logic. It was true. Gretchen was no more. The unexpected part of that equation was that he didn't care.

"Don't listen to her," Andre said. "She's fine. And you're out! I've freed you at last."

Hotspur had been imprisoned in the Eastern State for more than a decade, but he didn't appear very much different than he had when he went in.

"It seems as if they've treated you kindly," Andre said. "You look well."

Hotspur ignored Andre and turned to Clara and Wade. "What's happening outside?"

"Just your basic mayhem," Wade said. "Nothing we can't handle."

Hotspur nodded his approval of the situation.

"Does he know?" Hotspur asked them.

Clara and Wade looked at each other, then back at Chance.

"He has no idea," Clara said.

Hotspur raised an eyebrow in surprise—it was a big secret, one he thought sure would find its way out—but there it was. He turned to Andre. "You've been a good soldier. Very good indeed. You've played a vital role in

shaping the future of the world. It's going to be remarkable. We're going to fix it my way. The right way. This is
good information. Dwell on it, down through the ages."

Andre laughed awkwardly, as if he didn't quite
understand what was being said, and then Hotspur
moved his eyes to the left in a sharp, flitting line. Andre
lifted off the ground, flew through the air, and slammed
into the wall over Meredith's head. As he slid down in a
heap on the floor, Meredith rose up to the ceiling in the
way of a floppy-armed sock puppet and hit hard, then
back to the floor she went, hitting with bone-crunching
finality. The two bodies lay in a grizzly hug, limbs
entangled around each other, faces nearly touching.

Andre could feel the life ebbing out of him as
Hotspur came close, leaned down, and spoke.

"Gretchen was never yours. She was only ever mine.
She was loyal to the end, as you have been." He paused,
looking once more at Clara and Wade, then back at
Andre, who was fading fast. "I feel you should know;
these children are not yours. They are, of course, also
mine. My perfectly engineered seconds. But I thank
you for watching over them in my absence. That was a
kindness."

Hotspur Chance knew everything Andre had
known, because Andre was a first-generation Intel. Their
minds were connected, which had served an important
purpose during all the years Hotspur was imprisoned.

There would be no need to get Hotspur Chance up to speed. He already knew what had been happening in the world outside through the lens of Andre's mind.

Hotspur turned his head toward Meredith and breathed deeply the cool air of freedom.

"You should not have betrayed me. I'm afraid the boy will have to go."

Meredith felt a jolt of air enter her lungs. It would prove to be one of her last breaths, but enough to knock a single tear free from her eye and feel it rolling down her cheek.

"I'm sorry," she said.

She was speaking to Andre, not Hotspur Chance.

"I appreciate you saying that," Hotspur said, standing as he looked out and saw shadows moving across the spires of the Eastern State. "But I don't forgive you. Penance must be paid. I'll see to it."

Hotspur looked again out the window, as if calculating the outcome of different events. "Clara, you bring me out, move me to the safe house. Wade, remove that young man from the equation."

Wade, though reeling emotionally from all that was happening around him, relished the idea of killing Dylan Gilmore. It felt like the one thing that could take away all the pain and confusion he was feeling. He did have one nagging problem with the idea.

"What about the prison?"

Hotspur gave Wade a cool stare and answered without the slightest hesitation. "Move it off the city. Can you do that?"

Wade's true father, a man he hadn't seen but had surely felt for a decade, was giving him a chance to be a hero.

"Hell yes, I can do it."

"I believe you can. Just make sure you take care of Dylan in the process. We can't have him out there, not anymore."

Wade soaked up the praise and responsibility like a sponge. He had two tasks to occupy his mind, both with the capacity to please his father. It was exactly what he needed.

A moment later Hotspur, Clara, and Wade were gone. The room was quiet, and with the last of her strength, Meredith pressed the sound ring on her ear. She used up her breath to speak to her son.

"He comes only to kill, this man without a heart. Now you must run."

When her hand fell away, it landed softly on Andre's chest, where it remained as they both drifted up and out into the arms of eternity.

Chapter 18

The Last Light of Day

All the nights of standing outside Faith's window had been a kind of trial by fire for Dylan. He was thankful for it as he heard his mother's voice and felt a surge of strength return to his mind. She had ordered him to run; and if that's what she wanted, then that's what he would attempt to do. He had no way of knowing Meredith was dead; no one on the sound ring did. And he didn't know that Andre had perished as well, a fact that would later prove troubling in ways he didn't expect. In the span of a few seconds and without the slightest idea that it had happened, Dylan was orphaned on the face of the earth.

Unrelenting rocket fire had blown a quarter of the prison free, which was a few hundred thousand pounds less for Dylan to hold in the air. There was still a massive, almost incalculable weight beneath him, but he could feel the difference. Hawk, who was at his best when multitasking, had tapped into the drone command center and hard coded the system to attack nothing but falling debris and do so with brutal force. Like a classic arcade game of Asteroids, one of Hawk's favorites, drones blasted falling chunks of concrete into smaller pieces no bigger than watermelons. The fallout still inflicted damage, but nothing like a slab as big as a bus would have. Hawk was orchestrating a huge save from the edge of a forest more than a thousand miles away.

When Dylan made his first attempt to move, sliding sideways toward the edge of the Eastern State, he knew instantly it was a mistake. The prison dropped precariously fast on one side, then Dylan flipped upside down and the whole building started spinning out of control. The prison wasn't falling, but it had been torn off its center like a gyroscope, flipping and turning in wild directions. If it free-fell now, it would do even more damage, like a giant, spinning mace cut loose from its chain and launched at a china shop.

Dylan righted his position, held steady, and slowly brought the prison back to center.

I can't move, and I can't leave this thing here, Dylan thought. *How am I supposed to run?*

He had been trained to remain cool under pressure, but the sound of Hawk's voice and the message he delivered pushed Dylan right to the edge.

"Whatever you do, make it fast. I think Clara and Wade are on the move. I'm calculating under a minute if they're heading your way."

Dylan glanced to one side, where drones were flying everywhere. He was within a few hundred yards of the outermost edge of the Eastern State. Three football fields; it was a long way off, but not insurmountable. Dylan put the force of his mind into a new kind of thinking, in which he imagined himself as the top of a pendulum that would not move, no matter how much weight shifted underneath him. Dylan forced the prison to rock one way, then the other, like one of the old rides at Six Flags that was shaped like a Nordic ship at sea, slashing through the air. The prison rocked up on his right side, and he felt the strain of incredible weight. Then it lowered beneath him and rocked high on the other side, toward the edge of the city. Back and forth, higher and higher, the weight like a magnet pulling against Dylan's will. One last rock in the direction of the inner city, then back under and hard to the outside, and Dylan let go.

He hadn't fully realized the weight of what he had been holding on to. This fact was quadrupled because the prison was made of the one thing that could kill him in the end. It was a suffocating burden, and the release was like a giant gasp of pure oxygen. His strength returned in a wave of power that heightened every color and sound.

The prison flew up and out, not nearly enough to clear all the buildings, and Dylan moved like lightning underneath. When it came down on his hands he was already driving upward, pushing his mind to places it had never been, forcing everything he had into the weight of a stone monster that threatened to kill millions of people below.

Wade was out of the spire and up in the air, where drones remained as thick as a swarm of mosquitoes. He couldn't believe what he was seeing, but there it was. The prison was being carried across the sky by the guy he hated more than anyone else in the world.

Off in the distance, Hotspur and Clara were already far from the Eastern State. Hotspur watched with interest as Dylan did the job he'd sent his son to do. The prison was moving fast, like a freight train across the sky, as Hotspur took Clara's Tablet in hand and relayed a message to Wade.

"Looks like he's done your job for you."

Blood surged in Wade's head. He'd never been so angry in his life, and that was saying a lot for Wade Quinn.

"Let's see if you can finish half of what I asked you to do before the sun goes down."

Dylan delivered one last push, giving it the full thrust of his mind, and launched what was left of the prison over the final spires. The mass of stone and metal tumbled end over end, a quiet moment of strange splendor before it hit like a meteor falling from space.

"Dylan!" Hawk yelled. "You have company. Better make a run for it."

But it was too late for that. Wade slammed into Dylan's back before he could turn around. He was so exhausted from the effort of the past hour, and so used to the counterweight of something so large, that he couldn't stop Wade from pushing him. Wade stayed a few feet back, held on to Dylan like a tractor beam, and pushed. Fifty, a hundred, two hundred miles per hour and heading straight for the crash site. At that speed, if Dylan hit all that concrete, he'd never live through it.

There was simply nothing left in his engine. All the gas was gone, and Dylan's mind sloshed with confusion as if heading into a dream. Wade turned sharply toward the sky, pushing for the clouds.

"Let's make absolutely sure this does the job," he

said, driving Dylan up into the blue.

Hawk was already at work, his fingers flying across his Tablet, trying desperately to rearrange a sequence of drone codes. With only a few seconds to spare, he tapped out the final command. Every drone in the air space above the Eastern State angled out of the city on a collision course with the prison. They were capable of speeds topping four hundred miles an hour, and Hawk set them to red line. As Wade turned in the sky and started down, the power of his mind flipped Dylan end over end. He pushed Dylan past two hundred miles per hour and stayed right behind him.

"Come on," Hawk said. "Faster."

A hundred drones were coming in hot, gathered like a swarm as they charged for the prison. They hit with a violence that rocked the buildings in the Eastern State, one after the other, demolishing the prison in a great cloud of dust. Wade stopped short, but Dylan was still regaining his bearings as he disappeared into the plume of debris. The drones had blown a hole fifty feet deep, clearing away all signs of concrete or stone. When Dylan hit, it was the cool impact of dirt on his skin that finally broke through. Like being slapped in the face, the contact with something as pure and fresh as earth itself fired his senses back online.

Wade watched, waiting for the dust to clear, but it

was a massive cloud and patience was not one of his virtues. He dived into the fog of dust and debris, hoping to find a lifeless body he could bring up to the surface like a trophy, something he could wave in front of his father and say *Look! I did this!*

"Dylan," Hawk said. "If you can hear me, now would be an excellent time to get the hell out of there."

A split second later Dylan burst from the cloud on a path leading directly away from the Eastern State. Before Wade reappeared from the dust cloud, Dylan was already a mile away and gaining speed. No one, not even Wade Quinn, was going to catch Dylan now.

Wade didn't have the heart to call Clara and report what had happened.

After a decade apart, it had taken him less then fifteen minutes to fail his father not once, but twice.

Clooger breathed a sigh of relief in the operating room. No one else had made it out, or so it seemed, but at least Dylan had escaped. There were no windows here, but because they were in a hospital, there were backup protocols when the grid went down. Somewhere in the bowels of the building there must have been a generator or two with enough gas to power the lights, but even that was fading fast. The bulbs were burning at about 20 percent, which made him feel as if the sun was going down though it was only one o'clock in the afternoon. A few short hours and so much had changed. It was, he thought once more, the way of war. It could turn on a dime like that and really surprise a guy.

Faith was out cold. The fresh blood and Clooger's handy stitching work had saved her, but she was exhausted in any case. Clooger had only rarely seen a second pulse with an injury, but when he had, the healing was always fast. Hawk had surmised that this was because a second was protected from everything outside the healing process. No germs or viruses could interfere, no infection could set in. Once the threat was removed—in this case titanium—the healing was efficient and rapid. Clooger had given Faith a sedative against her wishes, but it was for the best. She needed to sleep through the day, long enough for Dylan to return so the three of them could leave together under the cover of night.

Only Clooger knew where they were all going and how desperate the situation had become. Meredith, despite her constant deflecting, had told him plenty over the years. He alone knew that Hotspur Chance wouldn't waste any time setting the world on a different path. It was a lot for one man to carry, but then again, he was the only adult left. It came with the territory.

Hawk had waited until Dylan was clear of the

Eastern State and Faith was sleeping before making a certain death official.

"Meredith's sound ring has gone cold. She's gone. Sorry, guys."

Dylan and Clooger were both in that strange state of mind where they had already known it was true. They knew intuitively, before Hawk verified the fact, that Meredith was dead. But somehow hearing it made it ten times more real. Neither of them spoke as they endured the news in the cocoon of their own thoughts.

Thinking of his mother, Dylan felt confused and alone. She'd been driven by forces he'd never fully understood. It was as if she'd been given the knowledge of some future catastrophe only she could prevent. Whatever it was, his mother had risked everything to try to stop it. And it appeared that she'd failed. That was the hardest part of knowing she was gone. Meredith, who had always seemed invincible, had failed.

"You might as well know," Hawk went on after a long silence in which he watched a line of deer move into the field in front of the HumGee. "All our single pulses are gone. And Andre, too. I'm tapped into the Eastern State security system, so I'm getting this firsthand. Someone they're calling Prisoner One is out. And they're reporting four unidentified flying people—that's gotta be Wade, Clara, Dylan, and this Prisoner One;

they're saying those four have been deemed the most wanted people on Earth."

Hawk knew Prisoner One was Hotspur Chance, but somehow saying it made it more real than he was willing to admit until they were all together again. It was a secret he would hold on to for a few more hours.

"Dylan, I'm sorry about Meredith," Clooger said, his voice cracking as he pressed his sound ring and tried to zero in on what good remained. "But you know I've got Faith right here. She's fine. She's waiting for you."

Night was approaching as Dylan flew low, down the middle of a street in a deserted neighborhood. When he found the house he was looking for, the one with the red door and the yellow trim, he pressed into the sound ring.

"I'm here. Where do I find her?"

Dylan quickly maneuvered around all the nearby houses, searching for signs of life.

"Door is dead bolted," Clooger said, pressing his sound ring. "The window on the left has a latch you can turn. She's upstairs, farthest door on the right."

"Unless she got up and started scouting the neighborhood," Hawk said. "I wouldn't put it past her."

Clooger had moved Faith farther away from the Western State and locked her away, and then he'd fled to find Hawk. The clock was ticking, and Hawk had been stranded in the HumGee all alone. Without Clooger he had no protection, and officials from the Western State would almost certainly discover the missing prison before long. It would be one of the first places they would look once the pieces started falling together.

"We've moved about twenty miles up into the middle of nowhere," Clooger said. "Way up into the forest. Soon as it gets dark we'll put some miles behind us."

"When are you telling me where we're going?" Dylan asked, pressing his sound ring as he came around to the front of the house again, satisfied that no one was nearby.

"For tonight you're not going anywhere. Just stay put once you find Faith."

"Lucky." Hawk pressed into the sound ring. "I'm stuck with Clooger. But we're watching *Modern Family*, so I'm surviving."

"Let me know if she's okay," Clooger said. "Other than that we're going silent on the sound ring for the night. You two need some peace and quiet."

Dylan had a familiar feeling as he landed on the front porch of a two-story house in a zeroed town a hundred miles outside the Western State. Faith's second pulse should have put an end to situations where he sat by her side, waiting for her to wake up from an injury he felt somehow responsible for.

He found the window and, turning the latch with his mind, raised the glass out of the way. Inside it was cold·and silent. A few birds and some mice had found their way in over the years, but it was surprisingly well kept for having been vacant for such a long time. Whoever had lived in the house had taken down all the personal stuff and left behind the furniture. The last light of day fell upon the stairs as Dylan quietly scaled them one at a time. His nerves were shot, and he was more exhausted than he'd ever been in his life; but his adrenaline was pumping from a combination of excitement about seeing Faith and the fear of an intruder having beaten him there.

He arrived at the door and ran both hands through his hair. It had turned thick and wavy from hours in flight without the advantage of a bullet suit to protect him. He was suddenly aware of how cold he was—chilled to the bone.

He opened the door to a small, dark room with the curtains drawn. A small shaft of light split the curtains in two, the last remains of the daylight leaking into a secret space. There were so many comforters and blankets layered on top of the bed that it was hard to tell if anyone lay beneath them. He moved in, closing the door behind him.

"Faith?" he whispered as he knelt down near the sleeping figure. He leaned in close and felt her warm breath. She was alive, this much he knew, and that was enough to close the sound ring for the night.

He pressed in and turned away from the bed.

"She's okay. We're safe. Signing off until tomorrow."

Clooger pressed in: "We promise not to bother you. Get some sleep, both of you."

"Talk tomorrow, buddy," Hawk said. "I'm looking forward to seeing you both."

"Me, too," Dylan said, pressing his sound ring for the last time that day.

He took a deep breath and walked around to the other side of the bed. Shoes were removed, and he slid in under the heavy coat of blankets. The sheets were cold on his side, but as he inched closer, the warmth of Faith's body comforted him. She stirred, rolling her head toward him.

"Dylan?" she asked, dreamy.

"Yes, it's me. I'm here."

"Come closer, just be gentle," she said. "The wound is on my side, here."

She took his icy hand in hers and guided it toward her. Faith's hand was warm and soft, and as he felt the place along her side where the damage had been done, she flinched.

"It's okay," she said, smiling but tearful. The wounds of loss and the happiness of being together again were swirling her emotions into something she couldn't begin to control. She felt doubt and regret and love and triumph.

Faith pulled Dylan's arm around her as she slowly rolled toward him. Dylan's eyes had adjusted to the softness of the waning light. She was the most beautiful person he'd ever seen, and touching her face with his cold hand, her eyes brightened.

"We're going to need to warm those up before you touch anything else."

He kissed her and she drew him near, Dylan's body beginning to warm. Faith felt the coolness of his lips and the soft, dark stubble that had filled in his face. Her senses stirred as she looked into his dark eyes—he was her one and only, come back to take her in his arms.

Dylan held her as tightly as he could without hurting her, and he thought of all the things he could say. He could start down the long road strewn with doubts and losses, but instead he chose not to say anything at all. He touched her soft hair and wiped a tear from her face, and then he kissed her again. They settled into a cup, he behind, and he smelled the flowery blossom of her hair.

"I'm never leaving you again," he said.

Dylan lay awake as he felt Faith drift back into a deep sleep, the sedative working its magic once more. It felt to him like the safest place on Earth, there in the cold house in the zeroed town under all those blankets, holding her close. He took comfort in more than just Faith. It had been a very bad day, the worst one of his life. He'd lost both parents, one he'd never known. They'd lost their entire army, meager as it was. But he had Faith, and he had his closest friends: Clooger and Hawk. It was the four of them now, and that would have to be enough.

There needed to be moments of silence in a journey this difficult. This would be one of them. Soon enough they would come together again. They were moving toward a time when they would regain their strength and formulate their plans. They would go to a secret place so far into the wild even Hotspur Chance couldn't find them. They would have a few weeks to recover, maybe a month.

After that, one way or another, the end would be upon them all.

Everyone Fears a Quake
Few Can Create One

Read on for a sneak peek of the final book
in Patrick Carman's **PULSE** series

QUAKE

Chapter 1

Flight

Hawk's breath fogged the glass of his Tablet as dawn broke on the world outside. He turned to Clooger, whose wide nose had turned a pale shade of pink in the chill of morning, and said a single word.

"Incoming."

Clooger's black eyebrow went up and he dug a finger into his ear. The up and down of the mountain drive had left him feeling as if he was underwater.

"Here or there?" Clooger asked.

"There. And stay on your side of the rig. Whatever you're finding on that ill-fated ear expedition is probably nuclear."

Clooger pulled his finger out and examined it. "Better make contact."

"You sure?" Hawk asked. "With this much activity so close, who knows? We might blow their cover."

Clooger leaned his huge shoulder closer to Hawk and looked at the Tablet.

"Cover's already blown. Call 'em."

Hawk nodded. At fifteen he was scrawny for his age, but next to Clooger's colossal frame, he looked like a four-year-old.

"Dylan? Faith? Can you hear me?"

Hawk's small voice traveled into the sound ring as he searched for Dylan and Faith. He pressed hard on the lobe of his ear and wondered if the communication system he'd invented had been damaged.

"They're coming for you, Dylan. Tell me you're hearing this. Get out of the house. Get out now."

Still no answer.

"Why didn't you see this sooner?" Clooger asked. He was tougher on Hawk than anyone, but he loved the kid like his own son.

Hawk glanced at Clooger as if he was crazy.

"We both woke up thirty seconds ago. How much faster were you thinking?" asked Hawk.

"You should have an alarm on that Tablet for situations like this."

"At least Wade and Clara aren't out there." Hawk

scanned his Tablet again. "I don't see them anywhere."

Clooger was starting to worry, flexing his muscles nervously as he gripped the steering wheel. He blamed himself for their falling asleep, but they'd been up for thirty-six hours in a row. It wasn't as if they could stay awake forever. "We should have slept in shifts instead of simultaneously passing out from exhaustion. I should have known better."

"They've got maybe three minutes, Cloog," Hawk said. His fingers danced across the screen of the Tablet he held in his hand. "I don't know how this group found the safe house, but they did."

"At least the town is zeroed," Clooger said, stepping lightly on the accelerator. The HumGee hovered a few inches off the deserted mountain road, turning back and forth between fir trees. "How many?"

"A full unit of Western State military army." Hawk paused and looked at Clooger. He was glad to have the big guy at his side. "Air and ground. They've surrounded the house."

Clooger sniffed the air like a wolf and stared intently out the window. He pressed the sound ring embedded in his ear and yelled.

"Dylan, if you can hear me, move! Now!"

Hawk tweaked out in his seat at the booming sound of Clooger's voice and banged his head on the ceiling of the HumGee. His Tablet went airborne and hit the dashboard, instantly shrinking to its handheld size as it tumbled to the floor.

"Think you could warn me when you're planning on going nuclear?"

But that was Clooger—a bull in a china shop—and he was never going to change.

"What is it?" Dylan asked. He was finally awake, rubbing the sleep out of his eyes in a room filled with darkness and narrow slits of light.

Faith rolled over and looked at Dylan. She felt her side, hoping she'd find it healed from Gretchen's titanium dart, a dart that had nearly ended her life a day earlier.

"It's too late," Hawk pressed in. "They've surrounded the house. And I mean *really* surrounded it."

"Could they hide?" Clooger asked. He didn't press his sound ring, so only Hawk could hear him ask the question.

"Not a chance. Those troops have heat-seeking tech. Unless Dylan and Faith can seriously play dead, they'll have to make a run for it."

"If you guys get caught now it'll be a disaster," Clooger said, pressing his sound ring. He veered the HumGee back onto the road and gunned it. "Head into Oregon. I'll relay more instructions once you figure out how to evade everything the Western State can throw at you. Whatever you do, don't get caught."

"Faith, how are you feeling?" Hawk asked, pressing into the sound ring. He used his Tablet to set the auto-pilot on the HumGee and nodded for Clooger to let the steering wheel go.

"Ready to roll," Faith said. She was standing next to the bed in a T-shirt and underwear, nothing else. When she lifted her shirt along the side of her body, Dylan saw in the faint light that the wound had healed into a jagged scar.

"Nice birthmark," Dylan said as he pulled a shirt over his head and stepped off onto the floor on her side. He pulled her in close and edged back toward the bed.

Faith pressed her sound ring and pushed Dylan away with a smirk. "This is escape time, not make-out time," she whispered.

"I'm good as new, plus one badass scar," Faith said. "And my abs on that side feel like I just did a thousand sit-ups. I can roll."

"Excellent," Hawk said. "I had a feeling your body would regenerate very quickly. Glad I was right about that."

Faith pulled on her pants and a second, long-sleeve shirt. She picked her Tablet up off the nightstand, sliding it into the back pocket of her jeans.

"Figure out how to get away from the army outside

and back into hiding," Clooger said. "We'll guide you from here."

"Okay, first things to know," Hawk said, scanning his Tablet for data. "You've got two dozen armed flyers with jet packs surrounding the house. They'll be able to keep up, and they may know you can't be stopped with bullets or bombs. It's hard to say *how* much they know. Overhead you've got a half-dozen hovercraft. Those are fast and very nimble in the air. And they have space for a lot of weaponry."

"Like nets," Clooger reminded Dylan and Faith. "If they know about your powers, they'll know they need to trap you in order to stop you. Remember that."

"Okay, we got it," Dylan said. He looked at Faith, pulled her close again, kissed her.

"You sure about this?" Faith asked.

"Does it matter?"

Dylan kissed her, longer this time. When Faith pulled away and saw the longing in Dylan's eyes, she thought of how much she wanted to stay in the safe house, just the two of them. But she knew their escape from reality was over. They both did.

"No, it doesn't matter if you're sure, not really."

"Then let's get this party started."

Before either of them could pull the curtains, the glass in the window exploded inward and a can of tear gas hit the floor, flooding the room with eye-stinging smoke. They both heard the sound of the front door downstairs being forced open with a ramrod as armed men entered and began shouting instructions.

"My system doesn't much like this tear gas. You?" Faith asked.

"Can't say that I love it," Dylan agreed. They weren't sure whether their second pulses would protect them from poisonous gas; they'd never dealt with it before. No sense taking chances. Dylan went first, then Faith, flying out the window and up into the sky. They stopped and hung in the air over the house long enough to see the trouble they were up against. Men wearing sleek jet packs were already taking off, heading toward them, and firing a barrage of bullets.

"Pretty cool tech," Dylan said, surveying the armed forces. "I'd love to get my hands on one of those jet packs and take it apart piece by piece. Imagine what Hawk could cook up with the parts?"

"Too bad they don't have any interest in capturing us. These guys are aiming to kill," Faith said, trying to keep Dylan from geeking out, as he sometimes did at the most inappropriate times. Faith had long understood that things like jet packs and flying saucers set off even the least nerdy guys she'd ever met. Ogling this kind of modern technology was in their DNA. She glanced skyward as she and Dylan flew toward the Oregon border, bullets pinging harmlessly off their second-pulse shields. Overhead she saw the circle of hovercrafts, each of them thirty feet in diameter. They looked like oversized bumper boats, round and flat with one pilot sitting in the center.

"Let's see if we can outrun them," Dylan said. "That would be the easiest way out. And I'm curious what kind of speed these things can do."

Faith nodded and they went into high gear, arching up toward the cloud line. But the bullets and rocket grenades kept coming and the men in jet suits stayed tight on their heels. The hovercraft were even faster, encircling them from every side, firing at will.

"Open space isn't working!" Faith said. "Try close to the ground?"

Dylan nodded and they dove toward an abandoned street with houses on both sides.

Several hundred miles away, Clooger and Hawk were keeping track of the action as they drove.

"Spread out, you two," Clooger said, pressing his sound ring. He was leaning toward Hawk, watching heat signatures on the Tablet as the autopilot swerved them back and forth down a dusty road. "Make them choose who to follow!"

The HumGee went fast into a turn and pitched sharply to the right, throwing Hawk into the door. Clooger's weight followed, smashing Hawk as if they were on a shoulder-crushing fair ride.

"Buckle up, big guy! You're killing me here."

"Don't be such a wimp."

"I'm not a wimp. You're huge, bro!"

While Hawk and Clooger waited for the next hairpin turn, Faith picked up an abandoned car with her mind and threw it over her head. The men in jet packs swerved admirably, but when they looked back, Faith had picked up ten more cars. She turned on the troops and they all stopped in midair, watching.

"Stop following me," she said. Faith had a way of saying things like this that could turn the most hardened army veteran toward home. But these guys were either stupid or crazy or both. The troops all moved forward slightly, firing off a whole new round of bullets and blasters.

"Don't say I didn't warn you, because I did. I warned you."

Faith moved the cars into a long horizontal line in front of her and then pushed them forward one at a time like pendants stuck together on a chain. By the time they started reaching their intended target, the cars were traveling at a hundred-plus miles an hour, spreading out and clobbering everything in their path. The troops bounced like bowling pins, spinning wildly out of control as the jet packs malfunctioned and pushed them all over the sky. The cars continued their journey, slamming into houses and streets on the ground as the flying Western State troops tried to right themselves in midair.

Dylan was a quarter mile to Faith's left, dealing with the hovercrafts, all of which had decided to follow him.

"Clooger was right on the money—these things have net bombs," Dylan said, dodging hard to one side as a bowling ball–sized projectile headed his way. When it was within twenty feet of where Dylan had been stationed, it burst open like a shotgun shell full of lead pellets, splaying out a wide net with golf ball–sized weights around its perimeter. A long wire connected the net to the hovercraft, and when the net missed its target, it curled back into a ball and returned to where it had come.

"We need cooler weapons," Dylan said, pressing his sound ring so Hawk could hear. "You gotta see this, Hawk."

"You do realize it's killing me not seeing this stuff up close?" Hawk said as he turned toward Clooger. He pressed his sound ring. "Grab whatever you can!"

Dylan nodded to himself, but he knew it would be a fool's errand trying to separate a Western State flyer from his equipment. He looked down and uprooted an entire house with his mind, raising it into the air from below as dirt and debris crashed to the ground. All six hovercrafts fired net bombs, surrounding Dylan as they exploded in a circle around him. Dylan shot into the air, raising the house as he went. The nets were beyond sticky, covered in something that adhered to whatever they touched. Dylan heard the pilots screaming, *"Release! Release!"* But they weren't fast enough. Dylan pushed the house back toward the ground, pulling the hovercrafts down with it. By the time the lines were all cut, it was too late and all six pilots had to abandon ship, taking to their emergency parachutes and brandishing sidearms.

"Let's make a run for it," Faith said. "Stay low to the ground, out of sight."

The jet-pack troopers were barely getting their bearings again, and the hovercraft pilots were totally out of the fight. Only two troopers followed Faith and Dylan into the trees.

"A couple of stragglers and we should be clear." Faith pressed into her sound ring. She looked at Dylan, saw what he was considering. "Don't even think about it. You are not going back there for a hovercraft or a jet pack. Let it go."

"Sorry, Hawk." Dylan smiled. "I'd have done it for you, but Faith is a little more rational than me."

Dylan moved in close, wrapping an arm around Faith's waist. They kissed and Faith felt Dylan smiling. She loved it when this happened. To touch his lips to hers when he was this happy, to *feel* his happiness and know it was because of how much he loved her—it was everything, all she needed, all she wanted.

"Man, it would have been fun parting out one of those jet packs," Hawk said, his voice all excited and bummed out at the same time.

"It was a search mission," Clooger said. "Now that they've found you they'll send more. You need to move fast and find some cover."

"Head for the Columbia Gorge," Hawk pressed into the sound ring. "A million acres of trees along there. They'll never be able to track you."

"Still two on your tail, but they're falling back," Clooger added.

The HumGee turned suddenly to the left, barely missing a cliff wall as it continued down a winding forest-service road somewhere on the border of Oregon and Idaho. Hawk lowered his shoulder and used the gravity of the turn to slam Clooger as hard as he could, but his shoulder missed and Hawk face-planted into a wall of Cloog.

"I almost feel sorry for you. *Almost*," Clooger said, laughing softly as Hawk felt around his head for missing parts.

"I think you broke my face."

Clooger glanced at Hawk and gave him a playful shove.

"All in a day's work for a military man, right, kid?"

Hawk went right back to his Tablet, all business. "Let's get these two out of harm's way before another State armada shows up. It's all clear for the moment."

But Hawk was about to find out how wrong he was.

Faith and Dylan were far from in the clear.